DETOUR TO LOVE

By the Author

Romance Novels

Mergers & Acquisitions

Climbing the Ladder

A Swedish Christmas Fairy Tale

Second Chances

Going Up

Lost at Sea

The Startling Inaccuracy of the First Impression

Fitting In

The Flight Series

Flight SQA016

Grounded

Journey's End

The Remember Me Series

Bring Holly Home

Keep Holly Close

The Around the World Series

The Road Ahead

The Big Uneasy

Mystery Novels

Huntress

Death Before Dessert

DETOUR TO LOVE

by
Amanda Radley

2021

ISBN 13: 978-1-63555-958-3

This Trade Paperback Original Is Published By
Bold Strokes Books, Inc.
P.O. Box 249
Valley Falls, NY 12185

First Edition: February 2021

CREDITS
EDITOR: RUTH STERNGLANTZ
PRODUCTION DESIGN: STACIA SEAMAN
COVER DESIGN BY TAMMY SEIDICK

Acknowledgments

I've written quite a few books. So many that I've actually forgotten the exact number. However, this one is special because it's the first one I will release with Bold Strokes Books, and it marks the start of a big change in my author career. I'm very proud of it and I hope that you'll find as much enjoyment in reading it as I did in writing it.

Thanks go to Sandy for being an organisational ninja, Ruth for being an insightful and respectful editor, and of course to Radclyffe for allowing me to join my new publishing family. As I'm discovering, Bold Strokes Books is a business with many talented individuals so a big thank you to all of them for helping me to bring *Detour to Love* to the world.

Special thanks go to my wife, Emma. No thanks at all to my cats who cannot decide if they wish to be in my office or outside. Getting up to open the office door for them added at least four days to this project.

For the readers.

Early Mornings and Upgrades

Celia Scott smothered a yawn behind her hand as she waited for the traffic lights to change from red to green. It was ridiculously early in the morning, one of the many reasons she despised flying.

Not only was she forced to sit in a metal tube that inexplicably floated in the sky, with a group of strangers that always included screaming children and people with concerning coughs, she was also asked to get up at the crack of dawn to do so.

She tapped her fingers on the steering wheel. The light had been red for a while, despite there being no other traffic around for miles. Clearly, no one else was eager to drive into Heathrow Airport at five in the morning.

She couldn't blame them.

She eased her foot up slightly from the brake pedal and allowed the car to edge forward. She didn't quite understand how traffic lights worked. Were there sensors? Had it detected her waiting? Was it broken?

The only science she was aware of when it came to traffic lights was that they consistently changed from green to red at the moment she approached them. As if her car was some kind of magnet for stop lights.

A police car pulled up beside her. She put her foot back on the brake and smiled over at the officer.

He smiled back knowingly.

After what seemed like forever the light changed to green, and she drove off at a much more conservative rate than she would have normally.

Celia looked at the abundance of signage that lined the road: the railway station, departures, arrivals, hotels, and a myriad of parking options—short stay, long stay, meet and greet, extra-long stay, premium.

She reached over to her leather satchel that sat on the passenger seat and rummaged for the pack of paperwork her assistant had given her before she left the office the previous evening. Thankfully, the first sheet told her she was booked into the meet-and-greet parking service at Terminal 5.

She tossed the paperwork back and tried to remember why she felt a familiar tingle up the back of her neck when she thought of Terminal 5.

A moment later she remembered: that was the terminal famous for losing baggage. Countless millions spent on conveyor belts and fancy scanners to sort luggage, only for it to break down and cause mayhem.

If she was lucky, it would happen to her.

The perfect excuse to not travel could be waiting for her. She couldn't very well travel if the terminal building somehow ate her luggage. Or if the aircraft had a fault of some description. Or if the staff decided to strike.

She sighed as she pulled off the main road and towards her designated parking area.

A travel-preventing disaster would be wonderful but was highly unlikely no matter how much she craved one.

She'd done everything she could to avoid it, but it was no use. She was just going to have to fly to Tokyo and accept the award.

❖

Lily Andersen tucked her thumbs into the straps of her rucksack and stared up at the enormous departure board. Flight numbers, faraway locations, times, gates, and check-in desk numbers all merged into one big mess.

"You all right, love? Where you off to?"

Lily turned to see a member of airport staff smiling warmly at her.

"Tokyo," Lily said. "Departing at—"

"Eight fifteen," the woman replied without missing a beat. Lily presumed she knew every flight by heart. "You want any one of the check-in desks over there."

Lily looked in the direction indicated and was relieved to see a row of near-empty desks.

"That's great, thank you so much." She grabbed the handle of her suitcase and wheeled it over to the nearest desk.

"Good morning," the check-in assistant greeted her brightly.

Lily wondered how all these people could be so chipper first thing in the morning. She was used to getting up early, enjoyed it in fact, but this pushed her limits. She smiled and swung her rucksack from her back to balance it on her suitcase.

"Morning," Lily greeted the assistant, digging for her passport and ticket confirmation. She handed over the documents and waited patiently as the woman typed details into her computer.

"We have availability in business class at steep discounts, if you'd like to upgrade?"

Lily had never flown anything other than economy, or cattle class as it ought to be known. The flight to Tokyo was long, and the thought of stretching out in a more comfortable seat was appealing. And she had just been paid for a large commission.

"How much extra is it?" Lily asked.

"It should be three hundred, but it's showing here as one hundred and twenty. That's a steal, if you ask me. You get the extra leg room, the comfy leather seat, a better meal service."

Lily had been anxious about the long flight, and the idea of melting into a large leather seat and maybe drifting off to sleep sounded heavenly. She could afford to splash out, and she deserved a treat after saving for so long to pay for the trip.

"That sounds like a lovely idea," she admitted. She pulled her credit card out of her phone case and placed it on the desk. "Let's do it."

Within a few minutes, her suitcase was whisked away, and she was being directed towards security. Apparently, now that she was in possession of a business class boarding pass, she could use the priority channel to get through security screening.

Lily had never been priority anything, and so it was with some excitement that she flashed her posh boarding pass at a tired-looking security officer and made her way to the special area that had been cordoned off for those with a little extra money to spend.

She put her rucksack on a conveyor belt and watched it disappear into the X-ray machine before walking through a metal detector that appeared to beep at everyone. After a flimsy pat-down by a woman called Sharon, who was more interested in her conversation with another security officer about cheese, Lily picked up her rucksack and was free to go.

Before she got to the departure terminal, she heard her phone beep from within her bag. She excitedly dug through the sketch paper, pens, books, magazines, her fluffy pencil case, headphones, and other items that she'd considered essential travelling equipment. It was only when she picked up the heavy bag that she started to question how essential the three books and her Kindle were.

As suspected, it was a text from Asami. Lily couldn't help the smile that blossomed on her face.

As usual, Asami's message was filled with excitement and heart emoji.

Lily couldn't believe it was finally happening. After five months of talking online and via text messages, she was finally on her way to meet the woman who had quickly become her best friend. And would hopefully become more, if all went well.

Lily knew not to pin her hopes of a long-term relationship on someone she'd met online, but Asami seemed perfect for her.

Lily had tried to be sensible, but if she was honest with herself, she'd fallen in love with Asami in just a few short weeks. She'd been pining to see her face to face to see if the connection would be the same in person as it was online. Lily was sure it would be; it was like they were made for one another.

She read Asami's message a few times, taking it all in before replying with her own sweet words of adoration and excitement. She was all too aware that, very soon, she'd be on a plane and out of communication with Asami for the longest time since they'd started talking.

Some people would probably consider it a little unhealthy, but they messaged each other all day long and had done so for many months.

About to find some breakfast and then I'll be boarding the plane. Can't wait to see you! I'll text you before we take off xx

Lily tucked the phone into her back pocket and put her rucksack back on. She blew out a nervous breath. It was finally happening. She was finally going to Tokyo and meeting Asami. It had been a long time coming, but in less than a day they would finally be able to hug each other.

A mixture of nerves and excitement had hung over Lily with ever-increasing weight as the day had come closer. Now it was the final leg of the race, and she felt every emotion acutely and all at the same time. It was exhausting, but ultimately she knew it would be worth it.

"Just a few more hours," she murmured to herself.

Send in the Clowns

Celia blinked. "I'm sorry, could you repeat that?"

"It's a different aircraft, I'm afraid, so there are fewer first-class seats available," the woman at the check-in desk explained for the second time.

"I really don't see how that affects me," Celia replied haughtily. "I've paid for a first-class seat. I will have a first-class seat."

The check-in woman—*Dawn* if her name tag was to be believed—looked from her screen to Celia and back again with uncertainty. In Celia's experience, a degree of confidence was often the only thing required to resolve these situations. Dawn could fix the issue if she really wanted to; Celia had every faith in her. She just needed to provide her with the right motivation in the form of a steely glare and a pout.

"Is there a problem here?"

Celia turned to see a young man in an ill-fitting suit. He looked to be around fifteen, which presumably meant he was some kind of manager.

"We've had a last-minute change of aircraft," Dawn explained. "We don't have enough first-class seats."

"Dawn here is about to turf someone out of a first-class seat so I can have it," Celia said, smiling at the young woman.

"It's the Tokyo flight, Mike," Dawn told him, an edge to her voice.

Something was communicated between the two of them that went over Celia's head.

"Oh," Mike said. "I might be able to do something about that. They haven't checked in yet."

"Yes, but—" Dawn started to argue.

"It'll be fine."

"Does someone want to let me in on the secret?" Celia asked.

She didn't want to go to Tokyo, but she certainly wasn't going to be doing it in an economy-class seat. The last time she had flown economy was for an emergency meeting in San Francisco, and she'd been placed in the middle seat of a row of three for eleven hours.

There and then she promised herself to never, ever fly economy again.

Dawn and Mike shared another silent conversation, which caused Celia to let out a long sigh. It was far too early in the morning for this kind of nonsense. All she wanted was her boarding pass, one for the first-class seat that she knew was booked for her, and to get through to airside so she could have a well-deserved drink.

She knew she was being a little harsh, but she didn't think she was being entirely unreasonable in simply requesting her original seat. If they knew what kind of year she'd had, then they'd reupholster it in gold leather, of that she was quite certain.

"We had a large group booking," Mike explained. "HorrorVille."

Celia blinked again. "Excuse me?"

"A circus troupe. They specialise in, well, horror. Scary clowns, that kind of thing. They have all twenty first-class seats and ten in business class. However, they haven't actually checked in yet, so I could ask if one of their performers would mind a seat in business class," Mike suggested. "I'm sure one of the group would be willing to switch."

Celia pinched the bridge of her nose between her thumb and forefinger and leaned against the check-in desk. "Let me get this right. The entire first-class cabin has been filled with scary clowns."

He nodded.

"But you're going to ask one of those scary clowns to give up their seat for me. Meaning *I* will be in a confined cabin with the aforementioned group of scary clowns?"

"I can offer you a seat in business class," Dawn suggested, clearly detecting the chill to Celia's tone.

"Is there another flight?" Celia asked.

"The next one with availability would be tomorrow," Dawn apologized.

Celia let out a long breath. There was no point in getting upset—the aircraft had been changed, and availability was clearly limited. Challenging Dawn any further would just cause her to be put on some kind of list of difficult passengers, which Celia was sure existed.

"Fine, fine. *Downgrade* me to business class," she said. "But, please, do *not* put me near one of those damn clowns."

Mike wisely took his leave, and Celia waited as Dawn tapped away on her keyboard. The small-talk pleasantries they had enjoyed when she had first arrived were long forgotten.

Celia was glad for the silence; it allowed her anger to stew. Not only was it ludicrously early in the morning, but now she was discovering that she'd been kicked out of first class because the circus was literally leaving town. She supposed it was just her luck.

Her mobile phone rang. She pulled it out of her coat pocket and sighed as she caught the name on the screen. As she suspected, it was her boss.

"Good morning, Howard," she greeted him, attempting to sound as if she believed it was actually a good morning.

"Celia! Are you at the airport?"

"I am, just checking in now."

"Good, good. What a turn-up for the books this is!" Howard sounded excited and full of life, which was to be expected considering he'd just returned from a three-week holiday.

"Yes, very much so." Celia hoped she sounded as pleased as she ought to.

"I wanted to offer you my congratulations before your flight," Howard continued. "It's an enormous honour to win this award, as you know. You worked hard, Celia. You deserve this. Well done. Enjoy every moment. Oh, I wish I could be there, but there's this deal to sign and...well, you know. But I absolutely had to say well done."

Dawn silently held out her boarding pass and passport. Celia took them, offering her a tight repentant smile before walking away from the check-in desk.

"Thank you, Howard."

"I hear they're streaming the ceremony this year. Maybe we'll be able to watch you accepting your award here in the office. I'll have to do some math on the time difference. Technology, eh?"

Celia's heart sank. It was hard enough to have to fly all the way to Tokyo for a slab of glass that she didn't even want. To have the entire office watching back home was a horrible thought.

"I think it's very late at night," she lied. "I've not looked into it. It was a bit last minute."

"Yes, it was! I thought they'd at least warn me as I nominated you, but it seems they're getting very serious about their secrecy after all the leaks in previous years."

"It seems so. Look, Howard, I hate to cut this short, but I have to go through security."

"Of course, of course. Well, there's not a lot else for me to say. Congratulations again, Celia. Enjoy Tokyo."

"I will," she lied.

"Excellent, excellent. Speak soon."

He hung up the call. Celia slowly lowered the device from her ear and stopped dead in her tracks on the way to the security area. This was it; there was no turning back now even if she wanted to. She had to keep up appearances.

Damned appearances.

Beside her, an extraordinarily long shoe slapped impatiently against the polished marble floor. She turned to see a clown, arms folded and staring at her intently. His white face paint and drawn-on tear on his left cheek just infuriated her all the more.

"Oh, bugger off," she told him.

Sandwich Fingerer

L ily stared at the enormous array of sandwiches and snacks on offer. She'd never been on an eleven-hour flight before and had no idea what to buy to keep her going for that time.

She knew the airline would provide meals, but what they were and when they would come was always a mystery. And, right then, she felt as though she could eat a filled baguette the size of the Boeing 777 that was going to take her to Japan.

She reached out and picked up an avocado wrap and examined the back of it. She liked all the ingredients, but somehow it didn't seem quite right.

She put it back in the chiller, her hand hesitating before she finally let it go.

A club sandwich caught her eye, but she sadly remembered that she'd recently decided to cut back on white bread. She'd hoped that she'd have gotten older than twenty-five before her stomach started to rebel against certain foodstuffs.

Sadly, it wasn't to be the case. White bread made her bloat, and it had to be removed from her diet. Which was a shame because it was probably one of the tastiest things on the planet.

An egg mayonnaise sandwich on brown bread seemed appealing. But would it be filling enough? She picked it up and looked at it.

"Please, do let me know when you've finished fingering every sandwich in the shop."

Lily jumped, dropping the sandwich into the open chiller cabinet. She hurried to pick it up and put it back on the shelf.

"Um. Sorry." She stood to one side, allowing the important-looking, middle-aged businesswoman access to the chiller.

"No, by all means, carry on. There's a salad over there that you haven't prodded. We wouldn't want it to feel left out."

Lily wanted to take offence for the rude tone, but her proclivity for an older woman in a suit caused her brain to briefly cease functioning. The stare, the confident cock of the head, the immaculate hair and make-up all combined to make Lily want to blush and break eye contact.

But the woman *had* been rude, and Lily wasn't about to let the matter go without at least a sarcastic comment.

"No, no. I insist. After you, your majesty." Lily bowed deeply and gestured towards the sandwiches.

The woman smirked and took a step forward, efficiently plucking a sandwich from the shelf without checking any of the details. She snatched up a bottle of water and then stepped around Lily and stalked towards the counter.

"Rude," Lily murmured to herself. But hot.

❖

Lily heaved her rucksack off her back and placed it on a seat facing some large windows. She flopped down into the chair next to her bag and decided that one wrap, two sandwiches, two mini cakes, two cereal bars, and three drinks was probably too much. Especially for someone who was flying in business class, where food was probably plentiful.

She was only flying to Japan, not the moon.

But she couldn't decide what she'd fancy eating over the next few hours and had ended up panic buying.

Well, it was done now.

She opened her bag and pulled out her sketchpad and some colouring pencils. She'd wanted to take her brush pens but had read online that they often dried out during long flights, and she didn't want to take the risk. She usually preferred wet colours, but it would be good for her to practise with dry for a while.

She dug around in her bag for a while longer until she found her Bluetooth headphones and set about connecting them to her phone. She had small AirPods, but much preferred the larger headsets for their sound quality and comfort.

There was something strangely pleasing about being gently squeezed around her ears as happy tunes floated into them.

Headphones on, pencil in hand, and sketchpad balanced on her crossed legs, she looked out the window for inspiration.

Down on the tarmac she saw row upon row of parked planes preparing to depart. In between the planes were a variety of vehicles, from tugs to security, to food delivery and luggage trolleys.

She tapped the pencil against the pad in tune to the eighties pop music that played from one of her many Spotify lists.

Artists had been finding human features in vehicles for years. Cars, trains, planes, and even boats all had characteristics that could be manipulated into faces.

Lily looked at the nose of the nearest plane. The windows above would make great eyes; the wings could be arms. She giggled to herself at the thought of the wheels being tiny, stumpy legs.

With an idea of a character in mind, she started to scribble her character in rough.

Forty-five minutes later, the sound of her alarm interrupted her music, and she knew it was time to check for further boarding information. She always set alarms when she was working—otherwise there was a very real possibility that she would sit and work for hours on end.

She briefly looked at what she had been working on before gently removing the pages from the pad, sliding them into the back, and packing her things away. With a sigh and a grunt, she heaved her backpack on and looked around for a departure board.

The terminal building was pretty empty, probably because it was still incredibly early for most people. But Lily noticed a single figure at the champagne bar.

She rolled her eyes upon realising it was the same rude woman from the sandwich shop. She was sipping from a champagne glass, which didn't seem to be the first one she'd indulged in that morning, her mobile phone in her hand as she gestured wildly and chatted loudly.

Lily couldn't quite make out what she was saying, but the woman was being loud and typically obnoxious, just as Lily expected a drunk, middle-class businesswoman would be. She stared for a moment, safe in the knowledge that she hadn't and wouldn't be seen. There was something about her. Something that Lily wished she didn't find compelling. For reasons Lily didn't quite understand, she found that kind of woman impossibly attractive.

She didn't know if it was the fact they were older and that often meant wiser and more grounded, or maybe it was the suit and the feeling of security and power that flowed off them in waves.

The woman laughed loudly and nearly knocked her glass over,

only just catching it before no doubt expensive champagne tumbled to the floor.

"Someone's going to have a fun flight," Lily mumbled. She shook her head and continued her search for the departure board.

❖

Celia swigged from another glass of Taittinger. If she was going to travel over eleven hours on a flight, there was no way she was going to be sober for it.

Sleeping on a plane was utterly impossible unless inebriated. No matter what cabin class, there was always a stream of people needing to use the facilities or having loud conversations. Not to mention that the seats were not exactly designed for a casual nap but more so the airline could wedge as many bolt upright seats into a compact space as possible.

So if sleep was to be achieved, alcohol was to be imbibed.

While the airport pub was closed, and the other restaurant wasn't serving alcohol, Celia knew one could always rely on the champagne bar to be open and willing to oblige.

She didn't care that she was the only one at the bar, which was located right in the middle of the terminal's main pathway. The long, cylinder-shaped bar cut through the centre of the path with stools dotted around it at regular intervals.

It wasn't discreet, but the service was excellent. In fact, having the sole attention of the bartender was the best thing the day had brought her so far.

The time when it was acceptable to call colleagues in Europe had arrived, and so she filled her time by chatting to and networking with people before they headed off to work for the morning.

She emptied her glass and shouldered her mobile phone to glance at the drinks menu. She was fairly familiar with most of the vintages on offer, but there were a couple that were new to her that she wanted to try.

She continued her conversation with Marco, her counterpart in Italy, while gesturing to the bartender what she wanted from the menu.

"I thought the award was mine this year. Was sure of it," Marco said, a hint of sadness in his tone.

"So did I," Celia replied softly.

It was hard to speak to Marco; he'd won the Golden Arrow Award four years in a row. And it was always well deserved. He was excellent at his job, continually went the extra step, was respected by everyone in the company, and was rewarded with the coveted trophy for his efforts year after year.

But something had gone horribly wrong this time, and Celia had been announced the winner, despite not even wanting to be nominated. Damn Howard and his meddling in things he didn't understand.

Not only did she have to fly halfway around the world to pick it up, she had to seem happy about it. No more so than when she was speaking with Marco.

She had to finely balance a line between being empathizing with him and pretending to be happy that she had won the award. Nothing could be worse than having an award you thought was yours given to someone else, especially if that person clearly didn't want it.

And so Celia had to act. Something she'd never been particularly good at.

"I'm glad it was you," Marco said kindly.

Celia bit her tongue. She wasn't. In fact, if there was a way she could have secretly spoken to the organisers and had the award given to Marco, or anyone else, she would have.

"Thank you," she said. "It was just luck."

"Five point three million euros' worth of it," he pointed out.

"Expensive luck," Celia agreed. "Anyway, how is little Maria?"

Marco jumped at the chance to talk about his daughter. Celia took it all in, even though she really didn't care much about any of it. When clients and colleagues spoke to her, she remembered the names, the dates, the facts, and the figures, but she never really cared about them.

It was purely business.

Knowing the name of a client's child or pet was second nature to her. It was a way to connect with someone on a more personal level.

It was a tool, little more.

A glass of champagne appeared in front of her, and she took a quick sip. If her mood had been better, she might have appreciated the expensive, flavourful bubbles popping on her tongue.

Instead she listened to Marco and desperately wished she could be anywhere else. She hadn't even departed, and she was already counting down the hours until she'd be back.

TIME TO BOARD

L ily waited by gate B41. She hated how airlines always called the boarding gate well before they were ready to board. And frequently, the departure board would display messages such as *boarding now* or *last call*, which would result in her rushing to the gate only to find that they weren't boarding at all.

It was all a con.

A con because some people left everything until the last minute. If people were a little more considerate of others, airlines wouldn't have to resort to such sneaky tactics.

She shifted uncomfortably from one foot to the other. There were still a few seats empty, but she didn't take one as getting her rucksack on and off her back was becoming increasingly difficult. She didn't know what had possessed her to get two more magazines, a bar of chocolate, and another can of drink.

More panic buying, she assumed.

She sucked in a breath and slowly blew it out again. Soon she would be on the plane, the doors would close, and she would finally be on her way. Then it was just a matter of waiting. In a luxurious business-class seat, with a mountain of food and some great movies.

A Perspex door slid open, and a member of staff appeared. Lily felt everyone gathered around the gate become a little more alert, ready to run for the gate the moment boarding was called. The member of staff lowered her clipboard to the desk and started to tap away on a keyboard. Everyone seemed to watch each single keystroke she took, ready to pounce.

After a few moments she reached up for the microphone, paused, and then went back to typing.

The tension was palpable.

She slowly reached out towards the microphone again, her eyes still focused on the screen.

The crowd of people leaned forward, holding their breath as they waited.

Long seconds ticked by, and then, finally, she started to speak.

"Good morning, ladies and gentlemen, and welcome to Flight 87 to Tokyo. I'm pleased to say that we are on time and will begin boarding soon, starting with our passengers requiring assistance and those travelling with small children. After those passengers have been seated, we'll ask our first-class passengers to come on board, followed by our business-class passengers, our premium economy passengers, and finally our economy passengers. Please listen out for your row number."

Lily stood to one side to allow the passengers who would be boarding ahead of her some more space. Unfortunately, in attempting to give them room, she ended up bumping into a person standing behind her.

"Oh, I'm so sorry, I…" The apology died on her lips as she saw it was the lady from the sandwich shop.

"Well. We meet again." The woman smirked.

"Yup. Lucky me," Lily muttered under her breath. She couldn't believe her bad luck. Of all the flights taking off that morning, she would be on the same one as *her*.

The woman swayed slightly and was very clearly drunk. Lily couldn't imagine what kind of person got blind drunk so early in the morning, and before catching a long flight too.

She secretly hoped that the cabin crew would notice her state and would kick her off the plane. It would absolutely serve her right.

"Is this gate B41?"

Lily nodded.

"Tokyo?" the woman clarified.

"Yes."

"Good." The woman clumsily walked over to a spare seat and all but flopped into it. A small man seated next to her was literally lifted off the seat at the force. He gripped the armrests in fear.

Lily shook her head and turned away. She waited as boarding started. People in wheelchairs boarded first, then those with walking aids, and then those with children.

After ten minutes first class were called to board, and a large group of people appeared from around the corner. Lily blinked at an enormously tall man, followed by a very thin man, followed by a man on a unicycle.

"Sir, that will have to go with the luggage, I'm afraid," a member of staff informed him.

He sighed and handed over the unicycle.

Lily blinked in surprise as more and more people came around the corner. Some were wearing intricate make-up, the likes of which she'd never seen before. One woman was walking on her hands.

Lily just stared as they all disappeared onto the air bridge to board the plane.

Well, she thought, that was different.

A few minutes later the business-class seats were called. Lily stepped forward and nearly collided with the drunk, rude woman again.

Lily stopped and gestured for her to go first. The woman didn't thank her or hesitate; she simply stepped in front of Lily as if it was her God-given right to do so.

Lily smothered a grimace and got in line behind her. They inched their way through the security checkpoint and down the air bridge towards the plane.

On board, they showed their boarding passes to the cabin crew, the drunk woman turned right, and Lily went straight on and was then guided right.

As she stepped closer and closer to her row, her heart sank.

The drunk woman had stopped, checked her boarding pass, and then looked up at the row number on the overhead bin. Satisfied she was in the right place, she flopped into her seat.

Lily looked up at the row number on her own side and then blew out a soft, frustrated sigh.

She took the seat right next to the drunk woman.

"Oh, come on, you've got to be kidding me," the woman drawled.

"I wish I was."

"And I thought today couldn't get any worse."

"It's no picnic for me, either," Lily replied, attempting to shove her overly full rucksack under the seat in front of her.

"Excuse me!" The woman flagged down a member of the cabin crew and peered at his name badge. "Martin, are there any other seats? This woman is stalking me."

"I am *not* stalking you," Lily defended herself.

"I'm sorry, we're operating a full flight," Martin apologised.

He glanced at Lily for a moment before returning his attention to the woman. "I could ask if anyone is willing to change with you?"

Lily wondered how they could be operating a full flight if she was offered a cheap upgrade but realised she probably had her answer there: last-minute sales fever to get the cabins full. If they were offering everyone a cheap upgrade to business class, then it was no wonder they were busy. And Lily couldn't imagine Martin would be foolish enough to offer the rude woman a downgrade to economy.

The drunk woman turned and regarded Lily with a pained expression. "We'll see how we get on. I'll let you know."

She dismissed Martin with a flick of her wrist; he seemed happy to leave. Meanwhile, Lily immediately felt as though she was back at school and on the cusp of being expelled at any moment.

❖

Celia couldn't believe, of all the people in the airport, she would find herself sitting next to the young sandwich jabber she'd first encountered in the airport cafe. *What is she doing in business class anyway?*

It seemed as though fate had conspired to make her trip as awful as possible. Not only was she condemned to fly around the world, but she had a choice between sitting in a first-class cabin that had literally been commandeered by the circus or next to someone who didn't look at all like they should be sitting in business class.

She attempted to subtly glance to her side. The young woman was wearing jeans, a T-shirt, and an unbuttoned plaid shirt.

She's cute, though, Celia thought in a drunken haze. She quickly shook her head to remove the errant notion. Turning away she watched a few more people board the flight. It wasn't long before her curiosity got the better of her and she looked back again.

Celia watched as her seat neighbour decanted countless snacks from her backpack into the seat pocket in front of her. Bags of sweets, chocolate bars, a can of drink were all removed like Mary Poppins removing a hatstand from a carpetbag.

Celia looked at the array of junk food; the amount of sugar would keep the average person awake for a year.

"Are you intending to eat all of that?" Celia asked.

"Maybe. Depends what I fancy. At least I have a selection."

"You certainly do. Enough to feed the cabin. You do know that they provide food on board, yes? This isn't the short hop to Málaga. There is a full menu." Celia glanced around and waved to a member of the cabin crew.

Martin came over and crouched down next to her. "How can I help, miss?"

"Scott. Celia Scott," Celia provided. "Do you have a menu? This poor dear seems to think that she's going to have to survive off packets of crisps and bars of chocolate. We must enlighten her. At once, Martin. Before she develops diabetes."

"I know there's food," the other woman complained. "Which, to be honest, you could certainly do with. If only to suck up some of the alcohol swimming around your body."

A light bulb went off in Celia's mind. "Good point." She turned to Martin. "Get me a glass of champagne, or whatever passes for it on board, please."

"Of course, Miss Scott. I'll be back in a moment."

Celia sat back in her seat smugly.

"I cannot believe he is getting you more alcohol."

"It's his job," Celia pointed out.

"To keep you tanked?"

"I'm not tanked. I'm merry."

"Do you often get merry at eight in the morning?"

"Depends on the circumstances. What's your name?" Celia turned to look at the young woman. She was obviously going to be a part of her journey, so Celia might as well have a name to use when she recounted the facts to friends at a later time.

Or maybe she was, on some level, looking forward to talking with her. She didn't wilt under Celia's tone like so many others did. If Celia was to endure this horrible flight, she might as well enjoy one aspect of it. And her seat mate was a sight to enjoy, even if Celia didn't quite understand why her subconscious kept pointing that fact out.

"Lily."

"Celia," she introduced herself.

Lily put some large headphones on. "Yeah, well, if you'll excuse me. I wouldn't want to be accused of stalking you."

Celia chuckled to herself. Lily certainly gave as good as she was given—Celia liked that in a person.

Martin returned with a tray of champagne flutes and a small paper menu. Celia took the menu and handed it to Lily and picked up a glass of drink.

Martin looked at Lily. "Would you like a glass of champagne, miss?"

Celia snorted at the notion it was actual champagne rather than sparkling wine.

"No, thank you, *far* too early for me," Lily said.

"If you have any questions about the menu, let me know," Martin replied.

"Will you be serving a hot meal quite soon?" Lily asked. "Only, Miss Scott here is clearly drunk and will need some sustenance to suck up the considerable amount of alcohol she's consumed."

Celia laughed and took another sip of champagne. "Whatever gives you the impression I'm drunk? My dear, I work in insurance. I can drink five times as much and still walk in a straight line while calculating your taxes."

"Around ninety minutes after take-off," Martin replied to Lily before wisely leaving them to their little spat.

Lily let out a sigh. She tapped the screen in front of her and started browsing through the entertainment on offer.

Celia hoped Lily wasn't going to be the type of person who watched back-to-back movies throughout the flight. While the screen was in front of Lily's face, that didn't mean Celia couldn't see it and be irritated by the flickering lights.

"Do you expect to sleep much on the flight?" Celia asked.

Lily glared at her. Celia decided she might have worn out her welcome with her earlier tone.

"Sorry I asked." Celia drank some more champagne. "I should let you know that I'm a very light sleeper. Any movement or noise may wake me. Also, I'm keen to get as much sleep as possible as I have a busy couple of days ahead of me in Tokyo."

Lily tapped her headphones. "Sorry, I can't hear you."

Celia narrowed her eyes at the obvious deception. She shook her head and turned her attention from Lily to focus steadfastly on the screen in front of her. The airline logo spun round and round while a small timer at the bottom of the screen, which had yet to start counting down, advised her of the interminable flight time that lay in front of her.

She downed the rest of the champagne in one go.

She turned to locate Martin and his tray of fake champagne, a slight wave of dizziness coming over her as she did. Perhaps she had imbibed a little too much considering the early hour.

Not that she cared. As far as she was concerned, that just increased her likeliness of being able to sleep. With any luck, she'd wake in time for the final meal served an hour before landing.

She made eye contact with Martin, and he promptly returned to her. She plucked a second glass of bubbly from the tray and thanked him.

DEPARTURE TIME

The snoring coming from the seat next to Lily was akin to something she had once heard in a zoo. Considering Celia Scott's airs and graces, she slept like an asthmatic pig. Not surprising, considering the amount of alcohol that was whizzing around her system.

Lily just wished the safety message would hurry up and finish, so she could put her headphones back on, crank the volume up, and not have to listen to the irritating din. It wasn't long after Celia downed the second glass of champagne that she'd promptly slumped into the world's loudest coma.

Lily had been relieved. The woman was difficult and almost angling for a fight, and Lily had no intention of giving her one. She was on her dream trip, to meet someone magical, having upgraded herself to business class. And no one, not even snobby Celia, was going to kill her buzz.

The video safety message came to an end, and Lily swiped to the movie she had chosen to watch first. It was a romcom from a year ago that she had wanted to see at the cinema but hadn't found anyone willing to go with her. She adored romantic comedies—the improbable scenarios, the mismatched characters who suddenly seemed perfect for one another, the humour.

Laughter was the perfect medicine for everything as far as Lily was concerned.

She started the movie and leaned back into her leather chair. There certainly was more room than in the standard economy seats she was used to. The seat was wider, and she had much more legroom. Best of all, she was separated from Celia's snoring form by large, padded armrests.

Out of the corner of her eye, Lily watched as the cabin crew prepared for take-off. She prided herself on being as little trouble as possible. Her bag was crammed under the seat in front of her, meaning her footwell was clear. Her seat belt was on and visible. She'd checked twice that her seat was fully upright.

Celia, on the other hand, was causing trouble even though she was unconscious. Martin took her satchel from her feet and forced it under the seat in front of her, then had to squint to check she had her seat belt fastened.

He didn't attempt to wake her, for which Lily was extremely grateful.

It's only a few hours, most of which she'll be unconscious, Lily reminded herself. *And then you'll be with Asami.*

She sighed with pleasure at the thought of finally meeting the person who had taken away her pain and managed to single-handedly light up her days.

The flight wasn't that long, and Celia wasn't that bad. She'd get through it all happily considering what awaited her in Tokyo.

❖

Something was wrong. Celia could sense it.

She opened her eyes with some difficulty. Somehow, her lids had become almost fused together. Probably something to do with sleeping with mascara on and the fact she'd drunk so much champagne it was practically leaching out through her eyeballs.

She pushed the thought to one side and forced herself to focus. She'd forced herself awake for a reason.

Something's wrong, she reminded herself.

She wasn't sure why she woke with the absolute feeling of certain dread, but she couldn't shake the sensation.

She sat upright and looked around the cabin. People looked concerned—some were very clearly frightened. The cabin crew looked serious as they marched up and down the aisles, giving instructions to people about trays and window blinds.

Yet again, she cursed not being in her usual first-class seat where she would be guaranteed a window. Now she was in the middle of the aircraft and straining to see beyond other passengers to get a glimpse out of the window.

When she did finally get a look, her stomach lurched.

She could see land.

The aircraft was banking sharply, and she could see land.

A glance at her watch told her what she already knew: it was far too early to be arriving. She might have been asleep, but she knew full well she hadn't been asleep for ten hours.

She couldn't remember exactly when they'd taken off, mainly because she was plastered at the time and almost certainly asleep. But if they had taken off on time, then it was less than two hours into the flight. Which could mean only one thing.

"We're dying," she whispered.

No one responded. Apparently her sleep-filled voice was so soft that no one heard her.

She turned to regard Lily. "We're crashing!"

Lily looked calm, eating potato chips and flipping through a magazine and apparently ignoring the dire situation unfolding before them.

"Welcome back. No, we're not crashing," Lily said without looking up.

"But…we're going down. I can see land! And we're not there yet. Unless this plane has some super-fast engine that has yet to be invented."

"If you'd been awake, you'd have heard the captain's announcement," Lily stated calmly. She popped another chip into her mouth.

Celia wanted to throttle her. "What did he say?" she demanded.

Lily let out a soft sigh. She slowly closed her magazine and turned to regard Celia. "He said that we're going to make an emergency landing in Copenhagen. That there's nothing to worry about, but there's a minor problem with one of the engines."

"None of those words are good," Celia informed her. "Why are you so calm? Are you insane?"

Celia grabbed for her seat belt; she needed to get up and speak to someone in charge. They were obviously all going to die, and the captain was attempting to keep the peace so utter anarchy didn't break out on the way to oblivion.

Lily grabbed at her hand, preventing her from releasing her seat belt. "What are you doing?"

"Getting out of here!"

"And going where, exactly?"

Celia didn't know. All she knew was that she had to get out of her seat and find out what was going on.

"Emergency landing," Celia spat. "Problem with the engines. We're clearly crashing. If you're not stupid enough to—"

Lily clamped her hand over Celia's mouth to silence her. Celia was enraged but far too drunk to do anything about it. Her coordination was a mess and her strength non-existent.

"Listen," Lily said, her voice a gentle whisper. "There's a lot of frightened people on this plane. And they don't need some drama queen like you making them even more frightened. We're not going to die. There's a minor problem. We're landing at the nearest available airport, and we'll be on the ground soon. Okay?"

Celia narrowed her eyes and glared at Lily.

"Okay?" Lily asked again, a stern edge to her tone.

Celia slowly nodded.

Lily removed her hand.

The moment she was free, Celia grabbed for her seat belt again, and Lily reached for her hand.

"Why are you like this?" Lily asked with exasperation. "Are you always like this?"

"I didn't even want to be on this plane," Celia said, frantically trying to shake off Lily's grip. "I don't want to go to Tokyo. I don't want to pick up the damned award. I never even wanted the award. And now I'm going to die for it. Dying for an award I didn't even want."

"Well, I'm sorry to be the one to tell you that you're not dying," Lily said as they wrestled for dominance. "We'll land in Copenhagen, get on a new plane, and you'll be picking up your stupid, unwanted award anyway. No one is dying here."

"Miss Scott, I'm going to have to ask you to calm down."

Celia forgot about fighting Lily for a second and turned to see the cabin steward, Martin, looking at her very seriously. No longer was he the smiling champagne delivery boy. Now he was in pure health-and-safety monster mode.

"We're going to die, aren't we?" Celia asked him.

"No. We're landing in Copenhagen."

"The engine is on fire," Celia argued.

"No. One of the engines has developed an intermittent fault. And so, out of an abundance of caution, we're landing to get it fixed. The other engine is fine, and we could fly on just the one."

"You're all lying to me," Celia said.

"Can we lock her in a bathroom for her own safety?" Lily asked.

"I'm not going to be locked in any bathroom," Celia responded.

"Just stay in your seat, Miss Scott. Or I'll have the police arrest you when we land." Martin stormed up the aisle.

"Can't arrest a dead person," Celia shouted after him.

"Oh, will you shut up?" Lily demanded, her voice icy cold. "There's a little boy back there, and you're scaring him."

Celia turned to see a small boy in a large seat clutching his mother's hand like a lifeline. He looked so much like her Andrew had at that age.

She sucked in a deep breath. If they were about to die, then it was best to do so with calm and decorum. Especially if there was a child nearby.

She sat up straight in her chair, leaned back into the headrest, and took some long, deep breaths. She closed her eyes and reached out for Lily's hand.

Once she had hold of it, she held it tightly and waited for oblivion to come.

❖

Lily didn't know why she was holding Celia's hand, but she was so relieved that Celia had finally stopped her mounting panic attack that she allowed it.

If she was honest, Lily wasn't exactly feeling calm about the situation. Although that didn't mean she was going to fly off the handle and act like Celia had done. No, she'd be sensible about it and accept her death quietly and privately if it was going to come.

She pressed back in her chair and appreciated the soft leather, wondering if it would protect her from a crash. Would her upgrade literally save her life? She snorted a laugh at the very thought. It wasn't as if half an inch of padding and a bit of leather were going to do much to cushion the blow of falling out of the sky.

Thankfully, they didn't feel as though they were falling out of the sky. However, it was clear they were descending at a fast rate. Lily's ears were already feeling stuffy from the sudden changes in air pressures, but that didn't prevent her from hearing the collective intake of breath every time the pilot banked the aircraft.

Everyone on the flight seemed completely attuned to every single movement of the plane.

The environment had gone from passengers lounging in their seats, watching movies and eating snacks, to everyone sitting bolt upright and holding their breath, wondering if every rogue sound was one of the wings falling off.

Lily found strange comfort in holding Celia's hand. Not that she seemed to have much choice in the matter. Celia wasn't about to let go, and Lily didn't mind that at all. Celia might have been a stranger, an occasionally rude stranger, but if she was about to die in one of the most horrific ways imaginable, then at least she wasn't entirely alone.

She desperately wished she could text Asami and let her know what was happening. Not that she knew exactly what was happening. What did you say to someone you thought you were in love with but had never met when there was a possibility you were going to die?

The plane banked steeply. A few passengers gasped; some let out a little scream. Celia held Lily's hand a little tighter, and Lily reciprocated.

Her heart thudded against her chest with such a force that she wondered if her ribs would be sore later.

If she survived.

She sucked in a deep breath and shook her head. She had to stop thinking like that. She *would* survive. Everything would be fine. They'd land safely in Copenhagen and then either fix the current aircraft or get on a new one.

God, she hoped they'd get on a new one.

She turned and looked at Celia. Somehow she looked peaceful and calm. Her eyes were closed, and her face was passive. She looked like she was casually asleep and not waiting for her own demise.

Lily wondered where the calm had come from. Celia didn't seem like the kind of person who was calm very often. She had seemed a powerhouse of energy and privilege, storming around the terminal building like she owned the place.

Her thick dark brown hair looked perfectly trimmed and styled as it rested elegantly on her shoulders. Her dark grey suit looked like it was bespoke tailored judging by the way it fit her like a glove.

She clearly had money, not a surprise considering her behaviour and the fact she was flying in business class. Lily thought about the award she had been babbling about and wondered what line of work she was in.

She had little to go on but found herself considering the matter with some depth, probably because the only other thing to think about was whether she'd be eating a famous Danish hot dog for lunch or if she'd be dead.

Celia could be a scientist or a doctor. Maybe she was picking up an award for some discovery she'd made. Or perhaps she was in show business, and she'd made an incredible film about the rainforest.

Recollection hit her—Celia had mentioned that she worked in insurance. Lily frowned. It all seemed rather boring compared to the flight of fancy she'd been on. And what kind of award could you really be given in the insurance world anyway?

Celia didn't seem like an insurance kind of person. They were all grey, old, and starchy, weren't they?

Celia wasn't like that at all. She was beautiful and under other circumstances Lily would love the opportunity to sketch her.

Lily tore her gaze away. She shouldn't be thinking things like that when she was on her way to see Asami. And she *was* on her way to see her, not about to die in a plane crash.

She hoped.

She closed her eyes, and with her free hand, she gripped the armrest of her seat and held on tightly.

LIMP LETTUCE

While the landing was relatively smooth, it instantly took a spot on Lily's list of the most stressful moments in her life, right up there with telling her grandmother she was gay.

The captain made an announcement welcoming them to Copenhagen and advising them that they would be deplaning shortly.

Lily had always considered *deplaning* a very strange word. You never detrained or deboated. Who decided you would deplane?

She didn't get much chance to think about it when Celia suddenly yanked her hand free.

"Are you okay now?" Lily asked her gently.

Celia hadn't said a single thing the entire way down. While it was a fast landing, it had still been fifteen long minutes of silence between them while they strangely held hands.

"Of course I am," Celia replied snootily. "How long do you think all this nonsense will take? This really is disgraceful."

"We're safe—that's the main thing," Lily argued.

Celia looked at her as if she was simple. "Of course we're safe. You don't think they'd actually allow us to take off if it wasn't safe, do you? No, of course not. Now, I want to know how they are going to fix this and get us on our way. There better be a standby plane waiting for us. I won't have a long delay. I just won't have it."

Lily turned away from Celia's ranting. It seemed that the calm, placid woman had vanished now that the question of their imminent mortality was settled. Now she was back to being an entitled bitch.

Lily did agree with her on one thing, though. Hopefully they'd get a new aircraft, one where she'd be allocated a new seat.

❖

"That's not acceptable." Celia folded her arms and stared at the airline employee.

"I'm sorry, there's nothing I can do." He tried to look strong, but Celia could tell he was starting to wilt under her gaze.

"I suggest that you get on the telephone to your head office and tell them that this needs to be resolved. Now." Celia tilted her head slightly, almost daring him to argue with her.

He clenched his jaw, swallowed, and then turned around and walked towards the small office he had appeared from. Celia had half a mind to follow him and stand over him while he made the call, but she knew she was just being cranky after her perceived near-death experience. And the fact that she suspected she had overreacted and embarrassed herself on the aircraft.

While her anger was real, she knew she should handle the situation better. It was just that there was so much swirling around her mind at the moment that sometimes the social niceties were the first things to be pushed out. Not that the airline was making it any easier for her to remain calm and pleasant.

She couldn't believe they were expecting her to stand around and wait for an unknown amount of time with no idea what was happening or when.

The relief she had felt when she'd finally gotten off the plane had been very short-lived once she'd discovered there seemed to be no firm plan to get them on their way again. The ground crew had advised passengers to keep an eye on the departures board for further information.

Which was completely unacceptable. Was she supposed to hang around the airport for hours, constantly checking in for information every ten minutes just in case they made a decision?

Celia had noticed the airline had a small information office at Copenhagen Airport and had made a beeline for it with every intention of making a nuisance of herself until she got some answers. Unfortunately, the only person present was some useless boy who had the authority of a limp lettuce leaf. All he could do was repeat the previous information she'd been given—to look at the departures board.

The only thing worse than having to fly around the world for an award she didn't even want was being stranded in an unfamiliar place with no idea how long her journey would now take.

She paced in front of the information office, waiting for the boy to return. She edged a little closer to the open door and was depressed to realise she couldn't hear the sound of him on the telephone.

A sinking feeling struck her, and she walked closer to look inside the office through the open door.

She sighed.

The room was empty.

The little snake had slithered away from her through another door. There was no one else to interrogate, so Celia turned away and decided to seek something out to keep her occupied.

The airport appeared to be very large, but Celia was mindful of not going too far in case she became disorientated and couldn't find her way back to the gate. She walked up the long corridor, which seemed to only lead to more and more gates and departure lounges. She assumed the main airport was ahead of her...somewhere.

Along the spacious corridor were a scattering of small coffee stands and food outlets. Since the emergency landing meant she hadn't slept off the alcohol, she decided it was a good time to have a coffee and some food before she started to feel sleepy again. She didn't want to wake up in a strange airport only to realise that her flight had taken off without her.

Or maybe she did?

She had been craving a problem with the aircraft that would stop them from getting to Tokyo. Technically, she had been granted her wish. She simply would have preferred it to have happened before taking off at all.

She stopped by a small coffee stand and got into the short queue. In front of her were two businessmen and a young woman. It was only on second glance that she realised the young woman was her seat neighbour, Lily.

Lily was happily conversing with the barista in another language, which Celia guessed was Danish. Her eyebrows rose in surprise. It seemed the dishevelled young woman had hidden depths.

One of the men in front of her answered a call on his mobile, then tugged the sleeve of his companion, and they both left. Celia took a couple of steps forward, placing her behind Lily.

She felt like she was intruding on a private moment between Lily and the barista, even though she had no idea what they were saying. The two women happily chatted away, laughing every now and then, seemingly unaware of Celia's presence.

Lily suddenly noticed Celia next to her and took a step back to allow her to be served.

"Sorry, didn't mean to get in your way *again*," Lily said.

Celia smiled as best she could. She didn't want to have another argument with Lily, especially after the embarrassing hand-holding incident.

"Sorry to interrupt." She turned to the barista and asked for a large filter coffee and a croissant.

"Did you find out anything new from the information office?" Lily asked, sipping from her takeaway mug.

"No, nothing. The child on duty assured me he would call head office, but then he ran away."

Lily chuckled. "Ran away?"

"Yes, there's another door in the office. He escaped." Celia shook her head at the thought. She should have listened to her instincts and followed him to the office.

The barista read off her order and the amount due, which seemed like a ludicrously high amount considering the currency differences. Celia held up her bank card to the machine—she'd just have to find out later if she had paid fifty pounds for the privilege of a drink and a pastry.

A queue of people had started to form, and Celia quickly took her items and walked away, surprising herself when she realised that she was following Lily.

Not that she had anywhere else to be.

"You speak Danish?" she asked, curiosity gnawing at her.

"Yes, my mother was Danish."

Celia heard *was*, put two and two together, and assumed Lily's mother had passed away. She decided to not mention it any further.

"So you must come here quite often?"

"Not as often as I'd like, but a few times," Lily said.

They approached a row of airport seats with small tables built in between each pair of chairs. Lily sat down and Celia followed suit.

"Do you think we'll get back on that same airplane?" Lily asked.

"I hope not, but I suspect so," Celia admitted. She set her drink down on the small table space and removed the cap to allow it to cool to a reasonable temperature. Why coffee shops insisted on centre-of-the-sun as a reasonable heat to aim for when making drinks was beyond her.

Lily got her phone out of her pocket, smiling the moment she looked at the screen, and started eagerly typing.

Celia was pleased to not have Lily's full attention while she ate her messy pastry. She enjoyed a croissant, but she was very aware that there was no dainty way to eat one. No matter how careful you were, it would end up all over your fingers and face. She wondered if it was some kind of French practical joke on the rest of the world. *Here's a delicious morsel, but you'll never be able to eat it without looking like a child.*

As she ate, she looked around the corridor. Her eyes landed on a nearby departures board. Their flight was listed, but the departure time was blank and the information area simply said *Please Wait.*

She imagined she'd be doing a lot of waiting, no matter how much shouting she did. She was very aware of how difficult it would be to get a replacement aircraft to them, which meant they were probably reliant on the Danish engineers fixing the problem with their current airplane.

How much did she trust the Danish engineers? Wasn't Denmark the home of a famous beer? Weren't they notoriously laid-back about things?

She shook the thoughts away.

"Why are you going to Tokyo?" she asked Lily, desperate for some kind of distraction.

"To see a friend."

"Ah. Very nice." Celia sipped her coffee. She winced. Still far too hot.

"I'm nervous," Lily confessed.

"Why?"

Lily lowered her phone and regarded Celia. "I've never met them before. We talk a lot. Like, *a lot.* And I think we have something…"

Celia regarded Lily with scepticism as she trailed off. "You've never met, and yet you're flying halfway around the world?"

"Yes."

"I presume you know this person quite well?"

"Yes," Lily replied defensively. "We talk all the time."

"How?" Celia asked.

"What do you mean?"

"Do you email or do you video chat?"

Lily hesitated a beat. "Mainly text and email. She doesn't like video chat."

Celia smirked. "Oh, doesn't she?"

Lily sighed and crossed her legs, now choosing to lean away from Celia. "I don't know why I told you anything."

"Me neither," Celia admitted. "But now you have. So, this woman—have you seen a photo of her at least?"

"Yes, of course I have," Lily exclaimed.

"And I presume you performed a reverse image search."

Lily frowned. "What?"

Celia sighed. "Did you search online for the image she sent you? To check it isn't someone fraudulently using someone else's likeness? Or a stock image."

"Who would do that?" Lily asked, clearly stunned.

"Use someone else's likeness, or check for the possibility? Either way, many thousands of people. You haven't checked? Why haven't you checked?" Celia reached down to her leather satchel and felt for her MacBook.

"I don't need to check." Lily sat up a little, anger clearly building within her. "Besides, I did chat to her on video once."

"A whole one time? Well, then she's definitely a real person—excuse my paranoia," Celia said with a chuckle. She pulled the laptop out of her bag, placed it on her lap, and opened the lid.

"Look, I know Asami is a real person. We have a connection."

"Let me guess, does she not like how she looks?" Celia asked.

"Well, no…as a matter of fact she doesn't."

"And so she doesn't send photos."

"As I said, I talked to her on video once," Lily pressed.

"Was it a long chat?"

Lily paused a moment before confessing, "Not that long, she had to go."

"Hmm."

"She's real. We talk all the time," Lily insisted.

"Of course, I'm being silly." Celia casually sipped at her coffee. She connected to the airport Wi-Fi and opened a new browser window. "I'm sure she's lovely, and you have a wonderful connection with her."

"I do." Lily nodded, her eyes still narrow as she presumably wondered if Celia was being facetious or not.

"Probably knows you better than anyone, what with talking online all the time," Celia continued. She typed a search into the search bar. "It would create a bond stronger than someone you only see once per week, for example."

"Exactly." Lily smiled, clearly happy to hear Celia was getting it.

"Lily, I'm going to tell you something very, very important," Celia said. She put her elbow on the armrest of the chair and cupped her chin as she looked intently at Lily beside her, suddenly very aware of how young she was. "Asami…is a man. I guarantee it."

Fury blazed in Lily's eyes. She reached down and grabbed her obviously heavy rucksack and struggled to put it on her back. When she had managed that feat of human strength, she plucked up her takeaway drink and looked down at Celia.

"You are *mean.*"

"Thank you," Celia replied. "But I'm afraid that doesn't change a thing. Asami is still a man. Sit down—I'll show you some research. This happened to a friend of mine a while ago. You'd be surprised to know how often someone is a victim of catfishing."

"Catfishing?" Lily asked angrily.

"Yes, it's when someone is lured into an online romance with a fake persona," Celia explained. She continued searching for the link she had shown Stephie a few months before when she had supposedly found a man in the US military who was head over heels for her but a little light on money to afford a flight to come and see her.

"I know what catfishing is. I'm not being catfished. Asami is real," Lily replied.

Celia looked up and couldn't help but smile at the bright red cheeks that met her gaze.

"Look, I know it's upsetting to think about, but this really does happen all the time. Just read this article. Ignore that it's from Age UK—it's just usually older woman succumb to this kind of thing. Actually, it's usually older men." Celia gestured to her screen. "This tells you all the warning signs."

Lily huffed and stalked off. She paused a few metres away and turned back. "She isn't a man!"

Celia regarded Lily for a couple of seconds. "Yes, he is," she replied after a moment of fake contemplation.

Lily made an angry face and then turned and left for good.

Celia exhaled and sighed. She hadn't wanted to upset her, but she couldn't keep her mouth shut sometimes. Really, who flew all the way to Japan for someone who they'd video called once? Classic fake-romance scam. She closed her laptop lid and picked up her coffee. Well, she had tried.

Doubts

L ily charged through the airport on a mission to get away from Celia. She didn't know why she had even bothered trying to have a normal conversation with her.

Celia Scott didn't know her. And she most certainly didn't know Asami either.

Not wishing to go too far away from her gate, Lily paused by a fountain with a small replica of the Little Mermaid. She took a seat on the tiled edge and took a few deep, calming breaths.

After a few moments she started to think back to a time when she'd had her own doubts about Asami.

Back when everything had seemed too good to be true.

Yes, she'd had concerns about her. Any reasonable person would have. It wasn't as if she had blindly walked into a relationship with a complete stranger as Celia had assumed. She'd done some due diligence, asked a few probing questions, and requested some photographs.

Asami had been a little reluctant at first, but Lily understood that she had privacy concerns. After a while, they'd gotten closer, and Asami had been more willing to share photos.

Only a few, though, because of her issues with the way she looked.

Which was ludicrous because Asami was stunning.

Lily paused and thought for a moment. Was Celia on to something? Was she being played?

She shook her head and pushed the thought down.

"No, no, no. You're letting her get in your head. She's just messing with you," she muttered to herself.

A young boy walked by and she caught him staring back at her, the curious woman slumped by the fountain, talking to thin air.

"Adults talk to themselves, kid. Get used to it," she told him.

He hurried after his mother.

She got her phone and reread the last message from Asami. It seemed normal, nothing overly concerning.

Or masculine.

She shook her head again. "She is not a man."

❖

Celia took the phone away from her ear and checked just how long she had been on the wretched call so far.

Thirty-two minutes and twelve seconds.

That was how long she had been talking to various useless people at the airline's UK head office. So far, no one was proving to be any help whatsoever.

There was a break in the terrible music, a pause, and then, "Miss Scott?"

"Yes, still here, still stranded and awaiting answers," she replied.

"Hi, look, I'm sorry to be the bearer of bad news, but I'm afraid it looks like you won't be continuing your journey today."

Celia blinked. "What?"

"The aircraft you were on requires a part that isn't available in Copenhagen. A replacement aircraft is being dispatched, but it's currently flying to London from San Francisco. It needs to stop there and then continue to Copenhagen. Or there's a chance the part will be expressed from France and fitted. But, either way, I'm afraid there's going to be an overnight stay and then a departure tomorrow morning."

Celia rolled her eyes and ran her hand through her hair. This really was the last thing she needed.

"Our hotels team will be in touch with you soon to arrange overnight accommodation."

Celia looked at the tip of her shoe, debating which scathing reply to go with of the selection that popped instantly into her mind. She took a breath and swallowed down the thought. It wasn't this poor call centre minion's fault. She needed to stop lashing out at people just because she felt she had the weight of the world on her shoulders.

Then something occurred to her.

Maybe this was exactly what she wanted, a reason to not go to Tokyo and collect her award. She'd been praying for something like this to happen, and now she had it. A way out.

Of course, it would have been nicer if it had presented itself before she arrived in Denmark, but beggars couldn't be choosers.

She was off the hook—that was all that mattered.

"That won't be necessary," she said.

"But—"

"I'll be returning to London." Celia disconnected the call and eagerly rang Howard.

It took a few moments for the call to connect.

"Celia? Aren't you supposed to be on a plane?" Howard asked.

"I was," she explained. "Technical issues, we landed in Copenhagen."

"Oh, for goodness' sake," Howard exclaimed. "Honestly, I had this last year when I went to Barcelona for that cruise. A problem with the windscreen, would you believe it? It's almost like no one maintains anything any more."

Celia swallowed down the mental image of a problem with the windscreen of an aircraft. That was something she really didn't need floating around in her mind's eye. "Yes, well, the real pain is that they can't get us on our way again until tomorrow morning. I've checked every other airline, and they are all fully booked," she lied.

"Tomorrow morning?" Howard asked.

"Yes, it's ridiculous. I'm probably going to have to turn back, which is such a shame." Celia tried to smother her smile of joy, to keep it from spilling into her voice.

"Well, it's still doable," Howard said.

Celia swallowed. "Well, yes, but it would be tight."

"Well, not exactly tight," Howard said. "You'd still have time to check in, catch up on some sleep, and get to the ceremony. Especially as you're staying in the hotel where they are holding the event."

Celia performed the mental calculation, and damn the man but he was right. She'd definitely get there in time—tired but in time.

"But—"

"I know you feel bad about the lost time," Howard said. "Knowing you, you were going to log in the second you landed and catch up on some emails. You should look at this like an unexpected holiday. A nice break from the office. Enjoy some time in Copenhagen, go to Tokyo, and enjoy being praised for your achievements. In fact, I'm going to pull your remote access codes—"

"What? No!"

"I'm doing it, Celia. No work for you. Seriously, enjoy your free time."

"Howard!"

He disconnected the call.

Celia wanted to cry. Not only was she going to have to go and get the stupid award, but she needed to kill an entire day in Copenhagen without access to her work files.

"Can today get any worse?" she muttered to herself.

❖

"I have a note on your file saying you don't need a hotel, Miss Scott?"

Celia picked up her paperwork from the customer service desk. "Oh yes, that. Well, I changed my mind."

"Ah. That may be a problem," the woman replied.

"Why would that be a problem? This is a city, isn't it? You presumably have hotels?"

"Well, yes, it's just very busy this weekend due to Eurovision."

Celia sagged. "What?"

"Eurovision. The final is this weekend in the city. Almost every hotel and guestroom is booked."

Celia opened and then closed her mouth. She shook her head with disbelief. "Are you telling me that not only did I have to give up my seat because the cabin was overtaken by clowns, literal clowns, but that now I don't get a hotel room because thousands of people have descended on this city for a music competition?"

"I can try Malmö."

"Where's that?"

"Sweden."

Celia blinked. "You want to send me to another *country*?"

"It's only thirty minutes away by train," the woman added helpfully.

Celia spun around and pointed to a huge building that towered over the airport. "That is a hotel. A perfectly adequate hotel, I'm sure."

"It's fully booked."

"You're not seriously telling me that Eurovision fans want to stay in an airport hotel that looks like *that*? Gay men have a lot more class than to want to stay in that soulless concrete monstrosity."

"I believe that's been booked by the organisers and some of the technicians."

Celia rolled her eyes. "Fine. I'm going back to England. Forget this."

She turned on her heel and stormed away from the customer service desk. Her phone was immediately in her hand, and she was calling Howard again.

Before he even had time to greet her, she was ranting. "Sodding Eurovision, Howard. Can you believe it?"

"I'm sorry, what?"

"Eurovision. You know, the annual opportunity for all of Europe, Russia, and even Australia to remind us how universally hated we are through the medium of song."

"I know what Eurovision is, and we have won it before, you know, Celia."

"Wasn't that in the nineties?"

"Was it ninety-nine?" Howard asked. "I'll google it."

"Anyway, back to the point, Eurovision is soon, and it's in Copenhagen. And that means there's not a single hotel room in the city. Or in Denmark at all, the way they are talking."

"Ninety-seven," Howard said.

"What?"

"Nineteen ninety-seven. Katrina and the Waves. It was a nice song, that one. I can't even remember what we're sending over this year. Probably deserves null point whatever it is."

Celia sat down on an empty bench. "Howard? Focus, please?"

"Oh yes. Well, that is a difficult one. Surely there must be somewhere?"

"They seem to think not." Celia sighed. "I'm afraid the gods are against me on this one, Howard. I'm going to have to come back."

"Such a damn shame," Howard muttered. "Maybe we could get you another flight from Heathrow."

"No, no. I think I'm done with this trip. I'm already exhausted. If I can't get on my way today, then I'd best not go at all." She faked a smothered yawn. "I'll shout at customer services one last time, a last-ditch effort. But if I can't manage anything, I'll head home."

Howard blew out a breath. "Yes, I suppose that is for the best. Still, such a shame."

"Yes, well, I'll go and try one last time. I'll let you know how I get on." She hung up and jumped to her feet, eager to find the first flight back to Heathrow she could.

She'd write off the terrible morning and short adventure in Denmark as a small price to pay for not having to go to Tokyo and accept the award.

Maybe things were working out for the best, albeit slowly.

On Second Thoughts

Lily hung up her phone and tucked it back into her jeans pocket. She looked down at the rips in them and let out a small sigh. Mormor wouldn't be pleased, and Lily would again have to explain how it was the fashion and not that she lived in poverty and had forgotten how to sew.

She looked around the large terminal building at the various shops and restaurants and wondered if she should have something to eat before beginning the journey across town to her mormor's home. It wasn't that far, but any excuse to delay arriving would be much preferred.

She spotted a Starbucks and walked over. As she got closer, she saw a familiar face standing by the chilled sandwich cabinet.

She smiled as a plan came to mind.

She quietly crept up behind Celia and watched as she picked up a sandwich, read the label, and then put it down again.

"Please, do let me know when you've finished fingering *every* sandwich in the shop," Lily said in a posh voice.

"Is that supposed to be an approximation of what I sound like?" Celia asked without even turning around.

Lily felt somewhat disappointed that Celia didn't jump as Lily had done when they'd first met.

"Yes, and it's a very good impression of you," Lily replied.

"I'll have to take your word for it." Celia picked up a sandwich. "I'll vacate the area so you can prod sandwiches at your leisure. Enjoy yourself."

Lily regarded Celia curiously as she walked by and started to look at the chilled drinks in the neighbouring cabinet. Something seemed different about her.

She seemed *happy*. Lily wouldn't have expected that from Celia following the news of the twenty-four-hour delay.

"Did you get a good hotel?" Lily asked, wondering if the airline had booked her into an expensive spa to keep her happy.

"Whatever for?" Celia asked without looking up at her.

Lily bit her lip. Was her luck so bad that she was about to have her head cleanly removed from her shoulders for being the unfortunate soul who had to inform Celia of the delay?

"The overnight stay," Lily said carefully.

"Oh, that. I'm not staying—I'm heading home." Celia picked up a bottle of water. She looked at Lily and sighed as if realising only then that politeness would dictate a fuller reply. "Did *you* get a good hotel?"

"Sort of," Lily said. "I'm staying with my mormor—I mean, grandmother."

Celia nodded slowly, looking Lily up and down as she did. "Ah, yes. Well, that's paid dividends, hasn't it?"

"Well, I'm not sleeping on a park bench. But that's about the only good thing about it, to be honest." Lily turned her attention back to the sandwiches but found her appetite had left her.

"Not a good relationship?" Celia guessed.

"Not really. She's old-fashioned." Lily didn't elaborate. She wasn't about to delve into it any further with Celia. Especially when she considered she'd have an entire afternoon and evening of it when she finally arrived in Valby.

Celia's mobile phone rang. She handed her sandwich and bottle of water to Lily as she got the device out of her suit jacket pocket. Lily didn't know why she had accepted the load or why she stood there like a servant holding Celia's things.

But she did.

"Howard?" Celia answered the call with a confused frown etched on her face.

Lily turned and looked at the chiller cabinet to afford Celia some privacy, without walking away with her lunch.

"What? No—I mean, that's…But—"

Lily chanced a look at Celia and was surprised to see she had paled. She wondered if she'd received some bad news.

"But really, Howard, a special ceremony isn't necessary," Celia said.

Lily had no idea what was going on, but whoever Howard was and whatever he was suggesting were not going down well with Celia. In fact, she looked downright terrified.

"Look, Howard, I've actually managed to find a customer service advisor who might be able to help me. Let me just see what she has to say. One moment." Celia lowered the phone and pressed a button, presumably to mute the call.

She let out a heartfelt groan and looked squarely at Lily. "There are no hotels in the city because of Eurovision. I'll pay you if you let me stay with you and your grandmother tonight."

Lily's eyes widened in shock at the sudden turnabout. "What?"

"I'll sleep on the sofa," Celia added. "I'll pay you a sizeable amount, and your grandmother. I just need somewhere to stay tonight, so I can get on that damned flight tomorrow."

"I thought you were heading home," Lily asked.

"Things are changing. Can I stay or not?" Celia's eyes bored into her, obviously wishing for a speedy and positive answer.

Lily considered it for a moment. Her grandmother wouldn't mind, there was room, and Celia seemed to be in a bind.

Part of her suspected that Celia would never have returned the favour if their positions had been reversed, but Lily knew that wasn't a reason to say no. Being the better person was a thankless job, but it was always the right thing to do.

"Yes, sure, okay," Lily agreed.

Celia tapped a button on the phone. "Howard, good news. I have a hotel for the night. I'll be in Tokyo for the event."

Knowing she'd done the right thing didn't prevent the sinking feeling in Lily's stomach.

❖

"Where are you going?" Celia asked Lily.

They had been walking side by side in silence since her disastrous phone call with Howard, making their way to Lily's grandmother's house. Wherever that was.

Celia briefly worried that she had made a terrible mistake in inviting herself into a stranger's house. For all she knew, Lily's family could be murderers. Or terminally boring.

At the moment, it was a risk she'd willingly take. Being killed, either through boredom or more direct methods, would be a far better outcome than Howard's scheme. She couldn't believe he had called the award organisers and begged them to send a delegation to the office for a special ceremony just for her.

Of course, the organisation was international and frequently held events all over the globe, but the thought of a special event in her honour, in London, was too much to bear. If going all the way to Tokyo to pick up the wretched award was a bad dream, the idea of a bespoke event in London was a fully fledged night terror.

As much as she desired to go home, she'd rather fight tooth and nail to get to Tokyo and accept the award and have it over and done with. An evening at an event and under sixty seconds accepting an award followed by her short acceptance speech would be infinitely better than an evening *dedicated* to her.

"The train station," Lily answered, pointing to a set of automatic doors that seemed to lead on a downward slope to the depths of the airport.

"I'd rather get a taxi," Celia said. There was no way she was going to drag her suitcase across town. She wanted door-to-door service.

Lily hesitated a moment. "Uh. Okay." She pointed in another direction. They both walked towards the exit, and Celia found she was relieved to breath fresh air again.

It had been a long while in airports or on board planes, and she hadn't realised what a luxury cool, fresh air was.

"So, where does your grandmother live?" Celia asked. She silently hoped it wasn't miles away or on a farm somewhere. She wasn't ready to be traipsing across some muddy field, nose constantly assaulted by the unique smells that could only come from a farm.

"Valby," Lily replied, clearly distracted as she had been since agreeing to let Celia stay.

"And that is?"

"Oh, sorry. It's not far from here, about a fifteen-minute drive. About fifteen minutes away from Copenhagen, too, if you fancy going into the city and looking around. Have you been before?"

Celia shook her head. "No. What do you recommend I see?"

Lily blew out a breath. "Um. Well, there's the Little Mermaid statue, you can get on a riverboat cruise, and there's loads of shopping, museums, and Tivoli."

"What's Tivoli?"

A smile lit up Lily's face. "It's my favourite place in Denmark, maybe even my favourite place in the world. It's like a theme park, but it's old and classy. Lots of twinkling lights and pretty gardens. It's fun."

Celia smiled to herself. It didn't sound much like her idea of fun, but Lily seemed to be taken with the place, and so Celia decided that she would keep her mouth shut on the matter.

It was not a trait she was necessarily known for, but needs must, dependent as she was. And truth be told, Lily was growing on her.

Just after Celia had spoken to Howard, Lily had called her grandmother to advise her to expect another guest. She'd done so in Danish, and so Celia had no idea how the conversation had gone. Lily's expression had remained relatively neutral throughout, but Celia got the impression that Lily wasn't too happy with staying at her grandmother's house herself, never mind with company.

"Anything I should know about your grandmother?" Celia quizzed her.

"Not really."

"Does she speak English?"

"Yeah."

"Good. That will make things easier all round," Celia said.

There was something definitely wrong, and Celia wondered what the issue between Lily and her grandmother actually was.

She suspected she'd find out soon enough, and she hoped she'd manage to stay out of it. All she wanted was a bed for the night.

AWKWARD FAMILY MOMENTS

As the car pulled up to the house, Lily sucked in a deep breath. She hadn't been expecting to see her grandmother, certainly not without a couple of weeks' preparation beforehand.

It wasn't that she didn't like the older woman; it was just that she had nothing in common with her. Furthermore, her mormor was old-fashioned and didn't understand, or wish to understand, Lily's way of life. No visit went without backhanded compliments or outright hurtful commentary.

But Lily was a martyr to the idea of family. She couldn't have lied and not mentioned her unexpected layover in Denmark, and if she hadn't stayed with her grandmother, then questions would have been asked, and Lily would ultimately be the one to feel guilty. It was a vicious circle with no real solution.

They got out of the car, and Celia paid the driver. Before Lily had another chance to steel herself, she heard the sound of the garden gate creaking open.

"There you are."

Lily turned around and hoped her smile looked genuine. "Here I am!" She opened her arms, and her mormor swept her up in a hug.

"You're skinny. And your jeans have holes in them."

Wow, Lily thought, that was less than five seconds.

"Mormor, this is Celia, who I told you about." Lily introduced them, suddenly very grateful for the distraction. "Celia, this is my grandmother, Anette."

Celia held out her hand and smiled warmly. "A pleasure to meet you, Anette. And thank you so much for letting me stay the night. I do hope I won't be putting you out at all."

Lily raised an eyebrow at this new, overly polite Celia. Where had this woman been hiding? Was this really the drunk who had been slumped beside her, snoring like a pneumatic drill? Was this the real Celia, and the person she'd met had simply been afraid of flying? There were so many questions, but Lily was too preoccupied with dealing with the current issue of her grandmother.

"It's my pleasure. Do come inside—I have made coffee."

Anette led the way, and Lily and Celia dragged their suitcases behind her.

"You called her something...*more*-something?" Celia asked Lily.

"Mormor, it means grandmother. Well, actually, it means mother's mother."

"Ah, so she is your maternal grandmother?"

"That's right." Lily didn't elaborate, not wishing to dredge up memories of her mother. Not now, when the day was already making her feel so unsettled.

They walked into the house and put their suitcases against the wall, shrugged out of their light jackets, and hung them up on the hook. Lily took off her shoes, and Celia followed her lead, causing Lily to wonder what kind of maniac wore a full suit and high heels for an eleven-hour flight anyway. Although, she had to admit she had been grateful for the view when she'd first encountered her in the sandwich shop back in Heathrow.

She shook off the thought and looked around the house; nothing had changed. The same photographs hung on the walls. The same ornaments sat on the shelves.

It felt as equally homely and unfriendly as it always had. Lily remembered a time when she would run to hug her mormor and enjoy every second spent in her home. She also remembered when things started to change and the feeling of not being quite welcome started to creep in.

Celia didn't wait for the tour, instead going straight into the kitchen where Anette was making drinks. Lily shook herself out of her mood and followed.

The kitchen hadn't changed either. The smell of her grandmother's perfume mixed with the smell of the lilac bushes outside the window. And there was something else familiar. Lily sniffed the air a little, and Anette grinned at her.

"I made cookies."

Lily smiled. She'd always loved her grandmother's sugar cookies. Mormor must have made them the moment Lily hung up the phone. They were another layer in the complicated cake of their relationship, filled with love but topped with disappointment. And very hard to swallow, no matter how delicious it looked upon first glance.

"I'm just going to go and use the bathroom," Lily said.

She left the kitchen, assuming that the new, sweet, and charming Celia that had hatched as she exited the taxi would be fine on her own for a while. Fishing her mobile phone out of her jacket pocket in the hallway, she made her way upstairs to text Asami and update her on the situation.

She should have been halfway to Japan by now. Instead she was in her grandmother's house with a strange woman who fluctuated between rude and pleasant as much as the wind changed direction.

Now she just had to count down the hours until she'd be back on her way and figure out a way to get through them.

❖

Celia watched Lily leave, wondering again why the young woman seemed apprehensive about seeing her grandmother.

Anette seemed lovely, a typical grandmother figure complete with apron, cookies in the oven, and children's paintings on the refrigerator door. The house was immaculate but well-loved with a beautiful garden to the back that looked like it was specifically made for children to run and play in while adults sat on the patio and watched.

It seemed idyllic, and yet Lily was clearly out of sorts.

"Coffee?" Anette asked.

"Oh yes, please," Celia said. She sat at the kitchen table and watched Anette potter around the space. "You have a beautiful home."

"Oh, thank you. I have lived here for many years. First with my husband, and now alone."

"I'm sorry for your loss."

Anette waved the condolences away. "It was a long time ago." She picked up the coffee tray and brought it to the table.

"Thank you. And thank you for agreeing to let me stay. I'm terribly sorry for putting you out," Celia said.

"Not at all. Lily said you were sitting next to each other on the plane, is that right?" Anette questioned.

Oh, so that was something she said in Danish, Celia thought.

"Yes," she replied simply, not wanting to say too much in case Lily had also explained just how rude Celia had been to her, and the complete basket case she had become when in her drunken haze she'd decided they were all going to die.

"Why were you going to Tokyo, if I may ask?"

"Work," Celia answered. "There's an event I have to attend."

"I hope you won't miss it."

I hope I do. "Me too," she said. "Hopefully we'll be back on our way tomorrow. That will give me plenty of time."

"Oh, good." Anette turned in her chair to look into the hallway. Was she checking to see if Lily was returning? "Lily tells me she is going to look at the art galleries. But I think it's something else."

Oh Lord, don't involve me in this. She sipped her coffee. "Really?"

"Yes. She doesn't tell me anything," Anette whispered. "But she's been different."

"Well, we only just met, so I'm afraid I can't be of any help. I have no idea why she's going to Tokyo."

Anette looked slightly displeased with the lack of information and sat back in her seat, a pensive expression now on her face.

"I take it you have grandchildren younger than Lily," Celia said, pointing to a finger painting attached to the fridge door by a magnet. "Unless that's her work?"

Anette chuckled. "I have two great-grandchildren. Sofia is three and Magnus is five. Lily's brother's children. Lily's drawings are much better. She's an artist, did you know?"

"Oh, is she? No, I had no idea. What kind of artist?"

Anette got to her feet. "I'll show you. One moment."

Anette walked into the living room and approached a large bookshelf. She started to flip through the volumes, occasionally taking one out and creating a small stack of thin books in the crook of her arm.

Celia watched with fascination. Anette returned with a variety of children's books and laid them on the table.

"She draws all of these," Anette said, the pride clear in her tone.

"Ah, she's a children's book illustrator, I see." Celia picked up a book about tigers and smiled at the depiction of a sleepy tiger in a pair of oversized pyjamas.

"She's always drawing," Anette explained. "Always was when she was a child too. I had to make her go out with me to the shops or to the park. *No, Mormor,* she'd say, *I want to stay here and draw.*"

"It's lovely that she's turned a hobby into a career," Celia pointed out.

"Sometimes she is a little too artistic, if you understand my meaning?" Anette said in a low tone.

Celia had no idea what meaning she was referring to, and so she ignored the comment and continued to look at the books.

"Oh, Mormor, you didn't," Lily said when she returned to the kitchen.

"I'm not allowed to show off your talents?" Anette asked casually, clearly not about to be told off by her granddaughter.

Celia looked up from a story about a tugboat and smiled at the rosy blush on Lily's cheeks. "You're very talented," Celia said with a smile.

"Thank you," Lily said, sitting down and preparing herself a mug of coffee.

"The cookies will be done, excuse me." Anette stood and went to the old Aga that took up most of the wall. She pulled out a tray of cookies and placed them on a cooling rack.

Celia looked from Anette to Lily and chuckled. Lily was staring lustfully at the cookies.

"Hungry?" Celia asked.

"They are the best cookies in the world," Lily said.

The doorbell sounded. Anette wiped her hands on a tea towel and went to answer it. "Do not touch them," she instructed Lily as she left the room.

"Yes, don't touch them," Celia said, "or I'll tell on you."

"Don't gang up on me with her," Lily warned. Her tone was light, but Celia had a feeling the words were serious.

"I won't," Celia promised. "She asked me if I knew why you were going to Tokyo, and I didn't say you were going to meet a man. So I've been very well behaved."

"She. Is. Not. A. Man."

"In his forties," Celia added. "Maybe fifties." Celia didn't want to be cruel, but if her words caused Lily to think twice and maybe spend a few minutes investigating her Japanese beau, then it would be worth any possible hurt caused.

"You're impossible."

"Why did you neglect to tell your grandmother that you're going to meet someone?" Celia asked, feeling as if she already knew the answer. Surely, deep down, even Lily must have understood the risks of flying to Tokyo to meet someone she'd never really spoken to or seen.

"She wouldn't understand." Lily leaned back in her chair, much as Anette had earlier, to check Anette wasn't about to return to the kitchen. "Please don't say anything."

Celia held her hand up. "A word shall not pass my lips. If you wish to die at the hands of a strange Japanese man while your poor family have no idea where you ended up, then that's your business, not mine."

Lily narrowed her eyes and glared at her.

Celia smiled in return and took a sip of coffee.

Anette returned, glancing first at the untouched cookies and then at Lily with a loving smile. Celia had to wonder if Lily would have sneaked a cookie if she hadn't been there to distract her.

"Any news from England?" Anette asked.

Celia kept quiet, assuming she wasn't asking as to the general political landscape or the weather.

"No, Mormor," Lily replied quietly. "Just the same as it was last time we spoke."

"No boyfriend?" Anette asked, her back to them as she scooped the cookies from the cooling rack onto a serving plate.

Fury flashed in Lily's eyes. "Mormor."

"It will pass," Anette said, a tension to her tone.

"It won't pass," Lily replied, her anger obvious.

Celia suddenly wished the plane had smashed into the ground and killed her. Then she wouldn't be stuck in a stranger's kitchen in what was obviously about to turn into a very sensitive argument.

"You are young," Anette added.

"Not that young," Lily argued.

"Young." Anette turned and held the plate out to Celia to offer her a cookie.

Celia politely took one and thanked her.

Anette placed the plate on the table, not bothering to offer one directly to Lily.

"I'm gay, Mormor," Lily said. "It's not going to change. I'm sorry, it's who I am."

"We'll see," Anette said.

Celia was about to say something to attempt to defuse the situation when Lily suddenly stood up and left the room. She listened to the sound of Lily rushing up the stairs and the sound of a door closing.

"The weather today is nicer than they forecast," Anette said, picking up a cookie and focusing her attention on the window to the garden.

Celia grimaced and took a bite of her cookie. It seemed the day could get worse and worse after all.

UNEXPECTED KINDNESS

Lily lay on the guest bed and stared up at the ceiling. She shouldn't have come here. She should have slept in the airport instead. Or gone across the bridge to Malmö and stayed in a hotel there. Anything but put herself through this nightmare for the umpteenth time.

Her grandmother wasn't *exactly* homophobic.

It was more the distance involved that bothered her. People could be gay—they just had to be somewhere else. Or *someone* else. Other people.

Her grandmother's favourite celebrity on the television could be gay and dating a lovely boy, and Mormor would be fine.

But when it came to her own flesh and blood, when it came to Lily, it wasn't acceptable to be gay. And that was what hurt most, the acceptance for some but not for her.

And if this semi-acceptance had to exist, couldn't it be the other way around? Why did being close to her grandmother mean Lily didn't get the benefit of her approval?

Why were film stars and musicians allowed, but Lily was confused and wasting her life?

The arguments were always the same: Lily was young, Lily was confused, Lily would change her mind. It was nothing outrageously homophobic but enough to constantly nag at her and make her feel like less of a person.

Most of the time, their conversations were pleasant, even loving, but certain topics would bring them back to the core debate that was slowly ruining their relationship.

Her grandmother couldn't let it go. Lily suspected that as Mormor got older, she felt more of a need to put Lily back on what she thought was the right path. A path that led to a nice man, some children, a mortgage, and what her grandmother considered normal and correct.

When Lily had been dating Angela, her relationship with Mormor had taken a colossal dip that she hadn't expected or been emotionally prepared for. When Angela had broken it off, her grandmother hadn't been unable to disguise her delight, much to Lily's frustration and sorrow.

But she knew Mormor loved her. She also knew that it would be impossible for her to break off all contact with her. She was her grandmother. They'd shared so much, and her childhood had been so vital in becoming who she was. To cut that tie would be like removing a part of her soul.

So Lily tried to keep the peace wherever possible and her tears as soft as she could when she failed. The balance wasn't perfect, but it was right for her.

She heard the creak of someone walking up the stairs and let out a sigh. She didn't want a second round. Nor did she want to be shamed for acting the way she had in front of a guest.

There was a soft knock on the door.

"I want to be alone," Lily murmured.

The handle clicked, and the door opened. Lily was surprised to see Celia in the doorway. She had a handful of cookies in some kitchen paper in her hand.

"I heard these were the best cookies in the world. I thought you might like some."

Lily slowly nodded, and Celia entered the room and handed over the cookies.

"Why are you being so nice?" Lily asked.

"Because your Japanese fraud will murder you tomorrow, so I thought you might as well have a nicer day today. Your grandmother has gone out to the shop, by the way." Celia took a seat on the small armchair in the corner that allowed for a view of the back garden from the Juliet balcony.

"I'm sorry you had to be there for that," Lily said. She sat up and placed the kitchen paper and cookies in her lap, breaking off a piece of one and slowly savouring the taste of it.

"I'm sorry you've clearly had to have the conversation more than once," Celia said.

Lily didn't have anything to say to that. The wounds were raw, and she didn't want to open them again, not any more than they had already been torn.

"I'm going to take a nap. Your grandmother showed me the downstairs guest room," Celia said, still examining the garden wistfully. "Then I'm going to go into the city for lunch and some general touristing. I wouldn't mind some company." She turned to look at Lily, a questioning expression on her face.

Lily knew it was an olive branch, but she didn't feel strong enough to take hold of it. Especially when she knew another quip about Asami probably lurked just around the corner.

"No." Lily shook her head. "Thank you."

Celia stood. "Very well. If you change your mind, let me know." She placed her business card on the bedside table. "My phone number, in case I've already gone out."

Celia left the room, closing the door behind her. Lily snatched up the business card, curiosity pushing her bad mood to one side.

The card informed her that Celia was a senior broker for an insurance company. Lily understood the words but didn't really know what that meant.

She supposed it meant that she now understood why Celia wore a suit all the time. She tucked the business card into her pocket and continued to pick at the cookies.

They were delicious, and that annoyed her.

A BREAK BEFORE AN ESCAPE

The room was small and clearly designed for young children to stay in. Celia placed her suitcase in the corner and looked at the small single bed, wondering when she had last slept in a single bed. Probably when she was a child.

Cuddly toys lined a shelf, and a tall chest of drawers was topped with an array of family photos, new and old. The wooden-framed window looked out to the garden, a small net curtain framing the window and rhododendron obscuring the view from outside to in.

She removed her suit jacket and hung it on the hook on the back of the door. Exhaustion was washing over her. There was the early morning, the alcohol, the adrenaline spike of the technical problem, and now she was staying in a stranger's home.

Her emotions were all over the place, a feeling she was becoming more and more familiar with. The last six months had been a strain, to say the least.

Thankfully she wasn't one for sleepless nights. Insomnia had been a problem for her for years, but when her life really began to fall apart, she'd started sleeping like a baby. Midday naps, early nights, forty winks on the train. Sleep suddenly came easily to her.

The one and only blessing karma had bestowed on her.

She sat on the edge of the bed and blew out a long breath, trying to shake off some of the stress she was carrying. When she realised it was a fruitless endeavour, she lay down and stared at the ceiling, controlled her breathing, and quickly drifted off to sleep.

❖

Celia woke to raised voices. It took her a few moments to remember where she was and figure out who the voices belonged to.

When her memory filled in the blanks, she let out a heartfelt sigh. Anette had obviously returned and had decided to continue her row with Lily.

She held her breath and tried to listen to the conversation, only to find that it was being held in Danish. She could only discern that the tone wasn't a good one.

It seemed that the voices were coming from upstairs, which presumably meant that Anette had sought Lily out in her refuge.

Not entirely fair of her, Celia thought.

She looked at her watch and was surprised to note that she had slept for an hour and it was now mid-afternoon.

Grateful for her forethought in packing an extra outfit, she got up and lifted her suitcase onto the bed. After a little digging, she pulled out a pair of smart trousers, a cap-sleeve blouse, and a thin cardigan. She grabbed her make-up bag and went in search of the downstairs bathroom Anette had mentioned when showing her the guest room.

A quarter of an hour later, she was changed and felt refreshed. Or as refreshed as she was going to get, at least. She'd brushed her teeth, touched up her make-up, and done something about her hair, which also wasn't a fan of early mornings.

Back in the guest room, she picked up her flats and took them to the shoe rack by the front door. If she was going to head out onto the streets of an old European city, she wasn't about to do it in heels.

"Did you sleep well?"

Celia turned to see Anette coming down the stairs, her cheeks a little red—either from the exertion of the impressively long argument she'd been having with Lily or from embarrassment at being caught in said argument.

"Like a baby," Celia said, neglecting to mention what had awakened her. "I was just going to head out for a while, get some lunch, and enjoy your beautiful city."

"I can prepare some lunch for you," Anette kindly offered.

"That's very generous of you, but I'd like some fresh air and a walk."

Anette nodded her understanding. "Yes, those airports and planes are very stuffy. Get some air while you can, yes?"

"Absolutely. I'll probably have dinner out as well, if that's okay? I don't want to be a rude guest."

"Of course, whatever you wish to do. I'll be in all evening, and I don't go to bed early, so do feel free to come back whenever you like. Would you like another coffee before you go?"

Celia debated for a moment before deciding that another hot drink would probably be a good idea before she embarked on her adventure to who knew where.

"That sounds lovely, thank you."

She followed Anette into the kitchen and tried to assist in making the drinks before quickly being told she was a guest and shooed away to sit at the table.

Celia watched Anette's tense form move around the kitchen. She was clearly upset.

Celia didn't know if she should upset her further by saying what was on the tip of her tongue. The path of least resistance was clearly to say nothing, accept the graciousness of her host, and then get the hell out of there as soon as possible.

"You really do have a magnificent garden. Does it take a lot of time to maintain?" Celia asked, feeling terrible that she was chickening out.

She wanted to say something, but it really wasn't her place.

MAY I JOIN YOU?

Lily might have purchased enough snacks in Heathrow to feed an army for a week, but they were useless to her in her bag by the front door, instead of in the room where she was hiding out.

Hunger gnawed at her, her stomach complaining bitterly about the fact that she had expelled a huge amount of energy in crying and fighting with her mormor.

She'd briefly considered popping downstairs to grab the bag, but the damned creaky stairs would give her away. She wasn't ready for another round.

She'd heard voices a while ago, Celia and her grandmother chatting in the kitchen. A short time after, she'd heard the front door gently close and assumed that Celia had headed off to explore Copenhagen.

Since then, she hadn't known what to do. Part of her wanted to run after Celia and get out of the house. But that wouldn't be fair to her grandmother.

Mormor had apologised in the end. It was one of those nonsense sort of apologies. A sorry-not-sorry. More a desire for the end of fighting now that the understanding had been reached that neither one of them would be moved from her position.

A temporary cease in hostilities, one that Lily and her grandmother had reached, and broken, time and time again.

But Lily wasn't ready to say sorry or to accept any apology. Especially one that wasn't real. One that would simply lead to another argument.

Lily had taken the opportunity to text with Asami, the only person in the world who knew how she felt. Asami had wisely said that Lily needed to look after herself, but also not cut herself off from her grandmother completely. One day, her grandmother wouldn't be there any more, and then Lily might feel bad about all the time they'd spent fighting.

It made sense, but the wounds were still too raw for Lily to see things that way. It was nice to talk to someone who understood, though. Asami had been through similar matters with her own family.

It was getting late in Tokyo, or late for Asami, who had to get up early in the morning to go to work at the hospital where she was a part-time cleaner, which meant that Asami would soon be signing off from their texts and going to bed. Which in turn meant that Lily would have no one to talk to about how she was feeling. And she would be stuck in the upstairs bedroom, waiting for her grandmother to return with some milk and cookies as if that fixed everything.

Worse, Lily would have to pretend that it *did* fix everything.

She had to get out of the house.

She looked at Celia's business card again, wondering if she'd been serious about wanting company. At this point, Celia's quips about Asami being a fraud were better than her grandmother's insistence that Lily wasn't gay. Which was quite a statement on the mess that Lily currently found herself in.

Picking up her phone, she quickly typed out a message. *Were you serious about wanting company?*

Lily checked the message for spelling mistakes and then sent it. A second later, she sighed as she realised that she'd forgotten something potentially very important. She typed a second message. *It's Lily, by the way.*

She checked the second message and then sent that. She didn't know why it was so important to her to make sure her texts were correctly spelt and used proper grammar. Celia just seemed to silently demand such attention to detail.

A moment later a text arrived back. *I'm not in the habit of saying things I don't mean. Let me know when you arrive in the city and we'll arrange a place to meet up.*

Lily considered writing a reply, but there didn't seem to be a need for one. Celia, as expected, had been to the point.

Now Lily just needed to use the bathroom and make herself a little more presentable before fobbing her grandmother off with some excuse.

She felt guilty, especially as she didn't see her grandmother that often. This was a sudden flying visit, and so surely she should suck up her feelings and spend as much time with Mormor as possible.

She bit her lip.

Then she remembered the fight and a few select sentences that fell from her grandmother's lips during it. Getting out of the house would be the best thing for both of them.

The sudden visit meant that neither of them had enjoyed their usual period of preparation before they had to meet. Their guest faces had not been attached in time, and the reality of that fact had stung them both.

Lily sat up and wiped at her eyes. It was time to go out. It was the right thing to do for both of them.

❖

Lily held her phone, turning it over and over as she waited for Celia to reply to her text. She'd grabbed the first bus into town and was heading for the central train station, assuming Celia would have done the same.

Except she now realised that it was highly likely that Celia had gotten a taxi or booked an Uber rather than getting on a city bus.

She'd texted to say she was on her way and asked Celia where she wanted to meet.

A text arrived, a photo. Lily frowned. It was a photograph of a road sign, a long street name containing several letters not present on the standard UK English keyboard.

I'm not going to attempt to type that. I'm here, window shopping.

Lily knew the street well. It was a popular shopping district in the centre of town. She replied to let Celia know she'd be there within the next twenty minutes.

Location dealt with, she sneaked some of the snacks out of her bag. It wasn't a real meal, but it would do. She snacked on a bag of chips and some chocolate-covered almonds.

She watched with interest as the streets of Copenhagen flew by the bus window. The scenery was so familiar and yet so foreign. She'd spent a lot of time in Copenhagen when she was a little girl, less as she'd gotten older.

Less the more she clashed with her grandmother.

It wasn't just her mormor—it was her brother too. Her brother was perfectly fine with her sexuality and even sent her a little rainbow flag emoji on Lesbian Visibility Day every year.

But he never stood up for her. Not once.

Each time their grandmother approached the boxing ring of their ongoing dispute, he disappeared to another room.

Not that Lily expected anything else. It was her decision, her battle to be fought. But the backup would have been nice once in a while.

She sighed and pulled a bottle of water from her bag.

Why did the damn plane have to develop an issue? She should be well on her way to Japan by now, not thinking about the family issues that haunted her every time she thought about her blood relations.

If they were still in the air, Copenhagen wouldn't have even entered her thought process. She'd be relaxing in a leather chair and enjoying all the trappings of a business-class lunch, watching movies, and eagerly counting down the minutes until she could finally meet Asami and be with someone who loved and understood her in a way no one else ever had.

But fate had a different idea.

Lily swallowed down some water. She leaned her head against the glass and tried to remember better times walking the familiar streets as they whizzed by.

She had enjoyed Copenhagen once. With an attitude adjustment she could do so again. At the end of the day, she was giving her grandmother the ability to ruin her time here, and she knew that was wrong. She needed to take back control of her own mood, life, and destiny.

It was time for a change, she decided. Time to push everything to one side and try to have a nice afternoon and evening in a city that used to be so dear to her heart.

She sat up a little straighter. She could turn the day around if she tried hard enough.

GETTING TO KNOW YOU

Celia tilted her head to the side and examined the blazer on the mannequin through the window.

"It would suit you," a familiar voice said from behind her.

"It's garish," Celia replied.

She turned towards Lily, giving her a quick once-over. Lily had also gotten changed and looked a great deal better than she had when Celia had last seen her.

"It's Scandinavian," Lily corrected. "They like their weird pastels."

"Hmm." Celia looked over her shoulder at the blazer. "I'd be laughed out of my office."

"I doubt that," Lily said. "I'm sure you look great in anything. And you're too scary for anyone to laugh at you, surely?"

"You've not met my work colleagues. Have you eaten?"

A light blush touched Lily's cheeks. "Yep."

Celia regarded her. "Have you eaten real food? Or did you strap your rucksack to your face and consume all the chocolate and sweets like a horse?"

Lily rolled her eyes. "You're really rude."

"Yes. But am I right?"

"Yes, but that doesn't change the fact that you're rude."

"Hmm. Doesn't change the fact you haven't eaten properly either."

Celia put her hand on Lily's shoulder and turned her around and gently pushed her to encourage her to start walking down the street. "You have to eat, if only to keep your strength up for when we go back to your grandmother's house." She saw Lily tense up.

"I'm sorry about her. She's…old-fashioned."

"She's something," Celia agreed. It wasn't her place to talk negatively about Lily's grandmother, especially as Anette had been nothing but delightful to Celia.

Lily obviously wasn't going to say anything else, and so Celia allowed them to walk in silence for a while before they came across a cafe that looked reasonable.

"How about we eat here? My treat," Celia suggested.

"I don't need you to buy me lunch," Lily said defensively.

Celia smirked. "I'm well aware of that—I'm being nice. I know it's at odds with my personality, but I do occasionally give it a whirl."

Lily looked suitably chastised. "I'm sorry. I'm…having a weird day."

"What a coincidence—I'm having one of those myself. Shall we discuss it over lunch?" Celia gestured to the door.

Lily nodded, and they stepped inside. Celia was grateful that she'd only eaten a couple of pieces of fruit from a farmers' market she had passed on her way into town. It meant she could now sit down and have a proper lunch, even if it was a little later in the day than she was used to.

Thankfully there was waitress service, and they were quickly taken to a free table, where proper leather-bound menus were placed in their hands.

They sat in companionable silence for a few minutes until they placed their orders, both opting for pasta dishes.

"I love pasta," Lily said conversationally.

"I'd eat more of it if I could," Celia confessed.

"I can't cook it, though. It should be the easiest thing to cook, but every time I try, I seem to get it wrong," Lily continued.

Celia wasn't about to sit and talk about cooking pasta. She might have been killing time, but she wasn't that hard up for conversation.

"So, you're an illustrator?"

Lily glanced down at the table. "Yeah."

Celia frowned. She hadn't expected Lily to be embarrassed by her job.

"Your work seems very good," Celia added, trying to figure out what was making Lily uncomfortable.

She shrugged lightly and started to look around the cafe. "It pays the bills."

"Do you not like the work?"

Lily's eyes snapped up to meet Celia's. "Oh no. I love it. If I could

choose to do anything, I'd choose this. I just know that it's not very…
mature."

"Mature?"

The waitress returned and placed cups of juice and pots of tea
on the table. Lily watched her silently before whispering a thank-you
when she'd finished.

The silence between them grew.

"What do you mean by mature?" Celia prodded.

"I mean, it's not like it's a real job."

Celia frowned. "Do you get paid?"

"Yes, of course."

"Then it's a real job. Money in exchange for goods or services,
the very concept of paid employment. Why do you think it's not a *real*
job?"

Lily pulled her teapot closer to her and lifted the lid, examining
the water within. "It's just a bit…childish. I draw pictures for a living.
Usually silly things like trains with faces and personalities, or poop. It's
silly, that's all."

"While I'm personally not a fan of the increasing fascination with
the humanisation of *poop*, I'm sure your books make children happy.
You clearly have a talent that many people don't possess. Don't be
ashamed of that."

Lily put the lid back on her teapot and slowly nodded but said
nothing else.

That topic of conversation was over, Celia decided. She reached
for her own teapot and gave it a small swirl to aid the brewing process.
She couldn't abide weak tea.

"So, you're a senior insurance broker?" Lily asked.

"How did you know that?" Celia asked.

"Your business card." Lily poured herself some tea.

"Ah, yes."

"And you look like you work in insurance," Lily added.

"Am I about to be the punchline of a joke?" Celia asked.

Lily shook her head. "No, not at all. You just look professional.
Nice suit. That kind of thing."

"Thank you."

"And you won an award?" Lily asked, the tone of her voice
changing ever so slightly in an indication that she suspected it might be
a conversational point that Celia didn't wish to visit.

Which she didn't.

But they were having a nice lunch, and Lily didn't know any better. Celia wasn't about to ruin that. At the moment it was easier to be friendly than to be at odds with the girl.

"I did." She picked up her teapot and gave it another small swirl before pouring some tea.

"And you're going to Tokyo to pick it up?" Lily continued to fish.

"I am. Supposedly."

"What's the award for?" Lily came out and asked the question she had been skirting around.

"I won my company a very large contract," Celia admitted.

"How large?"

"Five point three million euros."

Lily nearly choked on her tea but managed to only splutter a little.

"That *is* large."

"It is," Celia agreed.

"No wonder you're getting an award."

"Hmm."

"That you don't want," Lily added softly.

"You really ought not lie to your grandmother about meeting someone in a foreign country. The fact that you have indicates that you know it's a dangerous thing to do. But I'm sure you don't want to discuss that, much the same as I don't wish to discuss my award." Celia held Lily's gaze for a few seconds to emphasise her point.

While she wanted to have a pleasant lunch without any of her usual acerbic comments, she needed Lily to know that she wouldn't be pushed. Not on this matter.

"Unseasonably lovely weather we're having," Lily commented.

"Absolutely, and not too hot either," Celia added.

The waitress showed impeccable timing by choosing that very moment to return with their meals.

❖

Following lunch and a couple of hours of window shopping, Celia found herself on a sightseeing boat, cruising around the canals and waterways of the Danish capital.

It had been Lily's idea, of course.

Celia had resisted the notion right up until Lily had suggested that Celia was scared of water. In some ridiculous attempt at disproving the ludicrous theory, she found the first boat tour company and purchased two tickets.

The open-top boats seated around fifty people in long rows. She and Lily had the back row to themselves.

While some of the journey was undeniably pretty, some was fairly dull. They were currently navigating a waterway that ran between many luxurious apartment buildings of various architectural styles that Celia knew she would appreciate more if she gave a damn about architecture.

Between the water and the buildings were gardens and grassy areas, often filled with people biking, walking, or picnicking.

"Isn't that building beautiful?" Lily enthused, pointing to a large, strangely shaped apartment block.

"Can a building be beautiful?" Celia asked.

"I think so."

Celia turned away and let out a sigh. Maybe booking the longer tour had been a bad idea. Boat tours always seemed like a good idea until you were actually on one. Then you were stranded, utterly at the mercy of the weather and whichever part-time employee-cum-student had the microphone to give a potted history of what you were seeing.

Usually information that you ultimately decided was made up on the spot by said student.

A man in nothing but a towel exited one of the apartment buildings and started to walk towards the canal. There was something about his expression that caused Celia to frown. He was smirking, a little spring to his step. Suddenly, he removed the towel to reveal he was utterly naked underneath.

A few of the other tourists noticed and gasped or chuckled at the sight.

Celia nudged Lily in the ribs to get her attention, not taking her eyes off the man.

He smiled and waved to the tourist boat and then performed a handstand, allowing everything to hang as nature intended.

"Oh my God," Lily mumbled.

"Your people are friendly," Celia said through a chuckle.

"He is not my people," Lily said. "He is…Well, I don't know what he is."

"Well, he's not cold," Celia pointed out.

"Oh God, don't look at it," Lily cried, looking away.

Celia burst out laughing at Lily's disgusted reaction. "Sorry," she said. "Have you not seen the delights of the male body before?"

"Once," Lily said. "Why do you think I'm a lesbian?"

"It isn't the prettiest of body parts," Celia agreed. "It's like the last chicken breast in the shop, the one that appears to have been run over and the skin is hanging—"

"I could have happily lived my entire life without that analogy, thank you very much," Lily interrupted.

"Are you squeamish?" Celia asked.

"No, I just don't want to talk about some old guy's junk. In public. With you."

Celia glanced back at the man. He was walking on his hands and laughing happily at the reactions he was getting. She chuckled and turned her attention back to Lily.

She was about to make another comment when her phone rang. She glanced at the screen and sighed at James's name.

"Sorry, I have to take this," she told Lily. "Hello, James."

"I heard about the delay. Everything okay?" he asked without preamble.

"Yes, I'm in Copenhagen overnight and will fly out tomorrow instead."

"Okay. Sorry to hear that. I know it…it's not easy for you."

Celia bit her tongue. If James had shown even one percent of this care and concern when they were together, then maybe they wouldn't have had to go through a very public and very painful divorce.

"No," she agreed. "I'm still intending to come back on the same day, so I can still sign those papers."

"We can push it back if you need to," James offered.

"No, we've waited long enough, best to get it done." She didn't want to delay the final signatures on the paperwork that would officially remove them from each other's lives.

While getting married had been an afternoon ceremony and a couple of signatures, getting a divorce was very different. Endless amounts of paperwork, discussions, divisions of assets, compromise, and arguments. She wanted it done and dusted.

And while James had recently found it in his heart to be somewhat understanding and forgiving, Celia didn't want to forget how he had been. Or how she had been.

The sale of the second home they had purchased in Ireland was the final thing that connected them. It had also taken many, many months to sell. While everything else had been slowly dismantled, the final component hung around like a bad smell.

Signing the paperwork would be the end of it. She wanted it done. She needed it done.

"Okay, if you're sure," he checked.

"I'm sure. I'll let you know if there are any further delays, but I'll either be on my way to Tokyo tomorrow morning, or I'll be returning home if the travel gods attack again."

She heard another voice in the background and assumed it was his secretary.

"I have to go. My next meeting is early," James said.

"Okay. I'll see you when I get back, as we planned."

They said a quick, perfunctory farewell, and Celia hung up the call.

"Work won't leave you alone?" Lily asked.

"That was my ex-husband," Celia said.

"Oh. Oh, I'm sorry, I shouldn't have been nosy."

"It's okay. I'm divorced, like many other millions of people."

Lily turned to look at her. "It's nice you're still talking, though, right?" She smiled.

"Not particularly," Celia said.

Lily's smile vanished.

Celia sighed to herself. Her go-to reaction lately seemed to be harsh sarcasm. Lily deserved better, and so Celia offered a small explanation to soften her words. "We're tying up the loose ends. Prying apart a twenty-two year marriage isn't the easiest thing to do. There's a lot of things to deal with."

Lily faltered a moment, and Celia felt sorry for her. Her shitty life wasn't Lily's fault, and Lily was just trying to be nice now that they found themselves thrown together because of strange circumstances.

"But you're right," Celia conceded, knowing it was up to her to ease her harsh words. "It could be a lot worse. We're lucky we don't have animosity towards one another. I just...want it to all be over."

"I bet," Lily said. "I'm sorry, it sounds rough."

"It was rougher," Celia confessed. "It'll be over soon enough."

They continued the rest of the boat tour in silence, Lily eagerly soaking up everything the tour guide told them as if it was gospel. Celia just watched the world go by.

They'd managed to kill a few hours, but there was still time to go. She had no desire to hurry back, and she was sure that Lily felt the same way.

It was strange how she'd seemingly gone from having no interest in spending any time with Lily, actually wanting her to be removed from her presence on the flight, to not being willing to leave her side now.

Lily was actually not such terrible company.

As long as they avoided such conversational topics as Lily's fake Japanese girlfriend, her grandmother, work, and Celia's award.

And the Danish man's penis, Celia reminded herself. And presumably the last chicken breast in the supermarket.

"What shall we do after this?" she asked, seeing the boat dock coming up in the distance and knowing that their time in floating purgatory was nearly up.

Lily shrugged. "I don't know. I'd not thought about it."

"You were the one singing all of Denmark's virtues not so long ago. There must be something we can do."

"There's a really interesting art gall—"

"No."

"You don't like art galleries?" Lily asked, astounded.

"I don't mind them, but I don't want to do that tonight. It's a lovely evening, and I want to enjoy it. There must be something outdoorsy that we can do."

Lily's eyes shone with excitement. "There's always Tivoli?"

Celia thought back. "Oh, the theme park you mentioned?" The idea of spending her evening in such a place didn't appeal.

"It's not *technically* a theme park. I mean, it's not like Disney or anything like that. It's nice. Classy. I really think you'd like it," Lily enthused, clearly eager to get Celia on board with the idea of a trip to Tivoli.

Celia decided to play with her a little.

"And what makes you think that you know what I like?"

Lily paused. She opened and then closed her mouth again. "I…I feel like I kind of know you a little."

Celia's curiosity was piqued. "And what have you deduced?"

"That you'd really love Tivoli?" Lily tried.

Celia laughed at that. "Does this kind of persuasion technique usually work on people?"

"I don't know—I only really have one friend," Lily admitted.

Celia was stunned. How could someone as intelligent, happy-go-lucky, and kind as Lily have only one friend in the world?

"I'm sure that's not true," Celia said.

"It is. Asami—not a man—is the only person who really gets me," Lily said with some confidence.

"Very well. Does Asami—most definitely a man—fall for this kind of persuasion technique?"

Lily rolled her eyes. She did it every time Celia suggested that Asami wasn't who Lily thought, but her reaction had become more casual and tinged with humour each time.

While the initial suggestion of Asami being a man had been met with venom, now it was met with little more than a sigh.

It was a positive step for their friendship, but it didn't stop Celia from worrying that Lily was a young woman flying halfway around the world to meet someone who was quite possibly a fraud.

But she wasn't going to press the matter any further. She knew that there was little she could say to convince Lily. Right now, it was just easier to keep the tentative peace they had fostered.

Hopefully her constant digs would allow a slight sense of hesitation to dwell within Lily, and maybe it would keep her from harm. If the little joke they shared gave Lily the slightest pause for thought, Celia would be happy.

"Yes, it does work," Lily said.

"Very well, let's go to Tivoli. I'll let you know if I like it as much as you assume I will."

"I'm sure you will."

"Like it or tell you my thoughts on it?" Celia asked.

"Both."

Celia grinned. The banter between them was actually rather enjoyable.

Not that she would ever have chosen the evening she was having, but if things did have to go completely wrong, and she did have to be stranded in a strange city with someone, then she had to admit that she was glad it was Lily.

An Oasis in the City

Lily had no idea how many times she'd been to Tivoli. It was like asking someone how many times they had eaten a hot dinner or been for a walk. It was impossible to count.

Her mother had taken her as a baby, she'd begged to go endlessly as a child, and she'd owned an annual pass as an adult.

Tivoli had been a part of her life for as long as she could remember.

Apparently, she said her first words other than *Mum* or *Dad* in Tivoli. When looking at the large fountain, she'd pointed and mumbled something that her father had sworn was the word *water*.

To say Tivoli was an important part of her life and held a special place in her heart would be an understatement.

Which was why Lily held her breath as Celia walked through the security gate.

Lily had to admit, she had cheated a little. Tivoli Gardens was a theme park right in the middle of the city, a large square of land sandwiched between main roads, the railway station, and the shopping district.

It had multiple entrances, and she had deliberately approached the park in a way that brought them to an entrance that she knew would be a lot quieter than the main gate. It was also, in Lily's opinion, prettier.

The busier main entrance was a grand archway, which led to a treelined road, flanked with gorgeous buildings that housed the box office and administrative offices. But that entrance also attracted the most people. Lily wanted to show off the quiet, reserved side of Tivoli.

She had done this because she had deduced that Celia wasn't one for crowds. Not that Lily really knew that much about Celia, no matter how she might pretend that she did. But she made assumptions based on similar personalities she'd met throughout her life.

That said, Celia had sometimes been exactly what she expected and other times completely surprised her. Which was, she supposed, what humans were all about.

She walked a little way into the park and stood by the popcorn shop. The smell of popped kernels and all kinds of sweet flavours filled the air.

Celia stood beside her in the narrow street, looking to the right where the street narrowed and trailed downward towards game stalls and restaurants, and then in front of them to a long flight of stairs that led to an open, grassy area.

"Not quite what I expected," Celia admitted.

Lily wanted to punch the air in victory.

At that moment, a trainful of screaming passengers from the roller coaster above them went by.

"*That* was what I was expecting," Celia commented, looking up to find out where the sound had come from.

"It's a roller coaster," Lily said.

Celia raised a questioning eyebrow.

She pointed to a fibreglass mountain facade above the popcorn shop. "It's up there. It runs above all these shops and on the other side. It's one of the oldest wooden roller coasters in the world, built in nineteen fourteen."

Celia looked suitably impressed. "And it's still running, I hear."

"Yes, it's fun. We should—"

Celia held up her hand. "I'm not a roller coaster person. Its having been built over a hundred years ago is not improving its chances of having me as a passenger."

Lily decided not to push her luck and gestured towards the stairs. They walked down the double flight, and she noticed a new restaurant had opened in the building on the left.

While Tivoli was great at preserving heritage, it was also good at bringing in new and exciting shops, eateries, and rides. And yet, somehow, everything fit together.

One of the things she adored was the greenery. Trees, flowerbeds, fountains, lakes—the park was an oasis of calm but also had bumper cars. It was like no other place on earth.

They got to the bottom of the steps and approached the large, central grassy area that was frequently used by picnickers. She stopped to allow Celia to look around.

To the left was a large outdoor stage for live open-air music acts, and to the right were the fountains that led to the concert hall. And in front of them, barely visible through the luscious summer foliage, was the glass house that featured a theatre that accommodated nearly a thousand people. Lily couldn't remember when it had opened in Tivoli, but like everything else, it was decidedly Victorian in its appearance and considered a historical marvel.

"Definitely not what I was expecting," Celia said.

Lily smiled as if a compliment had been given. She supposed, in Celia's way, it had.

A peacock walked by, squawking and showing off its impressive tail feathers.

"Is this also a zoo?" Celia asked.

"No, there are just peacocks here," Lily replied. "There's the Pantomime Theatre over there, which has this amazing curtain that's shaped like a peacock's tail. It unfolds from the top when the show is about to start."

Lily pointed towards the theatre, which was obscured by the open-air stage.

"I can't see a curtain," Celia commented.

"Oh no, that's the lawn theatre—they have all sorts of live performances there. The Pantomime Theatre is behind it."

Celia looked at Lily in surprise. "There are two theatres?"

Lily pointed to the glass house. "That's a theatre too." She then pointed beyond the fountain. "And that's a concert hall."

"There are *four* theatres?" Celia clarified.

"Yes, for kids, and rock music, opera, and plays. And everything in between."

Celia cocked her head to the side and looked thoughtfully at Lily. "I see. This isn't quite like an ordinary theme park, is it?"

"No. Although there is a ride called The Demon which has three inversions."

"I don't know what that means," Celia admitted.

"You go upside down," Lily explained.

"Three times?"

"Yes."

"How awful." Celia pointed to the stage. "Did you say the… peacock theatre place is behind that?"

She was already walking, and Lily hurried to catch up with her.

"Yep."

"Let's have a closer look, shall we?" Celia smiled, and Lily felt a rush of happiness that Celia also seemed to have fallen for the charms of Tivoli.

❖

Ninety minutes later and they had completed a very slow circle around Tivoli Gardens, past the lake, the pirate ship, the classic carousel, the Chinese market, the arcade, and more.

Celia had asked questions about the history of the park and what was behind closed doors the whole way around, and Lily had answered as best she could.

She spoke about restaurants that had come and gone, shops that had done the same, the rides, the introduction of more brands, the importance of the trees, the popcorn lights, and the general ambiance that visitors loved so much.

Now and then they passed a less-than-tame ride, and Celia would stare at it for a few moments as people screamed as they were whipped around like rag dolls. She didn't say anything, and they moved on.

Thankfully there were not many of those rides. Many were for the family or just for children.

"Thank you for bringing me here," Celia said as they walked through some manicured gardens by the central fountains. "It really is idyllic. I can't believe we're in the middle of the city. It's only now and then, when you look up and see a skyscraper or when you move away from the music and you hear the traffic, that you realise you're absolutely in the centre of Copenhagen. It's surreal."

"I'm glad you like it," Lily said. She held back a second comment that was on her lips—that maybe she did know Celia after all.

"So, I'm going to take a wild stab in the dark and assume you come here a lot?" Celia asked, a lopsided grin on her face.

Lily felt her face go red, realising that she had been effusing about Tivoli endlessly for over an hour.

"Maybe we should consider eating dinner here," Celia suggested. "There are plenty of places to eat, and by the sound of it you've eaten in most of them, so I trust you can find us a decent meal."

Lily nodded. "Yeah, sure. There's…well, there's most things." Her brain scrambled to think of something that would be Celia-friendly. Nothing in the food hall, nothing with limited seating, nothing quick service. Suddenly it seemed like an impossible job to come up with somewhere, despite the fact that Tivoli had well over forty different places to eat.

Often, Lily wouldn't eat a heavy meal if she was going to go on rides. A quick bite to eat at one of the many good quality fast-food restaurants was enough, or even just some churros and ice cream to keep hunger at bay.

Then she remembered when her mother had taken her on a surprise visit to Tivoli when she had passed her school exams with flying colours.

"The Promenade," she whispered to herself, a flood of memories coming back to her.

"And they do…?" Celia asked.

"Steaks, grills, burgers, fish, vegan. Bit of everything. It's a nice place. A little expensive, actually." Lily suddenly realised that she was suggesting quite a pricey option.

"Sounds perfect. My treat. Which way?" Celia asked.

Lily pointed to the two-storey building beside them.

"Convenient." Celia marched towards the door. "Come on."

NOT A DATE

Celia looked out of the upstairs window at the people enjoying an early evening picnic on the grass in front of the outdoor performance area.

Children of all ages played, parents and grandparents looking on in amusement. It really was the perfect place for families to hang out.

She felt a pang of sadness in her heart. She reached for her wine glass and took another sip of the delicious Cabernet.

When Lily had mentioned a theme park, Celia didn't think she'd be drinking some fine wine while a chef prepared her a piece of salmon on a bed of wild rice, but it seemed that anything was possible in Tivoli Gardens.

It was a theme park, but it was also so much more. And although she'd never fully admit it, she felt better for having seen such a heavenly place.

Lily sat opposite her, tapping away on her phone as she had done surreptitiously the entire day, no doubt in deep conversation with the mysterious Asami.

Lily must have sensed Celia's eyes on her because she placed her phone down.

"Sorry, I know it's rude," Lily admitted. "Just replying to a message."

"It's fine," Celia said. "You don't owe me your full attention—this isn't a date."

"No, but we are eating together," Lily said. "Anyway, I'm sorry."

Something occurred to her and Celia frowned. "Are you talking to Asami?"

Lily's expression darkened.

Celia waved away her fears with a shake of her wrist. "Not saying anything about Asami per se, just, isn't it awfully late there?"

Lily nodded. "It's two in the morning. She can't sleep because she's worried about me."

Celia didn't say the first thing that popped into her mind. She took a moment to sip some more wine before speaking again. "Being at your grandmother's?"

"At first that was what she was worried about," Lily confessed.

"And now?"

Lily hesitated for a moment. "She…she's worried that I've gotten cold feet. That I'm not coming after all."

Celia took another sip of wine to silence her first thought. At this rate she'd be blind drunk before the meal arrived.

Of course Asami was concerned, worried they had been found out, no doubt. Any good scam artist would be worrying that they had lost their prize, applying some extra pressure in order to guilt their target. Celia remembered every detail that had happened with her friend Stephie and then her subsequent research on the whole fake romance scam. Not that Lily would listen to reason—she'd been reeled in already. Celia wished she could save her but recognised that she wasn't going to be listened to.

"Well, they'll see soon enough that that isn't the case," Celia said.

She mentally patted herself on the back for not saying something wholly inflammatory as she had initially desired. It had been a long day, and she was too tired to get into the thick of it with Lily yet again.

"Yes, *she* will," Lily said, a slight inflection on the gender pronoun.

Celia decided to move the conversation onto safer territory. She gestured out the window. "You were lucky to be able to spend time somewhere so lovely as a child."

The smile was instant as Lily looked out the window. "Yes. This place has a lot of special memories for me. Do you have kids?"

Celia felt like she had been punched in the stomach. It was inevitable that someone would ask her, but this was the first time since the incident. She maintained as neutral an expression as possible, the only way to make sure she didn't fall apart in public.

"One son. He died not so long ago."

Lily's eyes widened and her face paled. "I'm so sorry," she whispered.

"It's okay," Celia replied. She looked out of the window. "Things happen. But he would have loved this place. If I lived near something like this, I would have taken him there all the time. And he would have no doubt been on that awful roller coaster with the eight reversions."

"Three inversions. And it's not awful," Lily defended The Demon. "It's actually quite fun. Don't knock it until you've tried it."

"Not after a bottle of Cab and a salmon dinner, I think," Celia said, happy that Lily seemed to be guiding the conversation to safer territory. "Have you seen many concerts here?"

"Loads," Lily enthused.

Celia settled into her seat and listened to Lily talk about her times at Tivoli. Concerts, rides, ice creams in the rain, getting sunburnt picnicking on the lawn. Celia revelled in the normalcy of it and asked Lily questions to get her to expand on her stories.

Dinner passed in a flash, but it had actually been well over an hour. They'd been deep in conversation the whole time, and Celia had to admit she'd enjoyed herself. Hearing Lily's family stories was just what she had needed to take her mind off herself.

"Oh, wow, I just talked and talked, didn't I?" Lily said as Celia paid the bill.

"I asked you to," Celia told her. "But we should probably get back to your grandmother's now."

Lily let out a sigh at the thought. Celia couldn't blame her.

"Don't worry, we'll be polite and then say our goodnights," Celia said. "We have an early start tomorrow morning."

"You're right. I just hate arguing with her. But I'm not going to just let her walk all over me either."

"Good for you." Celia thanked the waiter, picked up her handbag, and stood. "Don't let anyone walk over you. Even family."

"Easier said than done," Lily said.

Celia didn't say anything else on the matter. She wasn't exactly the best role model. Her own actions had caused a lot of pain and grief for a lot of people. It was probably best all round if she didn't promote her personal brand of behaviour.

They left the restaurant and silently made their way towards the park's exit. Celia walked a little slower than she would have ordinarily, allowing Lily the opportunity to stare in wonder at everything one last time.

Outside the main gates, Celia flagged down a taxi. Lily gave the address, and they sat back and silently returned to Anette's. Celia hoped that the animosity of earlier was in the past. She didn't want to play third wheel to another set of arguments. Nor did she want to see Lily so miserable again, not now that she was finally smiling.

She leaned her head back against the seat and watched as Copenhagen whizzed by the window. The day had been a strange, awkward, but eventually pleasant distraction. Tomorrow things would go back to normal. At least she had some good memories for now.

Leaving Mormor's

Lily stood in the hallway, heavy rucksack on her back and a hand on the handle of her suitcase. Celia was saying farewell and thank you to her grandmother, after they had played reverse tug of war with an envelope of money that Celia had tried to leave behind.

As suspected, Lily's grandmother wouldn't accept it, while Celia wouldn't accept *not* leaving anything as a token of her gratitude. Lily had silently watched as they'd spent the morning attempting to hand one another the envelope of cash, round and round like a sketch show.

Eventually, her grandmother had agreed to donate it to charity. Celia had seemed happy with that.

They'd enjoyed a pleasant enough breakfast together. Celia had expertly guided the conversation, keeping Mormor occupied with talking about her garden and her grandchildren—and avoiding any topics that could become controversial. Celia had done the same thing the night before, diverting her grandmother with small talk until it was time for bed.

Lily had silently thanked her with a glance.

Mormor walked towards Lily with her arms flung out. Lily hugged her back, and they said farewell. She promised to stay in touch and said she'd call as soon as she was back home.

Celia watched over them, and Lily found she was glad to have her there, watching, waiting, and ready to take action if needed. She'd never had that from someone before.

It was new. It was nice.

A last round of farewells were said, and Lily and Celia approached the waiting taxi. Suitcases were piled into the boot, and they sat in the back seat, letting out a sigh that they were finally on their way back to the airport.

"Take two," Celia said.

"Yes. I really hope it's not the same aircraft," Lily said.

"Would you be able to tell if it was?" Celia asked.

Lily considered the question. "Not if it was similar, no. I mean, if it was very different, then it would be obvious. But if it was the same layout, no. Would you?"

"Yes." Celia nodded with certainty.

"How come?"

"I tied a small hair tie to the seat back's pocket. Not something that would be noticed by cleaners, but I'll see it."

"That's very sneaky," Lily commented.

"Why, thank you."

"Some people wouldn't take that as a compliment."

"I'm not most people," Celia replied.

Lily had to agree with that. Celia was quite different to other people she'd met. And quite different to what she had expected when she'd made her initial judgements.

The previous day hadn't gone at all as she had expected. The aborted flight had been both a nightmare and a blessing.

On one hand, her grandmother was not prepared to have her gay granddaughter in town, and Asami was concerned that Lily had cold feet about them meeting. But on the other hand, she'd spent a great day with Celia in one of her favourite places in the world.

If someone had told her that morning that the rude sandwich shop lady would have turned her day from a pile of steaming crap to something quite enjoyable, she would have said they were insane. But somehow that was exactly what Celia had managed to do.

However, Lily was also very much aware that their connection was now at an end. They were just two strangers who had been thrown together by circumstance. After the flight, they would part ways, and that would probably be the last she would ever see of Celia Scott. She wasn't sure how she felt about that.

Technically, it shouldn't have mattered to her one bit. But there was something about Celia that she found curious. She had a hard exterior that seemed to be hiding a kind heart. She could be caustic with her words but sometimes balanced it with a dark humour that Lily couldn't help but enjoy.

And then there was the death of her son. Lily had taken very wide steps around that subject, detecting immediately that it was something to be very clearly avoided.

The crack in Celia's veneer at that point had given Lily another opportunity to see through the harsh surface that Celia seemed to protect herself with. In that brief second, she'd seen heartbreak and guilt, so raw and emotive that Lily wanted to do whatever she could to fix the wounds.

Lily pushed the thoughts aside. It didn't matter. Celia was just a person who would pass through her life, nothing more and nothing less. They'd share a flight and then would never see each other again. Which was a shame, because Lily knew she could use a friend like Celia in her life.

❖

Celia saw Lily standing around in the terminal building, nose buried in her phone as usual. She assumed that she was in text conference with Asami, as per usual.

Arriving at the airport had been slightly uncomfortable as neither of them had known what to do. They had spent a lot of time together recently, and it seemed odd to suddenly go their separate ways. But they weren't travelling together.

Celia had decided to take the bull by the horns and had walked off the moment her suitcase hit the ground. She tossed a casual goodbye over her shoulder to Lily and said she'd see her on board the flight. When she received a text advising her to report to the customer service desk, Celia had ground her teeth, thinking for certain that they were about to give her further bad news.

As it happened, they were upgrading her. The circus troupe had managed to get another flight, and first class now had availability for her.

For some reason, she'd hesitated before accepting the seat. Thoughts of Lily sitting alone floated in her mind, though she did her best to quickly shake them off.

What did it matter? Lily was an adult and could sit alone. Would probably prefer it. Just because they'd been thrown together by circumstance didn't mean she was in any way beholden to Lily. They'd have to go their separate ways eventually anyway.

But it would be right to tell her in person rather than let her board the plane and find out that way. And so Celia had sought out Lily, finding her—somewhat unsurprisingly—by a snack stand.

"Hello," Celia greeted her.

Lily looked up from her frantic typing on her phone. "Hey," she greeted in return.

"How is *he*?" Celia indicated the phone with a nod.

"Will you just stop?" Lily exploded.

Celia blinked and took a small step back. She thought they'd come to an understanding about the teasing joke, but clearly she had misread the situation.

"Why do you have to keep saying that? She is a *she*. Okay? Asami is a she. Okay? I'm not some idiot who got sucked in by some forty-year-old man, okay? Just…just stop."

Celia couldn't understand the sudden, volatile reaction, nor did she *want* to understand it. She wasn't used to being shouted at by people in public places.

"You're in for a shock," Celia stated coldly.

"I'm not. And I'm sick of having this argument with you," Lily said.

"Very well, we won't be having it any more." Celia turned on her heel and walked away.

So much for being nice and giving Lily a heads-up on the seat change.

So much for saying goodbye.

If that was the way Lily wanted it, so be it. Celia had better things to do than to converse with the immature young woman who was about to find herself face to face with a creepy man in his forties.

And serves her right.

No Time for Goodbyes

L ily stood on her tiptoes to look around the departure gate. Celia was nowhere in sight.

She swallowed nervously and shoved her hands into her pockets. She hadn't meant to shout at Celia; it was just poor timing.

Asami had been texting all morning to say that she wasn't sure about meeting up any more. For some reason, Asami had convinced herself that Lily had gotten cold feet and that the whole stopping off in Denmark thing was a ruse.

Lily had gathered all the data from various flight-tracking websites to prove that her flight had been delayed due to technical difficulties. She had sent selfies pouting under the terminal departure board. Anything to prove her version of events.

Asami hadn't outright accused her of lying. She just suggested that Lily's own fear was leading her to believe any ridiculous theory that her brain might come up with.

Lily could feel Asami slipping though her fingers and hated the very thought of it. She'd been frantically trying to get through to Asami, reminding her of their previous conversations and their plans for the future.

Tense didn't even begin to describe it, and she wanted nothing more than to arrive in Tokyo and immediately wrap her arms around Asami and assure her that everything was okay.

And, at the height of all that, Celia had appeared.

The little quip that fell from Celia's mouth so innocently—*How is he?*—had turned Lily's panic into rage.

Now, after having spent two hours placating Asami and promising that she would soon board a plane and finally be on her way to her, Lily wanted to apologise to Celia.

The problem was she couldn't *find* her anywhere.

She toyed with the idea of calling or texting her, but there wasn't much point because they were both ultimately going to the same place. In due course, she could deliver her apology to Celia face to face and spend a couple of hours of a long flight atoning if she had to.

Lily let out a sigh, her feet now firmly on the floor. Celia was nowhere to be seen, which was not entirely unexpected as Celia did seem the kind of person to appear to board a flight at the last minute.

More and more people were gathering by the gate; the wave of nerves and eagerness to get under way—again—was palpable. The area in front of the podium was becoming more and more crowded, and Lily was in the middle of it all.

Thankfully, boarding eventually started. As people started to move out of the way to let others by, Lily saw Celia in the distance. She tried to get closer but was forced backward by the crowd.

In the end, she gave up. It wasn't worth being trampled on just to get to Celia a few minutes early. They would see each other soon enough.

Business class was called, and Lily finally boarded the plane. It all looked very familiar, to her displeasure. She'd been so hoping for an obviously different aircraft, one that didn't have known engine issues.

She took her seat, testing it out with a little bounce. It felt like her seat. She looked at the footrest, the seatback screen, the air vent above her. It all looked the same, but she couldn't be sure.

With a sigh, she leaned over the empty seat next to her and looked at the seat back pocket. Sure enough, a small hair tie was wrapped around the netting.

"Damn it," Lily muttered and sat back in her chair.

As more people boarded the plane, Lily kept a watchful eye out for Celia. After a while, she realised they were boarding the economy cabin behind her. Considering the plane boarded from front to back, Celia should have been on board by now.

Lily wondered if she had been mistaken and hadn't seen Celia at the departure gate after all. Or perhaps Celia was going to appear a few seconds before the doors closed, takeaway latte in hand, chatting on her mobile.

A familiar steward walked by, and Lily looked up to get his attention. He stopped and looked down at her with a warm smile.

"Hey, um, the woman who was sitting next to me yesterday—"

"She's in first class," the steward replied. He seemed very happy about the matter.

"Oh." Lily didn't know what else to say.

"A few passengers cancelled or made other arrangements," he explained. "She was supposed to be in first class yesterday, but we had a booking issue. So she's up there now. You get some extra room."

Lily looked at the empty seat, wondering why she felt so sad about the fact. "Oh, okay. Thank you," she said, but he was already gone.

She didn't know why she suddenly felt a profound sense of loss. It wasn't as if Celia was a friend. She was just a stranger Lily happened to have met twenty-four hours earlier. But it stung that she hadn't even had the opportunity to say goodbye.

Which, in hindsight, was probably why Celia had approached her earlier.

Lily let out a frustrated sigh and leaned into her seat. She'd made a mess of things, but she wasn't about to barge into first class and attempt to explain herself. It was too late for that, and Celia probably didn't want to hear from her anyway.

They weren't friends. They weren't *anything*.

She just had to chalk it up to life experience. She'd reacted badly, and now she regretted it. At the very least, she would learn a lesson from it.

TOKYO

The flight had been just as awful as Celia had imagined it would be. Boring, long, bumpy in places, and for no good reason.

Even the trappings of first class hadn't served to appease her bad mood.

Since Lily had exploded at her for no reason, her mood had soured from bad to worse. Dwelling on the incident with Lily in Copenhagen had quickly morphed into irritation at needing to go to Tokyo at all.

She was back to being borderline furious about the whole award business. It was a waste of time and money for her to be picking up the award. An award which she desperately wished didn't even exist.

The seat belt light was switched off, so she undid the restraint and jumped to her feet. She gathered her belongings from the cupboard behind her seat and stood in the small queue of first-class passengers eager to disembark.

Getting off the stuffy plane first was one of the best benefits of flying first class in Celia's mind. The service was good, the food wasn't terrible, the seats could be considered comfortable if she hadn't been strapped in for eleven hours, but the ability to leave before everyone else was the best bit.

Getting a head start on the hundreds of other passengers was great, especially for someone who felt she had already wasted so much time on this pointless pursuit.

While waiting for the doors to open, she reset her watch. They'd left Copenhagen midmorning, and that meant that it was hideously early in Tokyo.

Thankfully, she knew there would be a car waiting for her, so she didn't have to worry about public transport. She'd already checked a map and knew it was around a twenty-minute journey from the airport to the hotel.

The ceremony was that evening, which meant zero time for sightseeing. Which meant her mood was even worse than it had been the previous day. At least if things had gone to plan, she could have spent a few hours looking around Tokyo and exploring some of the sights. The hotel was in an excellent central location and quite close to the Imperial Palace. However, the early hour, her exhaustion, and the fact she knew she looked as exhausted as she felt meant she'd need to spend the day resting and preparing herself for the evening event.

Speeches, dinner, drinks, and the ceremony. She'd need a solid four hours to prepare herself for the amount of fake smiling she'd need to do.

The door opened, and every passenger moved an inch closer to freedom despite the fact that the disembarking process had most definitely not started. The collective desire to get off the plane and on with the day was palpable.

Celia imagined she was the only person looking forward to boarding the flight *back* more than she was getting off the plane.

❖

Lily waited eagerly by the luggage carousel. The flight had been good, long but good. The food had been great, she'd eaten most of her snacks, the movies were fun, and she'd slept. If she'd had a Good Flight bingo card, she'd be a winner.

Sadly, her luck hadn't translated over to the time after the flight.

A long queue of people meant it had taken forever to disembark, passport control had another long queue, and now her luggage was taking its sweet time.

She hadn't seen Celia, unsurprisingly. She imagined she'd been the first to strut off the plane. Celia was probably the first to pick up her luggage too. Lily imagined that Celia's luggage was well-trained and among the first to emerge from the plastic tentacles of suitcase delivery.

Lily's bag wasn't well-trained. Nothing in her life was. She removed her rucksack from her back and placed it on a chair. Thankfully, she'd eaten most of the weight out of it, and it was now more reasonable to carry.

She opened a front pocket and took out a sheet of paper. Her

Japanese was non-existent. She'd tried, but language wasn't her thing, and she found it impossible to learn. The symbols meant nothing to her, but they were probably the most important symbols in her life at the moment: Asami's address.

Everything was suddenly becoming very real.

No longer separated by miles and hours, they were sharing the same space and time. Breathing the same air.

Lily stared at the bags slowly moving around the carousel. Every little thing felt like an interminable delay now.

Her phone pinged, and she nearly dropped it with the excitement of pulling it out of her pocket. She'd texted Asami the second they'd landed. She knew that was a bit naughty but assumed the plane wouldn't spontaneously combust because she'd sent a text.

Asami's reply was short and sweet. She was looking forward to finally meeting her and made her, yet again, promise to not be disappointed when they met.

Lily chuckled to herself. Asami's self-confidence was terrible, and Lily had promised herself it would be one of the first things she would work on. She'd spend all her free time making Asami feel like the exceptional individual she was, reminding her how beautiful she was inside and out.

Lily tapped back a message to say she was on her way. She'd mapped out the journey several times in the past and could do it in her sleep. It would take just over an hour to get to Asami's apartment in Asagaya.

She looked up from her phone to see that her suitcase had begun its journey around the conveyor belt, had passed her entirely, and was on its way around a bend.

"Damn it," she muttered as she dashed after it.

❖

Celia approached the arrivals area and squinted at the various boards for her name. Various taxi drivers and chauffeurs held up signs, scrawled in pen on a piece of cardboard, printed and laminated, or displayed on an iPad.

Celia felt a wave of relief when she saw a smartly suited young man holding an iPad with her name on it. She smiled at him and approached.

"Miss Scott?" he asked.

"That's me."

"I'm Shiro," he introduced himself before quickly turning off the iPad and snapping it back into a protective case. He took hold of the handle of her luggage and gestured towards a large set of automatic doors. "Please."

"Thank you," she said, casting one last glance over her shoulder before shaking off all thoughts of Lily.

"It takes twenty minutes to get to the Shangri-La," Shiro explained.

"Excellent."

He gestured towards a black town car and quickly dashed in front of her to open the rear door. She slid into the seat and let out a contented sigh as he closed the door behind her.

It was good to be back on solid ground.

And even better to be in control.

While suspended above the earth, she'd had little control over anything. Now she felt more secure, safe in the knowledge that she was mere miles away from where she needed to be. And hours away from the event she had been dreading.

All she had to do was wait as time ticked away. Then she'd attend the event, accept the award, be photographed, and make small talk. And then it would all be over.

Finally, over.

Shiro finished putting her suitcase in the back of the car and got into the driver's seat. He made eye contact with her.

"Are you comfortable, Miss Scott?" he asked.

"Very, thank you."

He nodded, and a moment later they were on their way out of the airport and towards the city.

Celia peered out of the window with interest. She wasn't going to see a lot of Tokyo during her whistle-stop tour, so she might as well catch a glimpse of it out the window.

As she'd suspected, sleep hadn't happened for her on the plane.

She'd always been jealous of those who could sleep on planes. Her usual course of action was to drink as much as possible. But the way her stomach had rebelled before she boarded the flight, she'd known better than to try that.

Besides, her liver would thank her one day.

Now she fully intended to sleep through the day before attending the ceremony that evening. Hopefully that way she would look slightly refreshed and not like someone who had been awake for longer than she could remember.

The current time, her body clock, the last time she had slept or ate were all in chaotic anarchy with one another. The best she could do now was sleep when she was tired, eat when she was hungry, and hope to get through the next twenty-four hours.

Shiro was true to his word, and twenty minutes later they pulled off a busy road, surrounded by towering skyscrapers and big, empty streets that Celia suspected would be crammed with people in another hour or so.

A quiet street in the middle of the city led to another and then to an entry port with the Shangri-La logo displayed in gold by a large set of glass double doors.

Shiro pulled up, and one of the doormen set about retrieving the luggage from the back of the car. Shiro turned in his seat and handed Celia a business card.

"I'm at your service. If you would like to go anywhere, then call me," he said.

Celia took the card. "Thank you. I suspect I'll spend the day resting. Tomorrow afternoon I return to London."

Shiro smiled politely. "If you change your mind, I'm at your service."

It was just like Howard to pay for a chauffeur service for her. She almost felt bad that she wasn't going to use it. But then she was utterly exhausted, and feeling bad was too much like hard work.

She thanked him again, tucked the business card into her handbag, and got out of the car.

A Life-Changing Meeting

Lily held her phone in front of her and slowly turned to the left and then to the right. The flashing blue dot that indicated her position on the map moved in one direction and then the other.

She'd successful navigated the monorail and then two different overground trains. She was pretty pleased with herself. Now in Asagaya, she was taken aback by how different everything was.

Of course, she'd known that Japan would be different to England, but the scale of the change was shocking to her.

From the station, it was a five-minute walk to the cafe where Asami said they should meet.

Neutral territory, Lily had thought. Very wise, even though they knew each other inside out after all the talking they had done.

But it would be good to meet up early on, before taking the two buses required to get to Asami's home.

Lily looked up and then back at her phone. She was heading in the right direction. Just five minutes and she would finally be face to face with Asami.

It seemed surreal that after all this time they were finally going to meet. Lily felt overwhelmed with emotions, from excitement to nerves. She practically shook with everything her brain was firing at her.

She'd slept a little on the plane, but she knew that it wasn't enough. In a short amount of time she was going to be utterly exhausted, jetlagged, and very much in need of some more sleep.

A grin curled at the corner of her mouth as she considered that, if she was very lucky, she'd sleep in Asami's arms. After being physically apart for the entirety of their friendship, the idea of being together was almost too much to process.

Many months and many miles had kept them apart, and now it was just five minutes to a coffee shop in Asagaya that would change her life forever.

A Rude Awakening

The rumbling noise pierced the silence of the room. Celia sat up in bed, disorientated and angry. It took her a few moments to figure out where the noise was coming from, a testament to how tired she was.

"Damn," she muttered as she crawled out of bed and walked over to the desk where she had left her mobile phone charging.

The number was from the UK but unfamiliar. She debated leaving it for voicemail, but her sleep had been disturbed, so she might as well find out by who.

"Celia Scott," she answered.

"Celia! Thank God!"

"Who is this?" Celia demanded, sitting on the corner of the desk chair and smothering a yawn behind her hand.

"It's Lily."

Celia struggled with the sleep fog for a moment. Jetlag had definitely kicked in, and she didn't think she'd recognise her own mother's name right then.

"From the plane," Lily added after a moment of silence.

It all came back in a confusing flash.

"Are you okay?" Celia asked, belatedly realising that was probably a stupid question. Lily sounded distraught and out of breath.

"You were right," Lily said.

"What?" Celia got to her feet and started to pace the room, willing her brain to wake up and fully engage with the conversation she found herself having.

"Asami was a *man*," Lily replied, her voice loud to combat the sound of busy traffic in the background. "A fucking man!"

Celia smirked. "Well, I hate to say I told you so—"

"Celia, I've been mugged!"

The fog started to clear, and Celia switched from confusion to action. "Are you safe?"

"I think so. They have my suitcase and my rucksack. All my money." Lily sounded more out of breath, and Celia wondered if she was running. "I managed to get away. I don't think they're following me. Celia, I'm scared. I'm sorry to call you—I just didn't know what to do."

"Lily, I want you to find a shop or a public place where you'll be safe. I'm sending someone to get you." She opened her handbag and poured the contents onto the bed, snatching up Shiro's business card.

"There's a coffee shop across the street. It looks busy," Lily said.

"Good, good, go there." Celia picked up the hotel phone in her other hand and quickly dialled Shiro's number. "Where are you, Lily?"

"I can send you my location via my phone," Lily said. "I'm so sorry."

"Don't be sorry. We all make mistakes," Celia said.

A few seconds later a location notification arrived on her phone, and she relayed the information to Shiro, advising him to go and find Lily and bring her back to the hotel.

"I'm running out of battery," Lily said.

"Okay. Listen, stay in that coffee shop. At least that way we can contact you if we need to. A chauffeur is on the way to pick you up. His name is Shiro. He'll bring you to me."

"I'm sorry," Lily whispered.

"I know. Lily, important question…" Celia began.

"Yes?"

"Was he forty?" Celia asked.

"More like fifties," Lily replied, disgust clear in her tone.

"Damn, so close."

"Celia!" Lily admonished.

"I'll see you soon. Stay where you are," Celia instructed her. They said a quick goodbye, and Celia hung up.

She tossed her phone onto the bed and shook her head. She'd known something was wrong with the whole Asami set-up, and while she had made small jokes about it, she hadn't attempted to really tackle Lily on the situation. She was kicking herself for that now.

Of course, she knew that not everyone online was a fraud; she had some very good friends she had met over the internet. She even knew people who had dated and even gotten married to people they met online.

But something seemed off about Asami. Some sixth sense had pushed her to think that something was wrong. Maybe because she'd recognised that Lily was so innocent and ripe for conning.

And now she'd found out she was right—something she usually enjoyed immensely—but this time it was bittersweet because she didn't want Lily to get hurt.

Certainly didn't want her to get mugged.

She worried her lip. Had Lily been hurt? What exactly had happened? What would have happened if she hadn't managed to get away?

She swallowed and shook the thoughts away. There was nothing she could do now. Shiro was on his way. It would take him just over an hour to complete the round trip and return. She would just have to wait until then to find out the details and figure out what to do next.

She looked at her watch. It was early afternoon, and ideally, she'd have loved a few more hours of sleep but knew that wasn't happening now. She was wide awake.

"Fifties," she muttered to herself. "Should have known."

❖

Lily exited the elevator and looked at the sign in front of her. Her exhausted brain took a while to figure out which way to turn for Celia's room. Numbers just weren't making sense to her. In fact, not a lot was making sense to her.

She took the corridor to the left and dragged her tired feet down the ultra-luscious carpet. She couldn't believe she was in the Shangri-La. She imagined it was one of the top hotels in Tokyo.

The building had well over thirty floors, with the hotel taking up the top few, presumably to allow for the best views of the city. Lily found herself wandering around the thirty-fifth floor looking for the room number that reception had given her.

It had been strange to arrive and be greeted by name. She had expected to have to call Celia again or to argue with reception to allow her entry to the building. But it seemed that Celia had planned ahead, and Lily was given immediate access and directions.

She suddenly found herself in front of the door she'd been looking for. Her desperation to get away from Asagaya and find Celia seemed to evaporate now that she was so close.

Lily didn't know what Celia was going to say, but she imagined it would be an almighty *I told you so*, delivered with that smirk that she loved to hate. She didn't feel strong enough for that, not after what she had just been through.

On the other hand, it wasn't like she had that much choice. She had a small amount of money, her phone, and her passport. She'd placed her rucksack in her suitcase for convenience and had never been so grateful to have kept hold of the three essential items that she'd stowed in her pocket.

The door opened and Celia stood before her. "Are you going to stand there all day?"

The dam on Lily's emotions broke, and she burst into tears.

Celia held the door open with one arm and held out her other. "Come here," she demanded.

Lily obeyed, walking straight into the hug and crying on Celia's shoulder. She was distantly aware of the door closing and of being enveloped in a strong comforting hug.

She didn't know how much time passed before Celia loosened her grip.

"Let me order us some lunch," Celia said.

"You don't have to do that," Lily replied, wiping at her tears with her sleeve.

"I've seen how much you eat—you must be starving," Celia quipped.

Lily wasn't going to argue again. She was hungry. And exhausted. And the bantering was nice, familiar and safe.

She was guided to a chaise longue in front of an enormous window with views of the city and the imperial gardens. Before she could appreciate much of the view, a room service menu was handed to her.

Lily picked the cheapest option, a sandwich, hardly looking at it.

Celia raised an eyebrow. "Come on, what do you really want?"

Lily shook her head. "Celia, I don't have *any* money. I can't afford any of this. I don't even know how I'm going to get home."

"I'm paying for your lunch—have whatever you like. Don't worry, we'll get this all sorted out, and you'll be home before you know it."

Lily didn't know why she believed and trusted Celia, but she did.

"Thank you," she whispered before changing her order to the burger and fries.

Celia crossed the room and made the call to room service. Lily turned and looked out the window at the impressive view. She'd been so excited about seeing Tokyo, but now she couldn't wait to leave the city.

It wasn't like it was Tokyo's fault, but Lily would be glad if she never heard of the place ever again.

She felt the chaise longue dip beside her and turned to see Celia looking at her with a concerned expression.

"Do you want to talk about it?"

She didn't, but she knew she had to. She needed to rationalise and process it for herself as well.

"We met at a cafe. It was her, the woman from the video chat and the pictures I'd seen. We hugged, but something felt off, like she was really uncomfortable," Lily explained. "I thought it was nerves."

She licked her lips and looked down at her hands in her lap. "She kept checking her phone, which I thought was weird. But again, I put it down to nerves. Then she suddenly said we should go. We walked through some streets, which I thought was strange because her home was a couple of bus trips away." She coughed. "Can I have some water?"

Celia jumped to her feet and went to fetch some.

Lily was only now beginning to realise how thirsty, hungry, and exhausted she was. The adrenaline she'd been running on seemed to have finally left her.

A glass of water was placed in her shaking hand.

"Thank you."

"Take your time," Celia instructed, taking a seat beside her again.

"I'm so stupid," Lily confessed.

"You're not."

"I am. And you think so too," Lily said. "Even you knew Asami didn't exist."

"I was further away from it than you," Celia said. "What happened?"

Lily swallowed. "She said she needed to stop off at a friend's house to pick something up. We get to this house that's really rundown, and this old guy opens the door and he just stares at me, and now I'm starting to feel scared. Asami goes to the bathroom, and then she doesn't come back."

Lily stopped and took a couple of small sips of water. She'd been reminding herself how lucky she'd been. She could have easily been overpowered, outnumbered, all kinds of things. Luck and nothing else had allowed her to escape.

"He's talking and talking, making no sense and saying that I'm pretty and that we should talk more. After a while, I kind of realise Asami's gone, and I know I have to get out of there. I made a run for the front door, but it was locked."

Lily's hand was shaking so much she worried about spilling the water. Celia took the glass from her and placed it on the coffee table, then took Lily's hand in hers.

"Go on," Celia said.

"He told me that I'd been talking to him. Admitted he was Asami, and the girl was someone he paid. He said that we belonged together, and we'd connected, and I shouldn't judge him based on what he looks like, it was the words we shared that…" Lily licked her lips and shook her head. She'd been such an idiot. How could she have fallen for such an obvious trick?

"Did he hurt you?" Celia asked, her voice deadly serious.

"No. I pushed past him and found a back door that was unlocked and ran out that way. I climbed over a fence. But he has my suitcase and my rucksack."

"Belongings are irrelevant right now," Celia told her. "As long as you're okay."

"I'm not okay," Lily whispered.

"You will be," Celia promised her.

Lily didn't know if she agreed, but she also didn't know how she was managing to stay upright, and so she didn't argue the point.

"I'm so sorry," she whispered again.

"I won't have you apologising to me any more," Celia told her firmly. "Enough."

"But—"

"No. No more." Celia stood up. "You were conned. Happens to many people all the time. These parasites prey on your perceived weaknesses. Don't apologise for what they did to you."

"I'm apologising for what I'm doing to you," Lily explained.

"I don't need your apology," Celia said. "I was in a bind last night, and you helped me out. Now it's the other way around. Such is life."

Lily really was too exhausted to argue with that.

It wasn't long before there was a knock on the door indicating the arrival of lunch.

The food arrived on a trolley that somehow expanded to become a table. Two foldaway chairs were placed at either end of the table, set by the two members of staff.

It was an elaborate production, but Lily imagined that was what you got when you paid Shangri-La prices.

Celia sat down and gestured for Lily to do the same.

"Do they have your passport?" Celia asked as they started to eat.

"No, thank goodness. I kept that with me."

"Bank cards?"

"They have them. I need to call my bank and get them cancelled." Lily sighed. "And the airline, see if I can get on the next flight home."

"That can all be resolved," Celia reassured her. "Eat."

POST-MUGGING ADMIN

After they'd eaten lunch, Celia gave Lily access to her laptop to find phone numbers for her bank, credit card company, and the airline. She'd then curled up in an armchair in the corner of the room with a book to try to give Lily some privacy. She was glad her company had opted for a larger room.

When she'd first entered the so-called deluxe space, she'd seen little point in the spacious room with two double beds, an enormous chaise longue, as well as a desk. Now she was grateful for the room to move about and not be in Lily's way.

While she was reading her book, she was still half paying attention to Lily's phone calls. The bank and the credit card company had seemed quite painless, but the airline was another matter.

Lily was closing in on tears again as she attempted to explain to whatever bozo she was talking to that she didn't have any money to pay for a new ticket. Or any money to pay the admin fee required to move her old ticket.

Lily was on the third attempt at explaining her situation when Celia had had enough.

She tossed her book on the chair, stood up, and held her hand out to Lily. Lily paused for a moment, a puzzled look on her face, before finally handing the phone over.

"Hello, who am I speaking to?" Celia demanded.

"Who is this?"

"I asked first."

"Katie."

"Do you have a surname, Katie?"

"Inglis."

"Lovely. Thank you. My name is Celia Scott, and I'm booked on a first-class journey with you tomorrow afternoon from Tokyo to Heathrow. I'm also standing in front of a young woman who has been mugged and needs your assistance in getting home. She's lucky to be alive and in possession of her passport. Now, let's work on getting her on the next available flight home before I call Johan Butler-Draper and tell him that you, Katie Inglis, were willing to leave Lily Andersen abandoned in Tokyo without a single thought for her safety and well-being."

There was a pause, and then Katie asked Celia to hold for a moment.

"Yes, I'll hold," Celia said.

Lily frowned. "Who's Johan Whatsit-Whosit?"

"The CEO of the airline."

Lily nodded. "A friend of yours?"

"Never heard of the man before yesterday—read it in the in-flight magazine," Celia admitted.

Lily's eyes widened. "What if she checks?"

"Do we really think Katie Nobody has a direct line to the boss?" Celia asked. "Highly unlikely."

"Miss Scott?" Katie's nervous voice resumed on the line.

"Yes?"

"I've managed to find a seat for Miss Andersen on your flight tomorrow. We don't have a flight leaving any sooner. Will that be acceptable?"

"Well, it will have to be," Celia said. "I'll hand you back to her to tell her."

Celia handed the phone back to Lily and returned to her book.

A few moments later Lily finished the call. "Thank you for helping with that," she told Celia.

"You're welcome."

Lily turned her attention back to the laptop and started typing. She leaned in close to the screen and frowned, scrolling and scrolling as she did.

"Problem?" Celia asked.

"I'm just wondering where I can stay tonight," Lily said. "Seeing if there's a cheap hostel that might agree to a stay now, pay later kind of deal."

Celia stared at her.

Lily could obviously feel eyes burrowing into her and looked up. "What?" Lily asked.

Celia pointed to the unused bed.

Lily looked at it and then at Celia. "I couldn't…I'm already imposing so much on you."

"I have two beds. I'm one person," Celia said. "Besides, I'm going to be at this event from six until God only knows when in the morning. It's not as if the room isn't big enough for two people."

Lily looked at the bed for a few silent seconds.

"Unless you want to sleep at the airport?" Celia added.

"No, no. I'm sorry. I'm being silly. I gratefully accept." Lily closed the laptop lid. "Thank you. I feel a little better now that most of that is sorted."

"It's not sorted—you need to call the embassy," Celia said.

"Why would I call them?"

"Because they need to know. You were kidnapped."

Lily scoffed a laugh. "I wasn't kidnapped."

"Did you or did you not find yourself in the house of a strange man? Led there by someone who was essentially paid to keep you calm and in line?"

Lily's face fell. It was obvious she hadn't considered it that way.

"I was kidnapped," Lily whispered, that part of the whole ghastly scenario only now registering.

"We don't know what his plan was, but either way you must report this to the embassy so they have a record of it," Celia said.

Lily quickly shook her head from side to side. "No, no. I can't. I…I can't. I can't go through it all again. Especially over the phone with a stranger. They'll think I'm stupid."

Celia abandoned her book again and snatched up her phone. "They most certainly will not think you're stupid. They'll think you are lucky. But if you can't do it, then I will. Let me know if I get any details wrong."

Celia didn't give Lily much opportunity to argue. The incident had to be reported to the local authorities, and if Lily was understandably reluctant to do that, then Celia would do it for her. It was hardly a hardship. And if it helped to capture the man who was responsible and throw him into a dark hole for the rest of his life, then Celia would assist with glee.

As expected, the embassy was helpful and understanding. Celia retold the events as best she could with occasional guidance from Lily. All the information they had was imparted, and the embassy took Lily's contact details with a promise to get in touch with her in a couple of day when she was feeling up to it.

Celia felt a weight lift in the knowledge that some justice might be served.

"I'm glad we did that," Lily admitted when the call was over.

"Good, I'm glad." Celia put her phone back on the charger and put the book away. "Feel free to get some rest if you'd like. I'm going to kill some time before I have to go and say hello to the organisers, and then I'll be getting ready for the ceremony."

Lily looked at the bed again, and Celia could see the exhaustion in her eyes. Her heart clenched for Lily; she couldn't begin to comprehend what she had been through that day. And right off the back of having a stressful day with her grandmother.

Not to mention that the whole Asami disaster had probably shaken her to her core. If they were as close as Lily had said, and had spoken for so long, then that was surely going to be a huge emotional shift for Lily to cope with.

"Actually," Celia said, "I should probably go downstairs and meet the organisers now." She crossed the room to the wardrobe and slid on a pair of flat shoes.

"You're not leaving on my account, are you?" Lily asked. "I'd hate to put you out. More so than I'm doing already."

"I'm not leaving on your account. As I said, I have to go and greet the organisers," Celia lied smoothly.

She hadn't intended to go to see them for another hour or so, but it was clear that Lily was utterly drained and could probably do with a few moments on her own to process what had happened.

"I'll leave the door card here." Celia placed the key on the desk. "I'll pick up a second one at reception while I'm out. I'll probably be an hour or so."

She picked up the perfectly wrapped gift she had for the organisers, which had been prepared by her assistant who had more of an understanding of Japanese traditions.

"Are you sure about this?" Lily pressed.

"Yes. I don't just randomly offer a bed to anyone I meet." She stopped and thought for a moment. "That came out wrong. I'm sure. Will you be okay if I head out for a while? Do you need anything?"

Lily shook her head. "I'm all good. Thank you so much, Celia. I can't tell you how much I appreciate this."

"It's okay. You'll find a way to pay me back." She smiled to demonstrate that she was joking before picking up her suit jacket from a hanger. "I'll see you later. Get some rest."

HONESTY

L ily looked around the hotel room. Celia had left her laptop, bag, and belongings behind.

She must really trust me.

It felt good to know that Celia trusted her. Good to know that not everything in the world was dark and scary.

She glanced at her phone, which was charging on the desk. It kept lighting up, and Lily knew it was Asami. Or whatever *his* name was. The man who had conned her and played with her emotions for months. The man who had hired a woman to pretend to be Asami, the fake persona he had created.

Lily felt sick to her stomach. She'd told Asami things she'd never told anyone else. Sent pictures, artwork, and voice messages.

She'd fallen in love with Asami.

But it was all a con.

She didn't know why he'd done it. Was it for kicks? Was it to rob her? To kidnap her? Was she part of a Japanese radio talk show? Was half of Tokyo currently laughing its ass off?

She didn't know, and she'd probably never know.

Still, she was safe, and now her brain could occupy itself with something new. The feelings of helplessness and loss were slowly starting to overcome the terror she'd been suffocated by.

What bothered her now was that she didn't know what to do next. It wasn't as if there was a manual for dealing with these situations.

She didn't care about her luggage—her belongings were unimportant in the grand scheme of things, considering there had been a moment when she felt sure that she was going to be killed and chopped into pieces or tied up in the basement.

Although she had to admit that she'd love a clean change of clothes right then.

That and to be able to forget it had even happened. To just go to sleep and wake up with absolutely no memory of it all.

What if this man had other girls arriving from the UK? She shivered at the thought. She'd reported it to the embassy, and they were forwarding it to people who dealt with this kind of crime. Because, as Celia had reminded her, many people fell victim to these scams, and as such departments were created to investigate them.

She hadn't wanted to admit what had happened, especially not to officials on the end of a phone. But Celia had been right that her story had to be told. If only to warn others. Not that she was strong enough now to recount every gruesome detail, and so she'd felt acute relief when Celia had taken the task on for her.

Celia who was surprisingly kind, soft, and gentle. Knowing when to push Lily and when to calm her.

Celia, whose perfume still lingered in the air.

Lily shook her head. It most certainly wasn't the time to be thinking of things like that.

She looked longingly at the bed. She wanted to sleep, but she felt so wired. Her fight-or-flight instinct meant that adrenaline was still streaming through her body in fits and starts.

One moment she could feel her eyelids closing, and the next she was so aware of her surroundings that she felt she could hear the heartbeat of the person in the next room. She hated feeling so on edge.

She stood and stretched her arms high above her head and let out a long yawn. Sleep would hopefully come if she made the effort to lie on the sinfully comfortable-looking bed. She pulled back the cover and slid between the sheets. She didn't know what it was about hotel beds that made them infinitely more comfortable than any other bed she'd ever slept in.

Lying down and staring at the ceiling, she chastised herself one last time for being so foolish before closing her eyes. A few moments later she could feel herself drifting off to sleep.

❖

Lily opened her eyes. She knew she'd slept, but she had no idea how long she had slept for. It must have been a while because Celia was clearly back, if the soft sounds of someone walking around the room were anything to go by.

She turned to check that it was Celia and not someone else; considering the day she had had, anything was possible.

Her jaw dropped open.

Celia was wearing a black cocktail dress, and her hair and make-up were perfectly styled. She looked devastatingly hot.

Thankfully she hadn't noticed Lily staring at her like she was the last chocolate in the Christmas selection box. Lily swallowed, shook her head, and looked away.

"Ah, you're awake," Celia said. "Sorry if I woke you. You were dead to the world when I got back, so I thought it best to let you rest."

"Thank you," Lily murmured. She sat up and looked around the room. Clothing had moved, Celia's case was open, and items were strewn everywhere. Two bottles of wine sat on the desk, one empty and the other currently being worked on.

Celia was standing in front of a mirror near the window, applying lipstick. Lily couldn't get over how great she looked. There was something about the way the dress clung to her and showed off her toned legs.

Lily tore her gaze away for a second time.

"Are you hungry? It's nearly dinner time," Celia said.

"I…don't know," Lily admitted. She was too tired and disorientated to think about food just yet.

"Well, if you do get hungry, then just call room service. It will go on my bill."

"You're very generous."

"My company is very generous," Celia corrected her. She stepped away from the mirror and picked up a wine glass and took a hefty swig from it. She snatched up a piece of paper and started reading it, pacing in front of the window as she did.

She seemed on edge. Lily presumed it was nerves before picking up an award.

An award she doesn't want, Lily reminded herself. "Did the organisers like their gift?" Lily asked.

"Hmm?" Celia looked at her in dazed confusion for a moment. "Oh yes, I think so."

Lily's eyes drifted towards the empty wine bottle. It wasn't the first time she'd seen Celia a little the worse for alcohol.

In fact, now that Lily thought about it, Celia drank a lot. She'd drunk first thing in the morning before the original flight; she'd drunk on the plane; she'd drunk over dinner the previous night. And not a small amount either.

Something about it nagged at Lily.

"You drink a lot," Lily said, hoping for a direct route into the conversation.

"I work in the financial industry—it's a requirement. Good with numbers, liver made of iron? You're in." Celia continued reading from her sheet of paper.

Lily sat up and rubbed at her eyes. "Have you drunk a whole bottle of wine while I've been asleep?"

Celia lowered the paper and looked at Lily with a tired expression. "You sound like my ex-husband."

"Did you drink a whole bottle of wine while he was asleep too?"

Celia demonstratively placed the wine glass down on a side table. "There. Happy now?"

"Why don't you want this award?" Lily asked. Her tiredness prevented her usual filter from stopping the questions and comments as they entered her mind.

Celia almost growled in frustration. "Why are you doing this *now*?"

"Because you seem out of sorts, and I want to know why. You said you don't want this award, and yet you've travelled all this way to get it. And you drink a lot, like, alone."

Anger danced in Celia's eyes, and Lily wondered if she'd pushed too far. She wondered if she should apologise and leave Celia to it.

"That award…" Celia stopped and sucked in a deep breath. "Never mind. Just forget it. We're not talking about it."

The peek into what was bothering Celia was tantalising, and Lily found she couldn't let it go so easily. "I am," she said. "I'm going to talk about it until you tell me."

Celia stared at Lily in disbelief and frustration.

Lily knew she should let it go, but she wasn't going to do that now. There was something about the way Celia looked at her, something in her eyes. Beyond the warning stare there was a helplessness and a story that Lily desperately needed to uncover. Something was up, and Lily wanted to help if she could. Helping others, even when it wasn't requested, was something she instinctively did. It had gotten her into trouble more than once, but the times it was worth it outweighed those by a long shot.

Celia had shown her such kindness, and this award business seemed to be a thorn in her side. If Lily could ease that pain in some way, then she would.

"Lily," Celia warned. "Do not push me."

"You've seen the day I've had," Lily said. "I don't think you can hurt me more than I'm already hurt. Maybe I'm an idiot, but I fell in love with someone, someone who doesn't exist."

"Lily—"

"And I don't know what they were going to do with me, or what I'll do next. Or even how I really feel about all this. But I do know that something is eating you up. And you hide it with snark and drink. But you can't bury it like that."

"Enough." Celia sighed, a shaky hand in the air. "Just…stop."

She'd gone from angry threats to exasperation. Lily took that as a good sign and wondered if she might be near a breakthrough.

"Why don't you want the award?" Lily repeated.

"Lily," Celia warned her again. She snatched up the wine glass and downed the quarter glass of liquid that was left. She slowly lowered the glass and stared at it, shock clear on her face as if only just registering what she had done. "Lily?" Celia asked, her voice quivering.

"Yes?"

"Would you please throw the rest of the second bottle of wine away? Down the sink, please," Celia requested softly.

Lily jumped out of bed, grabbed the bottle, and quickly did as she was asked. She watched it slowly bubble from the narrow neck and wash away down the plughole.

When she exited the bathroom, she noticed that Celia had taken a seat on the chaise longue and was looking a little shaky.

Lily placed the empty bottles in the small waste bin under the desk and sat beside Celia, giving her space but also staying close enough to maybe offer some comfort.

"Tell me," Lily requested quietly.

Silence stretched on between them for a long time, and Lily wondered if Celia would ever speak.

"This award…" Celia began before pausing again. "This award represents the fact that I am an abhorrent human being and mother."

Lily didn't speak. It wasn't her place to agree or disagree with anything Celia said until she was in possession of all the facts. She doubted very much that Celia was right, but any argument would fall on deaf ears.

"My son, Andrew, took his life not so long ago," Celia explained. "It was quite out of the blue. He was in university, and suddenly…he was gone."

Lily grabbed hold of Celia's hand and held it tight.

"The contract I'd been working on meant long hours, international conference calls, travel. I wasn't around very much for him. I hadn't seen him for weeks, probably the longest separation in our lives. I missed his calls, and sometimes I was too tired to return them."

Celia pulled away and stood up. She looked out the window, her arms wrapped around herself.

"The contract I'd been working on was a very big deal for the company. It meant promotion. It meant glory, money, and this award. This award is given to the broker who closes a particularly big or complicated deal. My office has never gotten close. The award does the rounds internationally, being won by the Italian office, the American office, the Danish office once, but never the British office. Not until this year. My boss put the deal forward for consideration. I didn't even know he'd done it. But he did, and we won. As the lead broker, it's my win."

Celia went to rub her face but stopped herself just before her hands connected with her make-up. She paused and frowned before slowly lowering them.

"I got the call that Andrew had taken his life precisely one minute before I was due to go into the boardroom to sign the contract to finalise the deal. A lovely policewoman called, and I can't for the life of me tell you what she said. She told me that Andrew was gone, and the rest was just a blur. He'd taken his life. I think we spoke for four or five minutes, but it is all just a complete blankness. I was numb. And then I hung up the call. And I went into the boardroom and signed the paperwork. We drank champagne to celebrate."

Celia looked down at Lily. "My son had just died, and a few minutes later I returned to work and celebrated with my colleagues. What kind of person does that? What kind of mother does that?"

"Why do you think you did that?" Lily asked without judgement. She could never imagine being in that situation, so she had no idea what she would have done in Celia's shoes.

"He was gone. In that moment I knew that nothing would bring him back. Running to Edinburgh University, going home, crying. Nothing would help. He was gone."

"You were in shock," Lily said.

"Maybe." Celia lightly shrugged. "I told my work colleagues about Andrew the next day. I lied to them, too ashamed to admit that I'd found out the day before. I told them it had happened that morning."

Celia turned from the window and perched herself on the edge of Lily's bed. "As the days and weeks went by, I wondered what possessed me. I had put everything into this contract. I had missed calls from my only son. Calls that maybe would have saved his life."

"You don't know that," Lily said.

"I don't. But my head still swam with those thoughts. I regretted all the work I had put into that contract, and I bitterly regretted signing it when I did." Celia leaned back onto her outstretched arms and chuckled bitterly. "And then I got the letter. The letter that said I had received the award. An award that I now didn't want because it represented what a despicable person I had become."

"Couldn't you, I don't know, decline it?"

"No. It's a much coveted award. Our company head office is here in Japan, and it would be considered very disrespectful to turn it down. My colleagues don't know about all this, and I've done my best to appear happy."

Celia sat forward and looked meaningfully at Lily. "So now I have to accept that awful damn award. I have to smile, give a speech, take the damn thing home, keep it in my office, and tell everyone how proud I am to have been bestowed such an amazing honour. I have to look at it every single day."

"I can see why you're drinking," Lily joked, unaware of what else she could say.

Celia laughed. "Get me my wine back," she replied in jest.

Lily felt a little overwhelmed with what she'd just learnt. She couldn't even begin to imagine what Celia was going through. It seemed too much for one person to stand. No wonder her personality flipped back and forth now and then.

"I started drinking to help me sleep," Celia confessed. "And then to distract myself. And then to forget. And then…just because I did. I don't think I've slipped that far yet, but I'm glad you helped me to identify that this is starting to be an issue."

"I'm so sorry that you lost your son. I know that's really meaningless in the grand scheme of things, but it's all I can say," Lily said.

Celia offered a small smile. "Thank you, I appreciate you saying so."

"And I'm sorry you have to collect the stupid award," Lily added.

"As am I." Celia stood and toyed with her necklace. "I keep telling myself that in a few hours, it will all be over. It will be done. And I can focus on getting back home and getting on with my life."

"Is there anything I can do?" Lily offered.

Celia shook her head. "No, I think you've had quite enough to deal with today. But thank you."

"Seriously, if you need me to do anything, just say." Lily wanted to feel useful. In fact she needed to feel useful right now. It would take her mind off things and also make her feel less like a weight around Celia's neck. "Please?" Lily added. "I'd like to do something if I can."

Celia looked as if she was about to decline the offer again but paused and tilted her head to the side as if something occurred to her.

"Would you listen to my speech?"

Lily nodded eagerly. "Sure. I can't promise I'll have much useful feedback, but I'll do my best."

"I just need to practise," Celia admitted. "I haven't really looked over it much. I've been busy burying my head in the sand, but I'm at the point where I only have a few hours. It's now or never."

"Now it is, then." Lily curled her legs beneath her to get comfortable and looked expectantly at Celia.

Celia picked up her speech and started reading from it. Lily didn't understand half of what was being said—it was all insurance and finance-speak and jokes that she was sure were funny if you understood the context.

She didn't mind listening. Celia had a rich, silky voice that she could listen to all day long. It helped that she looked stunning, and Lily was glad for an excuse to stare at her.

She smiled and nodded along with the speech, laughing at points that she thought were appropriate. In the back of her mind she cried with sorrow for what Celia had been through. To lose a child was one thing; to blame yourself was quite another. And to be awarded with something you just couldn't turn down, that would forever remind you of what had happened, was beyond heartbreaking.

Her own problems were diminishing in her mind, and she was now eager to focus on helping Celia overcome the enormous hurdle that she was fast approaching.

It was a welcome distraction, even though she desperately wished Celia didn't have to deal with any of it.

ALAN

I can't do it." Celia paced the small backstage area, her phone pressed to her ear. "I just can't. I feel sick."

"You can. You get up on that stage and act. I've seen you do it. You just put on a show, grab that award, give your amazing speech, and get out of there. You can do it!"

"I'm terrible at acting," Celia argued.

"You'll be fine. A couple of minutes, a few words which you know off by heart. Easy. I know you can do this."

Lily's pep talk was starting to dissolve her fear, but Celia still felt terrified. She had known it would be hard, but she had no idea it would be quite this hard.

The slow build-up was finally coming to a head. It could no longer be ignored or downplayed. It was here. After weeks spent ignoring the looming event, she was moments away from a golden envelope being opened and her name being read.

"Do you want me to come down?" Lily asked.

Celia seriously considered the offer for a moment. She hardly knew Lily, but already she was like an emotional rock to her. No longer some bright young thing who had been mugged due to her naive belief that people were fundamentally good and honest, now she was someone Celia depended on.

Without Lily there was no way she would have exited her room and gone downstairs to the dinner. She would have huddled on her bed and ignored the knocks on the door and phone calls as to her whereabouts.

She later would have pretended to have slipped in her shower, the inference that she was an old woman who fell in unfamiliar settings better than picking up the award.

"No, you needn't come down. They'll assume you're my high-class hooker." Celia teased her to lighten the mood.

"Oh, wow, you think I'm high-class?" Lily replied happily.

Celia laughed.

"I love it when you laugh," Lily said.

"Thank you for making me laugh."

"You sound like Mr. Burns from *The Simpsons* when you laugh," Lily continued.

"Why do I think that's not a compliment?" Celia asked.

But Lily had already changed the subject. "Ready to go and kick butt?"

Celia rolled her eyes. "Must we call it that?"

"Fine. Go and get 'em! Pick up Alan and then get out of there! Easy!"

"Alan?"

"Alan. The award. I've named him."

"So I see."

"I think we needed to take this step to identify with him on a more personal level. It will be much more cathartic to say *fucking Alan* than it will be to say *that fucking award*. Trust me."

Celia opened her mouth to argue but quickly realised that Lily was right.

She could see the chairman being welcomed to the stage and knew that very soon she'd be called to accept the award.

Or Alan, as it would now be known.

"I have to go."

"Good luck."

Celia hung up and practiced controlling her breathing. She just needed to get through the next five to ten minutes.

❖

Lily pulled on the fluffy white robe that she'd found hanging in the wardrobe. There were two, so she was sure Celia wouldn't mind. Besides, she didn't want to put her old clothes back on straight away.

Luckily, despite everything, she hadn't destroyed them too badly. She'd yet to spill on them, and they seemed reasonably fresh, but that didn't stop her from giving them a little freshening up in the bathroom with some complimentary body spray she'd found and a light showering. Her underwear she'd hand-washed properly, and the socks and panties were now hanging on the towel rail to dry.

The shower had been delightful, although it had to be said that the rainfall feature was a little bit what she imagined waterboarding to be like. After thirty seconds she was ready to confess that she had secretly opened and rewrapped the Christmas presents she found in her parents' wardrobe when she was a child.

But a little adjustment and the shower turned from torture to heaven. It felt good to wash away the day. It felt good to be safe, especially considering that she'd had a very real, very frightening moment when she hadn't been safe. That for the first time in her privileged life, she'd been in real danger.

It was a lesson she'd take to heart. She would never, ever put herself in that kind of situation again.

She walked back into the main part of the room. Her breath caught at the beautiful view. It was dark outside, and the lights of an energetic city sparkled like diamonds on velvet.

She sneered and pressed a button on the wall that automatically closed the curtains.

Tokyo, no matter how striking, was not going to get around her like that. She was still very angry with it, even though she knew that anger was completely misplaced.

Tokyo hadn't stolen her heart and pretended to be someone else. Tokyo hadn't stolen her suitcase. Tokyo wasn't a fifty-year-old man.

But she still felt enormous satisfaction at being able to mute the entire city at the press of a button.

It had been an hour since Celia's last call, which came minutes before she was due to go onstage. Lily had waited until the time Celia was scheduled to go on before she took her shower, just in case something happened and she was needed. Which seemed ludicrous— Celia was an adult who had done just fine without Lily her whole life.

But still, she waited just in case. When the time came and passed without incident, she assumed Celia had done what she had to do and would then socialise for a while as expected of her before returning to the room.

Despite the late hour, Lily wasn't tired in the slightest. Not surprising, considering her long afternoon nap and it being early afternoon according to her body clock.

She wondered if she'd be able to sleep that night. It felt strange to be sharing a room with someone she hardly knew. Especially considering that someone was Celia, whom Lily had recently decided was rather attractive.

"And straight," she reminded herself.

She blew out a breath and looked around the room for something to occupy herself. She'd already made the mistake of channel-hopping through some television and had been confused, horrified, and alarmed—in that order—by what she had seen. She'd heard that Japanese television could be interesting. Now she knew that it most definitely was.

She flopped on her bed and picked up her phone. It had recently occurred to her how the device was intrinsically linked to Asami in her mind. It wasn't just a phone; it was the way she communicated with someone she'd fallen in love with. It was how she accessed the scant few pictures she had of Asami.

At least now she knew why there were so few images.

She groaned out loud at the memory of the video call. Knowing now that the woman wasn't Asami was embarrassing, to say the least. She'd flirted her little heart out. And she'd misread the awkwardness, thinking that Asami was simply shy when actually she was an actress being paid to play a role. Even more embarrassing.

There was a click of the door being unlocked. Lily sat up a little and ensured her robe was decent.

Celia stepped into the room and held aloft a large glass award.

"I bring you...Alan," she announced grandly.

PENIS OR HEADSTONE

The award, now known as Alan, sat on the desk in front of the television. Celia lay on her front on her bed, chin cupped in her hand as she stared at the glass monstrosity.

Lily sat on the other bed, also on her front, with her head tilted as she regarded the award.

When Celia had returned, she'd kicked off her shoes, plonked Alan down, and then lain on the bed. She felt drained and relieved that it was, in many ways, over.

"Alan's..." Lily started and then trailed off.

"Hm?"

"He's, like, really..."

"Phallic?" Celia suggested.

"Yeah."

"Yes. Most awards are. Or like a headstone. I imagine you get a choice at award manufacturers: penis or headstone." Celia chuckled. "Circumstances as they are, I'm rather glad it's not the latter."

Lily didn't laugh. Celia guessed her very dark sense of humour wasn't apparent.

"But it's like...*really* phallic," Lily continued.

"You have a thing about the male genitalia, don't you?" Celia asked. "First that man in Denmark, now this."

Lily glanced at her. "Maybe I'm just a little fed up with seeing *them* everywhere I look. I mean, we're in a city filled with them. We're in a hotel that looks like one. You've been given an award that resembles one. That man in Denmark was obviously very proud of his. Don't you just get sick of it all?"

Celia shrugged. "I've never really considered it. I don't see a skyscraper and think it's shaped like a penis. I think it's shaped like a skyscraper. And I don't know what other shape it could possibly be."

"Okay, fair enough." Lily gestured towards the award with a tilt of her head. "But come on, that…"

"Oh yes, Alan is definitely shaped like a penis. Or what men would aspire to, at least."

Lily visibly shuddered, and Celia laughed at the reaction. A question flashed up in Celia's mind. She didn't want to be nosy but felt that they'd already shared a lot about themselves in the short amount of time they'd known one another.

"May I ask when you knew you were gay?" Celia asked.

"When I saw that Danish guy's junk." Lily laughed. "No. Um…I don't think there was an actual time. I think I'd always been aware of it. Even as a kid I liked some teachers and didn't quite realise why until much later."

"Have you ever dated a man?"

"Once. You know, to test it out," Lily replied. "Didn't feel anything. We kissed, and I remember thinking it was just a bit gross."

Celia laughed. "Gross?"

"Yeah, like, I don't know, I felt like he was trying to pump me up or something. We were teenagers and he was obviously hormonal, but I just wanted to make sure my lungs didn't explode."

"Teenage boys aren't known for their kissing skills," Celia pointed out.

"No. But I later found out that teenage girls were pretty damn good at it." Lily grinned.

"And that's when you knew?"

Lily thought about the question for a moment. "I don't know. I can't remember there being an actual time, just a gradual reinforcing of preferences. When did you know that you were straight?"

It was asked with a smile, and Celia chortled. "I'm sorry, have I been very rude?"

"No. It's just often a funny thing to ask a straight person," Lily replied with a cheeky grin.

"I have a crush on Gillian Anderson," Celia admitted.

Lily's eyebrows rose in obvious surprise. She quickly brought them under control again. "Gillian Anderson defies normal laws," she said seriously. "Everyone fancies her."

"Ah."

Celia didn't know why she had admitted to that fact. Did she want to send a little flare up to advise Lily that she could be persuaded, quite easily too? And if she had unwittingly done that, why? It wasn't appropriate when she'd offered to share her room with the young woman who had recently been through such a stressful ordeal.

Celia turned her attention back to Alan. She couldn't remember her speech or accepting the award from the chairman in much the same way she couldn't remember being in a car crash in her late twenties.

Her brain kindly repressed that kind of trauma, probably in preparation for it to come bounding out, all at the same time, when she was older. She wasn't looking forward to that day, but, for now, she was pleased to be done with it.

The applause and genuine smiles from the audience indicated that everything had gone as it should have. That was the main thing.

"Any others?" Lily asked.

Celia furrowed her brow. "Others?"

"Crushes. On women," Lily clarified.

Apparently this was a conversation they were now having. Celia had given Lily the chance to back out, but instead she had pushed forward. Interesting, Celia thought.

"Oh. I don't know, nothing obvious, but I can appreciate a nice-looking woman. Never really thought about it. I got married young." Celia flopped onto the bed and rolled over onto her back. She was emotional, and this direction of conversation was dangerous, so she decided to steer the ship back to safer shores. "Do you want to talk about the whole Asami situation?"

She heard Lily chuckle. "Not really."

"Where did you first meet her?" Celia asked, undeterred.

"A Facebook group," Lily replied.

"A lesbian one?"

"A grief one."

"Oh. I'm sorry."

"It's okay. My mum passed away a while ago. I'm speaking to a therapist about it, but she's pretty useless."

"So you felt the need to get real assistance from the faceless masses of social media?"

"Absolutely. Isn't that what everyone does?" Lily asked in obvious jest.

Celia wondered if Asami, whoever he was, had been deliberately hanging around grief groups to look for a suitable mark or if it had been coincidence. Either way, to focus on Lily when she was at her lowest and in need of support was sickening.

And exactly what people like him did.

Celia turned her head to regard Lily. "Why is your therapist useless?"

"Not sure. She keeps asking me about my childhood."

"Looking for trauma," Celia said. "That's what they do. They root around for trauma and then blame it all on that."

Lily looked at her, a grin on her face. "Have you been in therapy?"

"No. I nearly spoke to someone when my husband left."

"Why didn't you?"

"I was rather worried they might suggest I try to get him back." Celia burst out laughing and Lily joined in.

Lily sat up and looked at her wristwatch. "Wow, it's eleven and I'm not even tired."

"Nor me. I'm still on UK time," Celia said. "And I don't see much point in making the effort to acclimatise as I'm heading home tomorrow afternoon."

"Good point." Lily adjusted her robe and flopped back down on her bed.

They didn't speak, and Celia could hear the distant sound of a bustling city, sirens, traffic, muffled music. Any other time she might have been eager to go and explore, but right then she wanted nothing more than to fast-forward to her flight.

"I met Asami after I'd had a bad break-up." Lily's voice was so soft that Celia nearly missed the comment.

"Oh?"

"I'd been dating someone—"

"A real person?"

"Yes, a real person."

"Just checking." Celia smirked.

"We lived together," Lily said.

"So, no chance he was a Japanese man in his forties?" Celia checked.

"Fifties, and no. She was definitely not a man."

"Was he bald?" Celia asked, noting that whenever she injected a little humour into their conversations, Lily seemed a little lighter for it.

"Who?"

"Fake Asami."

"Does it matter?" Lily asked, grinning widely.

Celia turned onto her side. "I just want to make sure I'm getting the right mental image of him."

"Yes, he was bald. Well, thinning. May I go on now?"

"Please proceed."

"Anyway, we were living together. But she wanted to end it. Which was hard, even though I knew she'd had her doubts for a while."

"Why was that?"

Lily stood up and walked over to the tea-making facilities and grabbed the small kettle. "Tea?"

"I'd love some."

Lily went to the bathroom to fill the kettle. "She was older than me, and she always thought that I'd get bored of her and leave. Turned out that was too much for her."

Celia raised an eyebrow in interest. "An older woman, eh?" Her heart fluttered at the thought, and she quickly reprimanded herself. Lily was sharing her heartbreak to someone she trusted, and Celia wasn't about to break that trust. Lily was attractive in an adorable kind of way that Celia couldn't ignore. But she could not, and would not, push her advantage when Lily was emotionally drained and at Celia's mercy.

"Yeah." Lily returned and put the kettle on to boil.

"How much older?" Celia fished.

Lily turned away but not before Celia caught the flushed cheeks. Celia sat up with interest.

"Oh, my, you're blushing. This is going to be good."

"She was…fifty—"

"Fifty?" Celia cried.

"Four," Lily finished.

"Fifty-four!"

Lily looked back at her and raised an eyebrow. "It's not unheard of, you know."

"How old are you?" Celia demanded.

"That's private," Lily replied, arms folded across her chest.

Celia stood and snatched up Lily's passport from the bedside table where she had left it with her charging phone.

"Hey," Lily said, laughing.

Celia looked at the date of birth and did the math.

"Twenty-five." Celia looked at her. "Well, well, well."

"It's not unheard of," Lily repeated.

"You'd fit two of you in one of her," Celia said.

Lily laughed some more. "I don't think it quite works like that."

"And have change left over," Celia added.

"How old are you?" Lily asked suddenly.

"Fifty-one," Celia replied, feeling a blush on her cheeks. She rarely admitted the truth that she had passed the mid-century milestone. She'd been forty-eight for two years and forty-nine for three. If she maintained her stop-start ageing strategy, in a few decades she'd be a positively haggard looking sixty-year-old, but that was a future problem.

"Wow, really?" Lily's eyes tracked over her body.

She felt the blush intensify. "How old did you think I was?"

"You look really good," Lily said in lieu of an answer. The kettle clicked, and she turned to focus on making drinks.

MAD WITH BOREDOM

Stop flirting with her, Lily told herself as she made two cups of tea. Then again, could telling someone who obviously did look good that they looked good be considered flirting? Maybe it was just a public service announcement? Or just being nice?

Lily didn't know. She was all over the place. Despite not feeling in the slightest bit tired, she was definitely exhausted. Emotionally and physically.

She felt Celia move closer and watched as Celia picked up Alan and examined him.

"I really hate this thing," Celia muttered.

"Alan," Lily reminded her.

"I really hate Alan," Celia corrected.

"Can't you just, you know, lose him?" Lily asked. She held out a cup of hot tea to Celia.

Celia put Alan down with a thud and took the cup. "Thank you. I don't know. I'm expected to have it in my office with my other awards."

"You have other awards?" Lily asked.

"Yes, the finance and insurance industry is so dull that they frequently have to reward people for the tiniest thing to keep us all engaged. Or we'd all quite simply go mad with the boredom."

"Do you actually like your job?"

Celia thought about that for a moment before shaking her head. "Not really. But it's a necessary evil. Like taxes. No one likes them, but we understand why they are there. I don't particularly like my industry, but I understand the need for it, and I'm good at it. It pays me well."

"That sounds dire." Lily picked up her tea and sipped at the hot liquid.

"We can't all be artistic," Celia said. "Some of us are just cogs in the boring machinery of the world. And less than one percent of us get to create and entertain the rest of us."

Lily knew that was technically true, but that didn't make it sound any less harsh. She went to speak but noticed that Celia was staring at the award, lost in her thoughts.

She looked so adrift and sad. Lily desperately wanted to pull her back from the dark thoughts that she knew were running through her head.

"Let's kill Alan," Lily suggested.

Celia slowly looked up at her. "Pardon?"

"Let's kill him. Get rid of him. It will be, I dunno, symbolic. Cathartic."

Celia barked a laugh. "And how do you propose we do that? And what on earth do I say to my work colleagues?"

"One thing a time," Lily said. "Look, it's nearly midnight in a foreign city. It won't be too busy out there, maybe just a few people milling about. But it's dark. It's, like, the perfect time to dispose of Alan."

Celia's eyes widened. "You're serious?"

"Yep. Think about it. You hate this award. It represents so much pain to you. Wouldn't it be good to just bury it? Or lose it on the subway?"

Celia looked at Alan and considered the proposition.

"Well, yes," she finally admitted. "However, it has my name on it. So if Alan does manage to get lost, he needs to be *really* lost."

Lily put down her cup and went to the window. She pressed the button and the curtains slowly slid open. Pressing up against the glass to see out into the darkness, she tried to remember the view.

"There's a river, isn't there?" Lily asked. "Do you think Alan can swim?"

Celia stood beside her and peered out the window.

"Almost certainly not," Celia replied. "But what do I tell my work colleagues?"

"Airline lost your luggage?" Lily suggested.

"My boss would request they send another."

"Tell them you want to keep it at home? They can't make you keep it in your office, can they?" Lily asked.

"Well, no." Celia seemed to be giving the matter thought, and Lily started to mentally prepare for heading out into the city for a clandestine mission.

"I've never done anything like this before," Celia confessed.

"What? Thrown an award that emotionally represents your son's death into a Japanese river under cover of darkness? *Psh.* This is like a normal Tuesday for me."

"Should we?" Celia asked. "I mean, should we really?"

"I can't answer that," Lily admitted. "This is down to how you feel. From what you said earlier, this award represents a lot of hurt for you. I don't think you're the kind of person who gets nervous going onstage or speaking in public, so your reaction is to this award and what it means to you. And I don't personally think that anyone should have to live their life with a constant reminder like that. If that is what the award means to you."

Celia was silent for a long time as she contemplated all that Lily had said. Lily thought she could hear the cogs turning in her mind.

"The contract and the award represent Andrew's death to me," Celia finally said. "And specifically, how I wasn't there for him. I don't want Alan staring at me all day every day. Let's kill him."

❖

At first Celia hadn't been sure about Lily's idea. It seemed strange behaviour to destroy an award one had just received. But the more she thought about it, the more she realised that it was the right decision.

The award meant nothing more to her than a reminder of a time when work dominated her life at the cost of her son's. If she could go back and change the past, she would. If quitting her job would have meant Andrew still lived, she would have done so in a heartbeat.

She was a workaholic but never at the cost of her family.

Work had just been something to occupy her time. There were always more projects to do, more boundaries to push, more phone calls to make. An international company was a company that never stopped.

Early mornings to speak with the Far East, late nights to speak with America—it was so easy to end up almost literally burning the candle at both ends. Office politics became all-consuming, wanting to beat the other team and take a victory every time you could. Celia had become obsessed.

When a shot at the contract of the decade came along, she wasn't about to let it go.

Now she wondered what had possessed her. She couldn't recognise herself when she thought back to the woman she had been during the nine-month-long negotiations.

Always one for details and statistics, she'd later trawled back through her phone records and emails to see how many times she had neglected to get back to Andrew when he contacted her.

Shame rested heavily.

She knew she was to blame. She wasn't going to blame a glass statue for the things she had or hadn't done.

But it was symbolic.

Her work had culminated in an enormous pat on the back from her company. Boiled down into Alan.

There was a direct line between her guilt and Alan.

And that meant Alan had to go.

"This way." Lily held her phone in front of her and frowned. She turned to the right and then to the left. "No...this way."

"Can you read a map?" Celia questioned.

Lily didn't respond. Instead she took off in the second direction she had indicated.

It wasn't cold out, but it wasn't pleasant either. Celia wished she'd had the forethought to get changed out of her black cocktail dress, but she'd been eager to get out. Thankfully she'd grabbed her coat and handbag. A handbag that she'd emptied completely to accommodate Alan.

She hoped she looked like an ordinary person out for a casual walk, but she doubted it. She was about to dump an award into a local river. Surely that was a crime? She doubted they'd end up in prison, but she had already donated to a Japanese environmental charity as a token pre-emptive gesture.

"It's another ten-minute walk," Lily said.

Celia frowned. "Are we going through the main train station?"

"Yep."

"Is that a good idea?"

Lily frowned. "Why wouldn't it be?"

"Because we're on our way to throw Alan into the river."

"And?"

"And we look suspicious."

Lily chuckled. "No. Well, you do, a little."

Celia gave her a playful smack on the arm with the back of her hand.

"We don't look suspicious. You're just being paranoid," Lily said.

"What if they find the award and then look at the CCTV from the station?" Celia asked.

"Do you have any idea how much crime takes place in a city? Do you really think they are going to be wondering how Alan got into the river? Do you think there's *CSI: Tokyo* going through all the CCTV in a main line station for a woman with a glass award in her bag?"

Celia rolled her eyes. "Okay, you can stop mocking me now."

"Boss, boss! The Golden Strangler's back in town. He's already killed eight people!" Lily acted. "Quiet down there, we're checking the ten *billion* people who have crossed through the station in the last six months to see which one of them might have dumped this statue."

"Are you quite finished?" Celia asked.

Lily continued to laugh. "Sorry."

"You can't say sorry while you're still laughing," Celia told her. "It really takes the edge off. Besides, I didn't know I was hanging out with some hardened criminal."

"That's me." Lily nodded enthusiastically. "I got a speeding ticket last year."

"Oh, my, what a rebel," Celia deadpanned. "Doing a hundred on the motorway?"

"No, I was doing thirty-five in a thirty."

Celia laughed. "Be sure to tell that story when you're sent to prison. It will definitely give the inmates pause for thought before they rough you up."

"I broke into a library once."

"I'm going to need context."

"I'd left my coat in there, so I climbed through an open window to get it." Lily gestured to her body. "It was this coat."

Celia looked at the coat and sneered. "You should have left it."

Lily smirked. "I can never tell when you're being actually mean or just sarcastic."

Celia didn't reply, just offered her a lopsided grin.

"It's a great coat," Lily added. "Big pockets."

They approached the station entrance, and Celia was surprised by the European style. If she'd been placed in front of it without knowing any better, she would have said the red-brick building with cream cornerstones was British. She was also surprised to see how busy it was despite it being late on a weekday. Lily focused on her phone and the map and guided them through the station expertly.

Celia silently followed and wondered just how Lily had gone from the random sandwich stabber a couple of days ago to someone she wholeheartedly trusted. She'd been in close quarters with other people before and had never felt so connected to them. Meanwhile, she and Lily playfully bantered as if they had known one another for years, asked probing questions, and supported each other.

It was surprising that in her five decades on the planet she had never before encountered someone quite like Lily. And more surprising that they had gone from strangers to what felt like best friends in a matter of hours.

She wondered what would happen in the future. Would the flight home be the last they saw of each other? Did Lily just connect well with everyone and have stacks of acquaintances in her wake?

Was Lily just one of those people who were blessed with being able to connect with others? And if so, why had she attempted to find love with someone thousands of miles away?

Soon they were out of the station and back onto the streets. It didn't take long before the crowds thinned out and they were walking through some relatively deserted areas.

Alan felt heavy in her bag.

She did want to get rid of him—she knew she did. But she also didn't know if that would be an end to her guilt. Her logical mind told her that most likely it wouldn't be.

When she was a child, her father had experienced a run of bad luck at work—from being accused of something he hadn't done, to being demoted, to being made redundant.

It was a terrible time for the family, and her father had quickly found himself at his wits' end. Around the same time that his bad luck had begun, he had found an old, broken record player in the street near the house. He'd had every intention of attempting to fix it up. But the stress of work became too much, and he started to consider that the inanimate object might be cursed. Squarely placing all the blame for his work-life problems at the door of the bashed-up old LP player, he decided to destroy it.

Celia could only remember her father heaving the machine into the garage, a hammer dangling from his hand. The sounds of wanton destruction followed for five minutes. Crashing, snapping, shattering, grunting. It went on for what seemed like forever. Afterwards there were a few silent moments before her father re-emerged. He didn't look like someone who had just engaged in a violent outburst. He looked lighter, brighter, relieved.

Her father had never, ever been a violent man. It was then, when she was in her early teens, that she had first seen him demonstrate any such behaviour. Celia had later on poked her head into the garage and seen that he had cleaned everything away. A black refuse sack in the corner was the only indication that anything had happened.

Logically, she knew that the record player wasn't cursed. And she was sure her father thought the same. But it didn't seem to matter because his mood changed after that evening. He got a new job, a better job. And the family fortunes went up and up from there.

Something had changed in her father that night. He had believed that his bad luck and heartache were somehow concentrated in the musical device and that destroying it had freed him. She just hoped that killing Alan would do the same for her.

"Here we are," Lily announced pointlessly, as they were now facing the river.

A pathway with a small single-bar metal fence ran along the side of the waterway, easy enough to get over or under, enough to stop someone accidentally walking into a watery mess but nothing more.

Next to the path was a road, but the midnight hour meant that it was empty of traffic.

"You still want to do this?" Lily confirmed.

"Yes," Celia said with certainty. She didn't know if Alan was her record player, but she'd made her mind up and was now eager to get rid of him.

"Great." Lily grabbed her hand and pulled her across the road. Seconds later they both looked over the flimsy bar and into the murky water.

Celia looked around and checked that they were alone before pulling Alan from her bag. She lifted him up, ready to throw him.

"Wait!" Lily cried.

She paused.

"Don't you want to say a few words first?"

Celia looked at her with incredulity. "Say a few words?"

"Yeah, this is symbolic."

"This is illegal. We don't have time for a speech and a dedication ceremony."

"Fine, have it your way," Lily said.

"Thank you. I will." She looked at the award one last time. "Goodbye, Alan. I didn't know you long, but I'll be so very glad to see the back of you."

She looked at Lily, and Lily grinned at her.

Celia rolled her eyes and then lobbed Alan over the fence and into the water.

Alan landed hard, causing a large splash. But rather than a satisfying bubbling as he sank, he just sat there, looking at them with defiance.

"What the…?" Lily mumbled.

Celia couldn't understand what she was seeing. Why had Alan not sunk?

Lily picked up a piece of broken paving slab and threw it into the water. It made a small splash and then sat there.

"There's no water," Celia realised.

"Or very little," Lily confirmed. "It must be a couple of centimetres at most."

They both stared at Alan, sticking up out of the shallow water and glinting in the streetlight.

"We have to get him out of there," Celia said.

"What? Why?"

"It has my *name* on it," Celia reminded her. "It's all well and good if he's going to be washed out to sea or processed by a sewage plant. But he's *there*. For anyone to see. With my name on it."

"That's true," Lily agreed.

"Well?" Celia pressed.

"Well, what?"

"Go on then." Celia gestured to the water.

Lily balked. "Why me?"

"Because I'm wearing a cocktail dress and heels," Celia said.

"I don't have a change of clothes," Lily reminded her.

"I'll take you shopping tomorrow," Celia said. She pointed to Alan. "Go on, before someone sees him."

Lily let out a sigh and looked up and down the street. She climbed over the bar and placed a tentative foot on the bank. She held on and lowered her foot. Her boot squelched into the mud.

Celia winced.

"If I die…" Lily said.

"I'll find someone else to get Alan, don't worry," Celia quipped.

"You have a terrible sense of humour," Lily said.

Lily let go of the bar and took a couple of steps further into the mud. Alan wasn't far from the bank, but right then it looked like miles. Car headlights flashed in the distance, and Celia did her best to look like she was casually hanging out by the water, hoping that whoever it was wouldn't stop.

The car went by, the dark windows meaning that Celia couldn't see if they'd been spotted or not.

"Hurry up," she whispered through gritted teeth.

Lily pulled Alan out of the mud and dashed back. She dumped him on the bank and heaved herself up.

"Done. Next time, let's check the water level first," Lily said.

"Next time?" Celia laughed. "Haven't you learnt a lesson?"

Lily picked Alan up from the ground. "Look, so our first murder attempt didn't go well. It doesn't mean we quit. There must be another way to kill Alan."

Celia looked Lily up and down. Her boots were covered in wet mud. She even had some on her face for some reason. This poor young woman who had been through emotional hell that day was still willing to do whatever she could to help Celia.

She wondered if it was to take her mind off what had happened with Asami. Or whatever his name was. Or was it something else? Was Lily just that kind?

"Let's get back to the hotel," Celia suggested. "We can come up with a new plan of action."

Regrouping at the Hotel

L ily was pretty sure the stench of the stagnant canal wasn't going to go away any time soon. She couldn't believe she had waded into the unknown waters with so little encouragement.

"I stink," she announced to Celia as they arrived back at the hotel.

"You do."

Lily just stared at her companion. "Thanks for making me feel better."

"Do you want me to lie?" Celia asked, pressing the call button for the elevator.

"Yes."

"You smell like a beautiful garden of roses," Celia said.

"Aw. Thanks." Lily sniffed the air and felt a little sick. "I'll need a shower when I get back to the room. Sorry."

The elevator arrived, and they stepped in, Celia swiping her door card and selecting their floor.

"Not a problem. Leave your clothes outside, and I'll have the hotel launder them."

"Can we do that?"

"It's the Shangri-La. They'd build you a fort out of chopsticks if you asked."

"Not if I'm naked. I'd worry about splinters," Lily said.

Celia rolled her eyes. "Shall I have your clothes cleaned or not?"

Lily felt her face flame. "Yes. Please."

Celia nodded and continued to stare directly ahead at the elevator panel. She'd been quiet since Alan had returned to them. Lily wasn't quite sure why, but she could guess.

The only contact Lily had ever had with suicide was when a boy at her school had taken his life. One morning they were called into an assembly and told by the head teacher that Peter Harding had hanged himself the previous evening.

Lily had felt grief beyond belief despite not even knowing the boy. He was two years younger than she was, and she only vaguely knew him because he'd been on the athletics team. But the loss had been real; the thought that a twelve-year-old had seen fit to end it all had left questions swirling in Lily's mind for months and years afterwards.

She couldn't imagine how she would feel if someone near to her had taken their life. The very idea that her own child, someone she gave life to—

She shook her head. It was too much to think of. Too much to bear. She didn't know how Celia could even manage to breathe. Not that she knew how Celia was supposed to grieve. Everyone had their own path, their own process to go through, but Lily had never considered herself a strong person.

The elevator doors opened, and they walked silently to the room, Lily refusing to look behind her to see the trail of mess she was leaving on the luscious carpets as she walked.

In the room, Celia handed Lily a laundry bag from the hook.

"Put your clothes in there, and leave it outside the bathroom door. I'll call reception to come and pick it up immediately. They have a sixty-minute service."

"Even at one in the morning?" Lily asked.

Celia gave her a look.

"Yep, Shangri-La. Got it." Lily put her phone on the desk, kicked off her shoes, and went into the bathroom. She quickly stripped down and placed her clothes in the bag and placed it outside the door before getting into the shower.

She was glad the Shangri-La didn't skimp on body wash or shampoo. She was also glad she remembered not to turn on the rainfall effect.

As she showered, she considered what a strange couple of days she'd had. It was times like these when she was glad that she didn't keep a diary. If she did, she'd need hours to document the last two days.

She scrubbed her hands until they were red, trying to remove any trace of the filthy water.

"Just a few more hours and you'll be home," she reminded herself.

❖

Celia handed over the bag of laundry to the steward, who faithfully promised it would be returned within an hour. She thanked him and walked back into the room with heavy feet.

She felt exhausted. Not ready to sleep, just drained. She kicked off her shoes and lay down on the bed. She picked up her phone and did what had become a habit for her over the past few months.

First, she listened to Andrew's old voice mails. She'd saved them on her phone just in case they accidentally got deleted one day. There were six in total, and after Andrew's death, she'd never been so grateful for being one of those people who never cleared her messages.

After she had listened to them, she scrolled through the albums of photos and videos that either she had taken or that Andrew had sent her. He wasn't one for being in front of the camera, but he did enjoy shooting videos, and often his voice could be heard in the background.

"Celia?"

She looked up, blinking the tears away. She didn't know how long she'd been caught up in media on her phone, but Lily stood at the end of her bed looking at her with concern.

"Should I leave you alone for a while?" Lily gestured towards the bathroom.

"No. No, that won't be necessary." Celia sat up. "I was just watching some old movies of Andrew."

Lily pulled the belt on her robe tight and sat on the edge of Celia's bed. Her hair was still slightly damp from the shower.

"May I see?" Lily asked hesitantly.

"Oh. You don't need to do that," Celia told her. "But thank you."

"No, really. I feel like I'd like to know him a little better."

Celia hesitated a moment before nodding. She manoeuvred herself so she was sitting next to Lily. Her mind raced to find the best video and the best pictures, eager to curate the best of Andrew into as short a time as possible.

However, as she showed Lily her prized possessions, she realised that wasn't necessary as Lily was eager to see more.

They laughed at the video of Andrew being beaten at tennis by his then-girlfriend, and Lily laughed at the video of Celia attempting to walk on the icy path from the drive to the house.

Lily asked questions, but nothing felt too probing or personal. They were just two people having a chat about things on Celia's phone as if they were simply holiday photos.

When there was a knock on the door, they jumped and stared at each other in shock until Celia remembered the clothes.

Lily went to retrieve the freshly laundered clothes, and Celia wondered where the hour had gone.

"Okay, this is awesome," Lily announced when she returned. She held up all of her clothes on individual hangers, all in a protective cellophane bag. "I want to live here. My clothes have never been so clean, not even when I bought them."

She passed some hangers from one hand to the other to get a closer look at her astoundingly clean clothes.

Celia snorted a laugh.

Lily followed her gaze and then blushed. "Well," Lily said. "That's…embarrassing."

A pair of lacy red knickers hung on a wooden hanger, perfectly pressed.

"Very festive," Celia commented. And very sexy, she thought before again reprimanding herself.

Lily gave her a look. "Shut up." She turned the hangers around so Celia couldn't make any further comments on her underwear.

"I think I might try for some sleep," Celia said. "I don't feel at all tired, but maybe it will come. And if I don't try now, I'll probably fall asleep during check-in at the airport in twelve hours."

"And then you'll miss your flight and have to stay another day," Lily said, hanging her clothes in the wardrobe.

"Don't even jest," Celia pleaded. "I'm desperate to get home. With or without Alan at this rate."

Celia had given the matter some thought and decided to not try a second murder attempt while in Japan. Instead, she'd go home and show Alan to her work colleagues before taking him home and finding some appropriate, legal way to dispose of him there.

At least she knew the depth of her local canal.

"Agreed." Lily closed the wardrobe doors. "Maybe we'll kill him in the morning."

"Maybe. We'll see how the day goes," Celia agreed, not wanting to get into the conversation right then. "Would you mind if we had the television on? If it's suitably boring it might help us sleep."

"Sure, although what I saw earlier wasn't going to help anyone get off to sleep," Lily replied.

"Ah. Well, maybe the news channel? Doesn't everywhere show

BBC Worldwide these days?" Celia stood up. "I'll just use the bathroom and get ready for bed."

She was glad she'd thought to bring pyjamas as she often slept in the nude. Although her reason for bringing them had been in case of an unexpected fire drill in the middle of the night rather than a stranger sharing her room.

It had been an odd couple of days.

In less than fifteen minutes she'd changed, scrubbed off her make-up, and was back on her bed watching the news. "What did I miss?"

"There's a war," Lily said.

"A new one?"

"I don't think so."

"Ah."

"Yeah."

They lay on their respective beds watching the screen flicker and flash before them. From puff pieces to serious, hard-hitting journalism, it all merged into white noise, and before long Celia fell asleep.

GOING HOME

A ny luggage to check in?"
Lily nearly laughed in the face of the poor check-in clerk.
"Nah," she replied.

An eyebrow was raised but nothing was said, and soon Lily was handed back her passport with a flimsy boarding pass inside it. She'd always wondered why they insisted on printing something as important as a boarding pass on something as thin as tracing paper.

Regardless of the quality, she and the precious item walked away from the desk.

Celia was waiting for her by the entrance to the security channel, having checked in at the first-class desk and been seen and processed in a tenth of the time it had taken Lily.

"Thanks for waiting."

"All well?" Celia asked.

"Yep. Except for, you know, my life." Lily sighed.

"Yes, well, nothing to be done about the sorry state of that," Celia said with a grin.

Lily rolled her eyes. "Let's get through security, shall we?"

"I'm a preferred traveller," Celia said.

"What does that mean?"

"It means I don't get processed with the riff-raff—I get my own security channel. I'm sure they play soothing music, and I doubt I'll be patted down. Not like the hell you're no doubt about the endure."

"You're enjoying this, aren't you?" Lily asked.

"Immensely. See you on the other side." Celia turned and walked towards a discreet doorway guarded by a severe-looking guard. A wave of her boarding pass and she disappeared from sight.

"How the other half lives," Lily mumbled.

She joined the queue in the main security hall, wondering why she needed to bother, considering she only had a handful of items in her pockets and no bag to check.

There was no one to ask, and so she waited, shuffling forward every now and then to fill the gap in front of her.

She'd woken that morning to the sound of someone attempting to be quiet. It was a very unique sound—soft footsteps, a whispered curse when something fell over. She'd kept her eyes closed for a few minutes longer as she'd put the pieces together.

Asami was a fake. Her life was in tatters. She'd been robbed. She'd failed to kill Alan. Oh, and she was flying home in a few hours.

The itching curiosity about the time was what eventually had her opening her eyes. From there she'd quickly gotten dressed, had breakfast with Celia, and then scrolled on her phone until it was time to leave for the airport.

It had been strangely pleasant. Not at all what she had expected sharing a hotel room with an almost-stranger to feel like. Not that Celia was much of a stranger any more.

Celia had said she'd stay with her until they boarded, and they'd meet up again when they arrived in London so they could say goodbye. Lily had been pleased when Celia suggested the plan, as it was something she had hoped would happen. She wanted to be able to say a proper goodbye and thank you to Celia. It was no exaggeration to say that she'd saved her life.

Lily finally passed through security and entered the departures terminal. She immediately spotted Celia sitting on a bench, reading a paperback. Lily took a moment to appreciate the view. Celia was the stuff dreams were made of—gorgeous, intelligent, generous, and very funny. If you enjoyed sarcastic barbs, which Lily did.

Lily approached. "I was patted down."

"Of course you were." Celia slid a bookmark into the pages and snapped the book shut. "You look incredibly suspicious. Who travels with no hand luggage?"

"People who've been mugged?" Lily huffed.

"Suspicious," Celia said. "And I have the solution."

She reached down to where her handbag sat by the side of the bench and lifted up a paper shopping bag.

Lily frowned. "What's that?"

"A present."

"Why are you buying me a present?"

"Do you always become argumentative when receiving gifts?" Celia asked.

Lily peered into the large bag and smiled. "A rucksack?"

"Yes. You can fill it with sweets and chocolate for the flight."

Lily took the rucksack out of the bag. It was a good brand and clearly expensive. "You shouldn't have, but thank you."

"Come on, let's get some lunch. Dinner. Whatever one eats at this time." Celia stood up and grabbed her handbag. "Then we can swing by a store and fill your rucksack with E numbers and sugar."

"Do you seriously not take a single snack with you when you travel?" Lily queried.

"I sometimes pick up a water bottle."

"That's liquid nothing. What about food?"

Celia shrugged.

Lily shook her head. The woman was a mystery in many ways.

They walked deeper into the terminal, hunting for a place to eat a final meal together before their flight was called.

❖

"So, do you think this plane will have a serious technical fault?" Celia asked casually.

They were sitting on a bench near the departure gate in a very quiet part of the terminal. Somehow, they had managed to breeze through the entire process and were now an hour early for their flight, with little else to do but sit and wait. Lily didn't mind, considering her company.

"Nah. It will be a delay." Lily opened a bag of unidentifiable gummy sweets and popped one in her mouth. "Like, not a long delay, but long enough to be really annoying. Want one?"

Celia ruffled her nose and shook her head. "Do you even know what they are?"

Lily chewed a little. "Sugar."

"Enlightening."

"I blocked Asami's number," Lily admitted, "and archived all their messages. Emails. Everything. Out of sight but recoverable if the police want it all."

"Good for you." Celia smiled, and Lily felt a little proud that she'd done the right thing. "I am sorry. I don't know if I said that before."

Lily closed the sweets bag, took a swig of water, and put both in her rucksack before flopping back in her seat. She wondered why all airport seats were uncomfortable, either bolt upright or at such a strange angle that the sitter was at ninety degrees. This one was almost like lying down.

"Thanks."

"Seriously. It was a terrible thing to do to someone. I hope the police manage to catch him."

"I just hope he isn't conning any other women," Lily said.

"You said you spoke all the time. I'm sure he didn't have the capacity to talk to anyone else at the same time," Celia reassured her. She leaned back in her chair. "Why are these blasted seats always so uncomfortable?"

"They don't want people sleeping on them and making the place look untidy," Lily said.

"And yet they are perfectly satisfied with us both lying here like a couple of drunks?"

"It's an aesthetic choice."

"You're very silly."

"Thank you." Lily beamed. Then she yawned. "I'm also very tired. What time is it?"

"Here or back home?"

"Back home."

"About seven in the morning," Celia said without skipping a beat.

"How do you just *know* that?"

"I don't know. I've always been good with remembering facts and figures. And good at maths. I suppose that's why."

"Do you really think I was the only one?" Lily asked, caught up in the previous subject again.

Celia turned and looked at her. They were now face to face, and Lily could tell that Celia was feeling tired as well. Small lines formed around Celia's mouth when she was tired, and her eyes dulled. Not much, but enough that Lily noticed. She'd like to think it was her artistic side that noticed these things, but as it had only happened since she met Celia, she supposed not. From one crush to another. She mentally rolled her eyes at herself. Typical.

"I think so. This kind of person may cast a wide net at first, but then they find their mark and focus their energies on that one."

"I feel so stupid," Lily said softly. "I was in love."

"I know."

"I bet you think I'm a right idiot."

"No. I think you're a big-hearted, caring young woman whom

someone took advantage of. You believe the best in people, and that's a quality that is becoming more and more rare, which is why you must keep hold of it. You're a very special person, Lily. Don't forget that."

Lily didn't know what to say. Celia had her serious moments and her joking moments, but Lily hadn't heard her say something so heartfelt—certainly not something directed at her.

The silence between them grew, and Lily didn't know who moved first as they slowly drifted closer and closer. The kiss was gentle, full of meaning, and completely unexpected. It was over as soon as it had started, both of them pulling back, sitting up, and looking away.

Lily couldn't fathom what had happened. Or who had initiated it. Or what would happen next. She didn't want to say anything that might make a suddenly awkward situation even worse.

"We better locate our gate," Celia said.

Okay, we're not going to mention it, Lily thought. "Good idea," she said. Lily struggled out of her chair and pulled on her rucksack. By the time she was ready, Celia was already walking away.

She hurried to catch up to her, not certain if Celia wanted her to do that or not. She was exhausted and emotional. Had she made a move on Celia without realising it? And if she had, why did Celia allow it?

Celia stopped suddenly, and Lily nearly collided with her.

"I'm going to the bathroom—those toilets on the plane are always questionable," Celia announced.

Lily suspected the first-class lavatories on board the plane were clean enough to eat off the floor but didn't say anything. Celia obviously wanted to escape the awkward situation.

She couldn't blame her.

"Okay."

"Don't wait for me," Celia instructed her, already marching in another direction. "I'll…I'll see you in London."

"Will I?" Lily asked, an edge to her tone. If this was goodbye, she wanted to know.

Celia paused in the middle of the busy terminal and turned to look at her. "Yes, you will."

Lily nodded. Celia returned the nod and then disappeared into the crowd.

Back to the Circus

Celia boarded the flight as late as she could. She was one of the last-minute stragglers everyone hated and liked to stare at.

It wasn't a deliberate choice; in fact it irked her. She'd paid for first class, which meant she should be one of the first people on board, people with special needs aside.

But because she needed to avoid Lily, she'd hung out around the bathrooms and then around the coffee shop until the last passengers were finally boarding.

She was glad that she knew Lily was at the rear of the plane. Apparently, the only seat remaining was a middle seat along the back wall by the toilets. Lily had kept a brave face about it, but it was obviously going to be a terrible journey for her.

Celia had itched to pay to upgrade her so they could sit together for the journey home. Some company would be nice, and she knew she could have suggested it under the guise of wanting to keep an eye on her. But she knew Lily wouldn't accept it or would demand to reimburse her, something she was sure a children's illustrator couldn't do.

Now, however, she was extremely grateful that she hadn't acted on her initial impulse. Now she was very glad to be sitting alone in first class.

She stepped into the cabin and stopped dead in her tracks.

"No," she whispered in horror.

"Welcome aboard, Miss Scott," the steward said, offering to take her coat.

Celia didn't acknowledge him. She was too busy staring at a first-class cabin full of clowns.

❖

Lily never thought she'd find herself hoping for engine failure, but being wedged between two businessmen, neither of whom grasped the concept of personal space, had her considering that an emergency landing would be nice. Or even a crash landing, for that matter.

She'd named the man to her left Window Farter. He sat next to the window and couldn't stop attempting to thwart the airplane's air circulation system with his own gas.

To her right she had Aisle Spreader. He clearly had a medical condition that meant that his knees had to be at least a metre apart at all times. It was almost as if two magnets kept his legs spread, the force too powerful for him to overcome.

He either was completely unaware that his knee frequently rested against hers, or he simply didn't care.

She looked at her watch. They'd been in the air less than two hours.

She thudded her head back against the headrest. It was going to be a horrendously long flight. Sleeping on an airport bench for a week suddenly seemed preferable.

Above everything else she wanted to see Celia, wanted to talk to her about the kiss. The kiss that was almost enough to allow her to forget about Window Farter and Aisle Spreader.

Almost.

Celia was attractive and just her type, but Lily didn't think that she'd ever just absentmindedly kiss her. If that was what had happened. She couldn't imagine Celia kissing her. The very thought seemed preposterous.

Someone had to have made the first move. It was just that Lily had no idea who had. Which was why she wanted to speak with Celia: to get to the bottom of what had happened and to figure out if there was the slightest possibility of it happening again.

But that seemed impossible at the moment. She was two classes, nine hours, and a hundred rows away from the woman who had the answers.

Cranking up the volume on the movie she wasn't even watching, she closed her eyes and wished for sleep to come.

MISTAKE

Celia stood by the luggage carousel worrying her hands. She hadn't planned this very well at all. They'd agreed to meet in Heathrow, but they hadn't agreed on *where*.

She'd been hurried off the plane shortly after landing, and the air bridge was no place to wait for Lily. Then she went straight to passport control, where it was illegal to loiter.

Thankfully, she knew she was ahead of Lily.

There was no way Lily could have possibly got from the back of the plane to the door before Celia. And she certainly hadn't passed her along the way.

At the luggage carousel, her suitcase was one of the first out, and she picked it up. Now she needed to wait for Lily.

She'd spent most of the flight delivering evil glances to the circus troupe, who insisted on performing in the small amount of space and talking loudly with one another.

But when she wasn't delivering silent judgement, she was thinking about Lily.

Specifically, about the kiss.

The kiss that she hadn't expected. The kiss that she didn't know if she was responsible for or not. She'd played the sequence of events over and over and was no closer to an answer.

But there was one thing she did know—whatever had happened, she couldn't let Lily think that she'd experienced some kind of gay panic or been disgusted by the kiss. Lily had already experienced heartbreak in Tokyo and homophobia from her grandmother. She didn't need extra pain from Celia.

She couldn't talk about what had happened because quite frankly she didn't really *know* what had happened. But she could pretend it hadn't happened at all.

It wasn't the best solution, but chatting to Lily as if nothing had happened would hopefully prove to her that Celia wasn't repulsed by the kiss.

Cowardly, but a good middle ground considering the circumstances.

She watched an acrobat perform a handstand and point to a piece of luggage with her toes. A huge man picked up the heavy-looking case with just one finger and placed it on a trolley that was being driven by a man in a full clown outfit—red nose, curly wig, and ridiculous shoes.

The sooner she was away from the airport, the better.

She stared at the cases slowly going around the carousel. A great many bags had been added and removed since she'd been waiting. People had come and gone, some waiting with exasperation for a few minutes before shouldering their way to the belt to pick up their bags. Some arrived just at the moment that their case was approaching and smiled at their good fortune.

It was a strange travel lottery.

Some were winners and some were losers; it didn't matter who you were or how much you paid for your ticket. You were now in the equalising room, a room where your case would arrive when it felt like it and might be in pristine condition or might have the handle missing and a footprint embedded in it.

Something itched at the back of Celia's mind, something that the exhaustion wasn't allowing her to process.

A clown passed her, glaring. She glared back. She'd not made any friends during her journey home.

She smothered a yawn. There was a chance that she might have been able to sleep if the commotion in the cabin hadn't been so loud. It seemed that the troupe were excited about a gig they had performed and wanted to talk about it endlessly, even going so far as to perform certain pieces of their act in the middle of the floor.

If she was completely honest with herself, her own rage had probably kept her awake more than the noise they created.

Something nudged at her brain. She frowned, wondering what was causing the strange feeling. There was something just on the tip of her awareness but not quite fully formed yet. Something knocking at her flagging consciousness. Something important.

Her eyes flew open in realisation. She grabbed the handle of her case and hurried towards the exit.

Lily didn't have any luggage to wait for. She'd completely forgotten that critical detail.

Why would Lily be waiting at the luggage carousel? She would have bypassed the room completely and gone straight into the arrivals hall.

Celia raced through the customs channel, silencing the customs officer with a stare. She'd never been stopped for a search at customs, and she certainly wasn't going to be stopped now.

She entered the arrivals terminal with absolutely no idea what she was looking for. Was Lily going to take the train, the Tube, a taxi? Was a friend picking her up?

"Damn," she muttered, wishing she'd taken the effort to finalise these details before they'd separated in Tokyo.

She walked a few metres in one direction before stopping, turning around, and walking in the opposite direction.

For the second time in a few minutes she was hit by a smack of realisation. She sighed at her exhausted confusion and fished her mobile phone out of her handbag.

She found Lily's number and called her. She might have not thought ahead to arrange a place to meet up, but she had bought Lily a spare phone charger to ensure she could keep her phone battery topped up while on the flight. She just hoped she had done so.

"Hello?"

"Hi, where are you?" Celia tried to keep the panic out of her voice.

"I'm with a friend. About to go home. I thought you'd gone."

"No. I'm in the arrivals hall. I was waiting for you by the baggage carousel. I'd forgotten you didn't have any."

"Are you sure? You're not just trying to get another dig in about me not having any luggage?" Lily sounded like she was smiling, and Celia chuckled in relief.

"I did have a devastating quip prepared," she lied.

"I bet you did. I'm sorry, I thought you'd…forgotten and headed home," Lily explained. "My friend is parked in the car park, and we're there now. I don't want to keep him waiting."

Celia could easily detect authenticity in her tone. They'd not arranged things, and they had simply passed each other by. It was a mistake, nothing malicious.

"It's okay. Maybe we can meet up sometime this week?" Celia suggested. "I'd like to know you're okay. We can kill Alan together."

A woman who passed at that moment stared at Celia. Celia smirked back.

"I'd like that," Lily said. "I'll text you."

"Do. Take care."

"You too. And Celia?"

"Yes?"

"Thank you. For everything."

"You're welcome. Speak soon." Celia hung up the call before realising that she should have offered her own thanks to Lily.

She hadn't comprehended that she needed a friend to talk to, someone to admit her shame about Andrew, someone to reminisce with, someone to tell her about her drinking.

Lily had helped in ways she probably was not aware of.

Celia felt a little shiver run along her spine at the knowledge that she was about to return to her normal life, a life that was missing some of the light she used to feel. Things were darker in her days lately, the strain of heartbreak weighing heavily on her at times.

She had a lot of work to do to change that.

CASSIE

L ily sat at her desk in her home studio. She had a job to complete, but she just couldn't focus on it. She tapped her pencil against her lip and looked at the sheet of drawing paper. She'd rough-sketched the characters, but by this point in the early afternoon she would have expected to have finished colouring.

She'd been home a week and hadn't seen or spoken to a single soul. If people knew she was home, they'd ask why she wasn't still in Japan, and that would lead to a whole world of embarrassment.

Some knew she was meeting Asami because she'd fallen head over heels for her. Some thought she was simply a friend but probably suspected more. And a few, mainly family, thought she was visiting art galleries.

Lily didn't relish the idea of telling any of them what had happened. Instead, she'd spent the week locked in her house, having groceries delivered to the door in case someone saw her in Tesco.

At first she'd thought she'd work on her portfolio and a few pieces that she had queued up for when she got back from her holiday. In the end she had eaten junk food and watched television for days at a time. She went to bed late and woke up late, and her mind swam with thoughts of how she was equal parts stupid and lucky.

She had no idea what might have happened to her if she hadn't met Celia. Would she have gone to the British embassy? Would they have even been able to help her?

The doorbell rang and Lily jumped. She resisted the urge to hide under her desk, barely.

"Just ignore it," she told herself softly. "You're not here."

"I know you're in there!" a familiar voice yelled through the letterbox.

Lily jumped off her stool, her gaze darting around her office in shock. Cassie was at her front door.

"Come on, don't leave me out here. I know you're in there," Cassie shouted again.

Lily racked her brain to try to figure out how on earth her friend could possibly know she was in the flat. She couldn't figure it out, especially with the continuous doorbell buzzing.

She had no other option—she had to open the door. Cassie was one of the most tenacious people she knew, and there was no chance she'd just give up.

Lily took a deep breath and walked through the hallway and opened the front door.

Cassie walked in the second the door was wide enough.

"Okay, I don't know what happened, but clearly you are home and have been for a while. I let you have a few days to sulk, but it's been six and I haven't heard from you, so here I am."

Cassie was already in the kitchen, so Lily closed the front door and followed her.

"How did you know I'm home?" Lily asked.

"Netflix."

"What?" Lily entered the kitchen where Cassie was taking ice cream out of a paper bag she'd brought in with her.

"Mint or fudge?"

"Fudge, obviously. How did Netflix tell you I'm home?"

"Honestly, your lack of technical ability worries me. We share an account, remember? So if you log on to the account in a new place, I get a little email going, *Hey, this person might be fraudulently accessing your account*, and I think, *Nah, it's Lily*."

Cassie got two bowls out of the cupboard and started scooping ice cream into them.

"So I saw you logged on in Tokyo, and then nothing for a while, and then a login at home," Cassie continued, "and I thought, *It can't be my best friend because she'd definitely tell me that she was home*. But I didn't want to block your access in case you had come home. So I checked and could see someone was watching a stream of every single tear-jerking movie Netflix has. And some documentary on pandas. And I know pandas make you cry."

"They're just so *cute*," Lily admitted, feeling herself welling up.

"So I gave you a few days to get over the ugly-crying portion of whatever happened, and now here I am."

Cassie stabbed a spoon into the mound of ice cream and handed the bowl to Lily.

Lily looked down at the bowl and sighed.

It was time to tell the whole story.

❖

By the time Lily had finished her epic tale of the events from last week, her ice cream had melted into a pool of mush. Not that she cared as she carefully spooned the strange mixture into her mouth.

They sat facing each other on the sofa in Lily's living room, a small pile of decorative cushions between them.

Cassie's face maintained the shocked and confused expression she'd adopted the moment Lily had started her story. Cassie had remained relatively silent apart from the odd gasp or muttered curse word.

Lily knew that wasn't likely to last. Cassie was never short of a word to say on any subject.

"Okay, I'm going to need a while to process this," Cassie said.

Lily snorted. "How do you think I feel?"

"What did he want with you?" Cassie asked.

"I don't know." Lily shivered at the thought. It had been a feature of her nightmares for a few days now. "Murder me? Imprison me? Ask for a ransom? I mean, fat chance on that last one with my family, but he didn't know that."

"Thank God you reported it," Cassie mused. "Wouldn't want anyone else having to go through that. I hope they catch him."

"Look, Cass, I…I really don't want to talk about it," Lily admitted. "It's really shaken me up. There were times I didn't think I'd ever get home. And now that I am home, I don't want to leave."

Cassie regarded her with a raised eyebrow. "You're not going to turn into a hermit, are you?"

"Yes." Lily gestured to the walls of her apartment with her spoon. "Meet my shell."

"Nope." Cassie shook her head. "Not happening. Because then he won."

Lily shrugged. "Don't care."

"Yeah, you do."

Lily didn't say anything. She hated how well Cassie saw through her sometimes. They'd been friends since art school, or rather Cassie had swept Lily into her friendship circle then. Lily had been perfectly satisfied to be the quiet student who didn't talk to many people.

Cassie wouldn't have that. She planted herself next to Lily on day one and introduced herself. Within a week they were chatting like old friends, going out to local bars, and having late summer picnics in the park.

Cassie was the first person Lily had come out to about her sexuality. It was an eye-opening experience, as Cassie immediately claimed that she already knew—something about Lily's walk.

Lily had expected a fallout from her announcement, but instead her walk was insulted. Aside from that, nothing changed in their relationship except that Cassie started to point out hot girls that Lily might be interested in.

Her friendship with Cassie heralded the first time in her life that Lily had started to feel comfortable in her own skin, realising that she had someone who would support her no matter what.

"So what disastrous rebound relationship are you going to have now?" Cassie smirked.

Lily rolled her eyes but couldn't help but smile.

"We had Lucy and then Angela and then Asami, all of whom you met within a day of breaking up with the one before." Cassie counted on her fingers. "Damn, you've broken the cycle."

"I kissed Celia," Lily admitted in a small voice.

"What?" Cassie nearly exploded.

"Well, I think I did. She might have kissed me. I don't really know who kissed who, to be honest."

Cassie windmilled her arms in front of her. "Wait, wait, wait. Why am I only now hearing about this?"

"Because it was a mistake, an embarrassing mistake. Celia literally ran away," Lily explained. Lily put her melted ice cream down on the coffee table, suddenly losing her appetite. She'd meant to call or text Celia, but she hadn't had the courage to do it. And every day that passed made it harder to do. Now she was reeling from the idea that she would never see or hear from Celia again. And it was all her fault.

"But she called you after? Like, when you were in Heathrow?" Cassie asked.

"Yeah," Lily whispered.

Cassie slowly nodded her head in understanding. "And you've not heard from her since?"

Lily shook her head.

"And you've not contacted her?"

Lily shook her head again.

"Why?" Cassie asked the question as if it were the simplest in the world.

Lily swallowed, grabbed a cushion, and held it to her chest. "And say what?" she asked. "I mean, this woman saw my life fall apart. And she knew Asami was a fraud from the second I mentioned her. Him. Whatever. So she naturally thinks I'm an idiot. She saw me not able to stand up to my own grandmother, so she thinks I'm weak. She then had to rescue me in Tokyo, so she thinks I'm pathetic."

"And yet she kissed you," Cassie added.

"Or I kissed her."

"Or you kissed each other?"

"Well, whatever, I've hardly shown a very good side of myself. I'm sure she was just being polite when she asked me to call. Or, like, she feels maternal towards me and wanted to make sure I didn't get myself into even more shit the second her back was turned."

"Sounds to me like you're projecting an awful lot onto this woman. Maybe she genuinely likes you and cares about you. Whatever, she deserves a call. If only to thank her for saving your butt."

Lily groaned.

She knew Cassie was right. Of course, she had thanked Celia multiple times, but another wouldn't go amiss. Perhaps one with a gift, considering the expenses Celia had happily paid for while Lily was with her.

"Is she hot?" Cassie asked, seemingly cutting right through the haze to what Lily was thinking.

Lily slowly nodded.

"And, I'm guessing, older?"

Lily nodded again.

Cassie sighed. "Well, I'm not going to remind you how things ended with Angela."

Lily wished that was true, but she knew Cassie was about to launch into exactly that.

"I know you have a thing for older women—I can't say anything because if certain actors in their sixties knocked on my door, then I'd be very happy. But the whole business with Angela really did a number on you, babe."

"I know," Lily reassured her. "It's not like I'm actually planning to date Celia. For one, she's straight."

"A straight woman who occasionally kisses women in airports."

"She was tired," Lily reiterated. That's what she'd been telling herself. She was tired, Celia was tired, the entire Tokyo was tired, and somehow there was a kiss. It meant nothing. Except it also could potentially mean a lot.

"You know, I've been tired, and I've never just—whoops!—kissed someone. Never. And I've been pretty drunk."

Lily finished squeezing the cushion and put it back on the sofa. "I just don't want to do anything that might hurt her, you know? She was going through a really rough time."

Cassie raised an eyebrow, inviting Lily to continue.

Lily ran a hand through her hair. She hadn't wanted to talk about the award and Andrew. But now that she was trying to explain to Cassie how she was feeling, it seemed relevant to help her to understand.

"There's something else…" Lily started.

MORALE BOOST

Howard knocked on the frame of Celia's open office door.
"Knock knock," he said.

Celia wanted to ask why he insisted on performing the action and saying the words. It was infuriating. One or the other was perfectly adequate.

Instead she smiled. "What can I do for you, Howard?"

"I wanted to get a photo of you and…" Howard turned to face the display cabinet and frowned. "Where is it?"

"At home." Celia picked up her pen and continued reading the contract she had been engrossed in before Howard interrupted.

"Why?"

"Because I want to keep it at home," Celia replied. "It suits my home office rather nicely."

She'd brought Alan into the office upon her return and kept him in the display cabinet for a few days so people could come by, congratulate her, and comment on how fine it looked.

Then she took him home and stuck him in a cupboard; out of sight, out of mind.

"I wanted a photo of you and the award for the next newsletter," Howard explained.

"No, thank you," Celia said politely.

Howard took a seat on the sofa, uninvited. "Oh, come on. It will be a great morale boost for the team."

"Morale boost?" She lowered her pen and gazed at him. "Tell me, Howard, are we at war?"

He chuckled. "You know what I mean."

"No, I don't think I do. There's scarcely a person in the building who hasn't been by here to offer their congratulations, look at the award, or even lift the award to check its weight. It's become a baby. I'm surprised I'm not drowning in romper suits for the damn thing. Everyone knows about the award—adding it to the newsletter would just be redundant at this point."

Howard maintained his gaze for a few seconds before slapping his knees and standing up.

"Well, bring it in when you have a chance, and we'll photograph it in the boardroom. No need for you to be there if you don't want to. One day next week would be best—no later than Wednesday, as that's when we go to print."

He smiled and left. She'd just been handed an order, and the injustice of it burned.

She tossed the pen down on her paperwork and shook her head. No matter how many rungs she progressed up the ladder, someone was always a few steps higher shouting down orders.

Quite often, they were pointless orders.

Celia was a worker.

She focused her mind on a task, ensuring that it was a worthy goal, and then she achieved it. But throughout her career she had encountered people who were disruptors. Disruptors often meant well, but they became stuck on pointless objectives and thus disrupted the workers.

Howard was a disrupter. Pointless photographs, interviews, and radio news slots occupied his vacuous mind.

He was too high up the food chain to worry about work these days. And so, he busied his time with things he thought to be absolutely essential but which were just disruptive to the actual workers.

It incensed Celia that she was sometimes forced to cater to his whims. Most of the time, she could ignore him and get on with whatever project she was working on. He frequently ignored her, as he knew she was bringing in the big bucks for the firm. But in between large projects, he nagged at her to do things that he viewed as important and that she viewed as pathetic.

Putting Alan in the company newsletter was just one in a long line of time-wasting initiatives.

She wondered if she would turn into a Howard if she climbed the greasy pole any further. Would she end up scratching around for things to do, ultimately useless to the organisation? Badgering busy people to pose for pointless photographs?

The thought itched at her.

He phone rang, and she snatched it up without looking.

"Celia Scott," she greeted the caller formally.

"Um. Hi, it's Lily. From the plane. Tokyo. No bag."

Celia smiled. "Yes, I vaguely recall you. It's been a week, not a decade. I'm not *that* old. How are you?"

"Pretty shit, you?"

"The same," Celia agreed. "Would you like to meet up for a drink? We can debate who is having the worse time of it. I warn you—I'm probably going to win."

"I just got busted by my best friend," Lily said. "I was pretending to still be in Japan, and she knew I was home because of my Netflix account."

Celia laughed. "Well, you're twenty-five, dear. You really need to get your own Netflix account. And stop fibbing to your best friend. I thought you didn't have any friends?"

"Well, I kinda do, but I'm not that close to them. Like, I didn't tell her I was home from Japan."

"Ah, I see. Friends you don't wish to confide in." Celia knew the feeling all too well.

"Yeah. I guess. What's making your week so bad?"

"I can't say—he just left my office," Celia replied.

"Oh, sorry, I don't mean to bother you at work. Should I call you another time? Or…not call you at all?"

Celia was struck by the reminder of how adorable Lily could be, especially when she was apologetic and indecisive. She wanted to scoop her up, make her stand tall and be more confident. Or simply tell her to never, ever change. She couldn't quite decide which.

"You're not bothering me," she reassured her. "How about that drink?"

"Sounds good to me. When? Oh, and I'm buying, as a thank you for everything."

"Okay, but remember I work in insurance and drink like a fish," Celia teased.

In reality she hadn't drunk a drop of alcohol since Lily pointed out what a problem it had become.

She'd desired to do so a couple of times but had realised what a very bad sign that was. Within twenty-four hours of being home, she had donated all her bottles of everything to her ex-husband, who had been confused but delighted.

"I've been saving up," Lily said. "I sold a kidney. I could have gotten more for a liver, but I guessed you might need that."

"Aw, you'd give me your liver?"

"Well, a bit of it. It grows."

"I see. Well, I can see the direction this conversation is heading. Shall we arrange a location and a time? I'm actually free this evening if you are."

"I'm sure I can move some things," Lily said in a tone that made Celia think there was nothing at all to move.

She hadn't realised how much she had missed Lily until they started speaking again. As the hours turned into days, she had assumed that the short friendship they'd shared was over.

She wasn't about to be the person to make contact if Lily had decided to end things. The ball had been left in Lily's court, and she'd decided to ignore it.

Until now.

And Celia couldn't be more pleased.

❖

Lily held on to the handrail of the enormous escalator and looked up at the sky, which was slowly coming into view at the top of the long shaft.

The journey to Canary Wharf had taken forty minutes via the London Underground, and she was glad to be able to see daylight again. Even if that light was at the top of a ridiculously long and scary escalator.

She looked to her left and her right, and watched as suited automata paraded up and down the other escalators. Some were obviously going home for the day, and some seemed to be returning to their offices.

She felt like a glitch in the matrix: underdressed, going against the grain, and entering the lion's den. But Celia had reassured her that there were some excellent bars and restaurants to be had, and she worked there so it was convenient.

The butterflies in Lily's stomach must have been wearing protective armour, given the force with which they bounced around. Her breathing was a little erratic too, and she tried to tell herself that it was from being underground for so long. She'd always disliked the Tube, but it was without a doubt the easiest, quickest, and cheapest way to travel across London.

In reality, she knew that her butterflies and shortness of breath had nothing to with the journey. It was about seeing Celia again.

She didn't know what to expect. On the phone, Celia had been friendly and funny, and they'd briefly chatted and joked as if no time had elapsed since their last conversation.

But Lily still felt guilty for leaving things for so long and wondered if Celia would bring it up. And what she might say if she did.

When she arrived at the top of the escalator, she stepped forward and into the central square. Once she was out of people's way, she stopped and looked around.

Mainly looking up.

Skyscrapers and large office blocks surrounded her, and yet they didn't seem too imposing or crowded. Now that she was in the thick of them, they looked so very different to how she had seen them before.

She'd never had cause to go to the financial district of London, instead merely knowing of it and seeing it from afar. She'd considered it a concrete jungle of buildings, lifeless and industrial. Now that she was in it, she realised she'd been so very wrong. There was space to breathe, space to walk, even space for gardens.

The buildings were all slightly different shapes and sizes, and many were plated in reflective glass to keep the sun out of the office space, which gave an appearance of shimmering colours from the outside. It was almost beautiful.

Lily smiled to herself as she thought about the ways she could apply some personality to the buildings. There was a children's book here, she was sure of it—skyscrapers with faces made out of lit-up windows talking to one another.

She didn't know how long she stood there plotting out the plan, but it had been enough time to get in some people's way. She apologised and got her phone out of her jeans pocket to bring up a map to the restaurant Celia had suggested.

The route looked confusing, and she looked from the 2D map to the very much 3D landscape in front of her. Stairs and buildings and more interrupted the apparent straight line that the map suggested.

"This place is weird," Lily muttered.

❖

After navigating some strange, underground labyrinth and getting lost several times, Lily finally spotted the generic sports bar Celia had suggested. Apparently Celia had come to the conclusion that this bar was the easiest to find, which was odd considering Lily had passed several other drinking establishments along the way.

Celia sat at the bar, sipping from a glass.

"This place is a maze," Lily announced as soon as she was close enough.

Celia turned and looked at her with a frown. "You didn't take the bridge?"

"What bridge?"

Celia pointed to a bridge that connected whatever island they were on to the main island a few metres away, the Thames's waters gently rolling below. In the distance, she could see the London Underground station she'd come from. It was a direct route, one she hadn't noticed.

"Nope. Never seen it before," Lily said, taking a well-deserved seat on the stool beside Celia.

Celia grinned. "Did you come through the shopping centre?"

"You mean was I near the bowels of the earth going up and down staircases trying to look for a way out? Then yes. Stop smiling." Lily grinned to herself. It was interesting to her that she actually enjoyed being gently teased by Celia.

Celia covered the smirk with her hand and coughed. Once she was in control of her almost laughter she asked, "Can I get you a drink?"

"I'm paying, remember?" Lily pointed to the almost finished drink Celia had. "What are you having?"

"Thank you. I'll have another orange juice, please."

"Orange and…?"

"Ice."

"Oh." Lily didn't want to say anything, but she'd assumed they'd be drinking alcohol as they were meeting at a bar. It seemed strange that Celia wasn't drinking alcohol, considering how much of it Lily had seen her consume before.

"I've decided to take a little break from alcohol," Celia said, a touch of a blush on her cheeks. "I realised you were right."

"Good for you," Lily said. "For realising that I'm right."

Celia chuckled, and Lily ordered two orange juices. She'd been expecting to drink a glass of wine, but she wasn't going to do that with someone who had recently decided to give up alcohol. And it would probably be a good idea to keep a clear head.

"So, you lied to your friend?" Celia asked.

"Wow, you just get straight to the point, don't you?"

"Okay, do you want to talk about why you didn't get in contact with me for a week?" Celia asked, grinning again.

"So, my friend is called Cassie," Lily explained, eager to avoid the elephant in the room.

Celia smiled and listened as Lily told the story, breaking only to thank the bartender and pay for the drinks. She didn't mention that she'd told Cassie about the kiss. She had no intention of speaking of the kiss ever again.

When she was done, she took a deep breath and then a sip of orange juice.

"I have questions," Celia said.

"I thought you might." Lily groaned.

"Why did you pretend you were still in Japan? What was the plan?"

Lily sighed. "I don't think I had one. And Cassie is a good friend—I might have even told her everything eventually. I think I just couldn't face it at the time, you know? I needed some time to myself to come to terms with everything."

Celia nodded with understanding. "And have you? Come to terms with everything?"

Lily shook her head. "No. I'm just as confused as I was."

"Watching television in your pyjamas didn't help?" Celia asked, a twinkle in her eye.

"I don't know why I confide in you." Lily couldn't stop the smile that grew and grew whenever she was around Celia. Yes, the woman was sharp and even downright rude at times, but she was also spot on and often quite funny. And she knew it too.

"No, I don't know either," Celia confessed. "But I am glad that you do."

"For your amusement?" Lily questioned.

"Naturally." Celia plucked the menu from the counter. "Have you eaten?"

"Ice cream for lunch."

Celia looked at her in horror. "I'll take that as a solid no. You must look after yourself, you know."

"I do," Lily promised her. "It's just been a weird day." She leaned forward and grabbed a menu for herself. "This doesn't seem like your kind of place."

"It was Andrew's favourite, and I have a few clients who are sports fans." Celia gestured to the television screens that hung over the bar. "They do a remarkably good vegetarian burger."

Celia returned to studying the menu. Lily suspected Celia knew it by heart and assumed her actions were more to hide her sorrow, visible on her face, at the mention of her son.

Lily bit her lip, wondering if she should say something or allow Celia time to come to her on her own. While Celia was acting bright and breezy, it was clear that something was weighing her down. She'd noticed something ever so slightly off when she arrived, and she didn't think it had anything to do with her.

"What's wrong?" Lily said, deciding to bite the bullet. Celia had often been direct with her, so it was worth returning the favour and seeing how the strategy panned out.

Celia looked up. "Wrong?" She did a good impression of someone who was fine, but Lily knew better.

"Something's wrong, I can tell."

Lily held her gaze. She didn't want to force Celia to talk to her, but she wanted to prove that she knew she wasn't okay. Celia might be able to fool others, but Lily wanted her to know that she was different.

Celia let out a sigh and lowered her menu. She took a quick sip of orange juice before saying, "I've heard from one of Andrew's old roommates. They are having some kind of a gathering to remember him, and they want me to attend."

"Oh, cool, when is it?"

Celia stared at her as if she was an absolute idiot. "Well, I'm not going, obviously."

"Why?"

"Because…because I'm the reason he is no longer with us. Why on earth would I want to be surrounded by his friends? They'd judge me, and they'd be right to." Celia bristled and shook her head. "No. I won't be attending."

"I don't think they would have invited you just to judge you. What would be the point of that?" Lily asked.

Celia shook her head. "I don't know," she admitted.

"Maybe going would be a good thing. Well, I mean, it will obviously be hard, but it might get you some closure."

Celia barked a laugh. "I don't think so."

Lily shrugged and turned back to face the bar. She returned her attention to her menu.

"I mean, what would be the point?" Celia asked.

"Dunno," Lily replied, studying the offerings and ignoring Celia. It was obvious that the invitation was playing on her mind, and she was fishing for Lily's thoughts on the matter. Lily had given them, and now she needed to wait for Celia to eventually agree with her. Simple.

"It would be a waste of time," Celia added.

"If you say so. Is the vegetable burger spicy?" Lily asked.

"All the way to Edinburgh," Celia continued, apparently ignoring her. "And then what?"

Lily waved towards the bartender. "Excuse me, is the vegetable burger spicy?"

He shook his head. "Nah, it's mild."

"Thank you." Lily closed her menu and looked at Celia.

Celia looked annoyed. "You think I should go, don't you?"

"I think you *want* to go," Lily replied.

"That's ridiculous. I don't know where you get your ideas from. And the vegetable burger does have a bit of a kick." She shook her head. "You can't trust him—he once gave me sweet potato fries when I asked for wedges."

"The monster." Lily picked the menu up again. After a week of takeaway, she was looking for something plain and nutritious.

"He's an idiot," Celia added.

"He can probably hear you."

"Probably. Can you hear me, Duncan?" Celia asked without raising her voice.

"Yeah, I can hear you," Duncan replied without turning to face them, continuing with his stock check.

"You're an idiot."

"Thanks, Celia." He chuckled.

Lily blinked and stared at Celia. "You are *so* rude."

"He used to work for me," Celia explained, "and then decided he wanted to give it all up to be a musician."

Duncan turned around and grinned at them. "And you got me my first gig."

Celia shrugged and turned her attention back to her menu.

Lily looked from Celia to Duncan. "Did you? Did she?"

Duncan nodded. "Asked one of her clients to give me a chance. He owns some London clubs."

"And now he serves me fries when I ask for wedges," Celia added.

"You asked for fries," Duncan told her.

"And that vegetable burger is spicy."

Duncan rolled his eyes playfully. "Give me a shout when you're ready to order, ladies." He walked down to the end of the bar to serve some other customers who had turned up.

Lily shook her head. Celia Scott was full of surprises. And kindness apparently.

"Go to Edinburgh," Lily said. "Meet Andrew's friends, and tell them about him. Show them your photos and videos. They'll appreciate it."

Celia hesitated before shaking her head. "I couldn't."

Lily smiled to herself. She was getting somewhere. They'd gone from it being a ridiculous idea to Celia saying she couldn't—a big step up.

"Why not?"

"Because it scares the hell out of me," Celia admitted. "I can't look his friends in the eye."

An idea popped up in Lily's head, and she wondered if it was too foolish to say out loud. After Celia's recent white knight undertaking in rescuing her, she felt desperate to return the favour.

The thought of being able to be the one Celia's leaned on in her time of need was intoxicating. Not just to rebalance the friendship but as a chance to actually be there for Celia and support her through what was clearly a terrible situation. The thought of having Celia look to her as someone who was strong and capable was exhilarating.

"What if I came with you?" Lily asked. "If I get the slow train and use my railcard, then I can afford a ticket to Edinburgh. I have a friend who would probably let me crash on their sofa."

Celia stared at Lily as if she had grown another head.

"I'm sorry, I'm overstepping," Lily said. She mentally chastised herself and turned back to the menu, hoping that the white-hot blush she felt on her cheeks would quickly fade. She couldn't believe she had just inserted herself into something so intensely private like that. They weren't friends. They hardly knew each other. Why on earth would Celia want her company?

"You'd do that?" Celia asked, her voice no more than a whisper.

Lily looked at her. She didn't seem mad, just confused. "Of course I would."

"Why?"

Lily didn't have a concise answer. It was tied up in her heart and in the million and one emotions that swam around her. "Because."

Celia seemed to accept the non-answer and nodded slowly, seemingly deep in thought.

"It's next Thursday," Celia said, her voice low. "I'd travel the day before. And I'd pay for your travel and accommodation."

"You don't have to do that. I can afford it," Lily said.

"But you shouldn't have to spend your own money. Not on this, not because you're accompanying me. I know you spent a lot going to Japan, and obviously..." Celia trailed off and looked up, sad eyes meeting Lily's.

"We travel next Wednesday?" Lily asked, not wanting to bring up Japan again.

Celia nodded.

"Great, count me in."

Celia smiled gratefully, and Lily swiftly turned the conversation to discuss the menu. They'd eaten together a few times now, and she trusted Celia's opinion.

She also wanted to get things off the hard topic of Andrew and onto something lighter. It was clear that Celia was still buried under her guilt, and Lily hoped that speaking with Andrew's friends might relieve some of that. She couldn't imagine that they would actually blame Celia for his loss. And if they did, certainly not to her face.

But Lily was happy to go with her and do whatever she needed to support Celia, in much the same way Celia had supported her. They were like a team these days, helping one another through the rough patches.

They ordered food, and Lily demanded to know more about Duncan the part-time bartender and his fledgling musical career. The conversation was easy, with plenty of laughs thrown in, and Lily made a mental note to thank Cassie for pressuring her to call Celia that afternoon. Even though the kiss still hung between them, undiscussed.

KING'S CROSS

Celia smothered a yawn behind her cupped hand. Why did going anywhere always mean dreadfully early travel?

It was eight in the morning, and King's Cross train station was heaving with commuters, most of them coming into London rather than departing as she was.

She'd woken up at five thirty in order to get ready, pack, and get to the station in plenty of time. Her nerves were frayed, and she thought, for the hundredth time that hour, that this was a very bad idea.

Not that it mattered; she was far beyond the point of cancelling. Lily was on her way to be her support for the trip, and Andrew's friends were expecting her.

She sipped from her takeaway coffee and looked down at the main concourse. Hundreds of people filed through the station in organised chaos, each knowing the quickest route from their train to their desired exit and forming lines through crowds of tourists who didn't know they were standing in the way of a well-oiled machine.

Celia knew all too well what it was like to be a commuter on a mission, which was why she immediately went to the upper level to grab a drink and watch from the quiet balcony.

She didn't get to King's Cross often and had been surprised to see the entire concourse had been redesigned, an enormous criss-crossed canopy now covering the area. It looked neat and modern but still protected the old charms of the venerable station. She briefly wondered if Andrew had ever seen the redesign. She had no frame of reference for when it had been completed but knew that Andrew frequently travelled by train to and from Edinburgh.

She often wondered about the things he had seen and the things he had missed. She didn't know if it was healthy, but she did it regardless.

"Morning."

She jumped a little at Lily's arrival.

"Sorry, didn't mean to scare you," Lily apologised.

"It's okay. I was miles away," Celia replied.

Lily wore jeans and a comfortable-looking sweater. Her hair was up in a messy bun, and her overloaded rucksack was on her back. She looked like she was backpacking around Europe for a week, not going to Edinburgh for a couple of days. Celia suspected the bag was full of painting supplies and sweets.

"Can I get you a drink?" Celia offered, gesturing to the coffee shop behind them.

Lily shook her head. "Nah, I'm looking forward to checking out the shop on board."

Celia smiled. "Preparing to buy your body weight in sweets and chocolate?"

"Yes. It's the only way to travel." Lily nodded seriously.

Celia couldn't express how pleased she was to have Lily with her for this painfully awkward trip. The distraction and the easy conversation were going to make a long journey and an even longer couple of days slightly more bearable.

"Well, we're in first class, so you'll be fed, at least," Celia commented.

"First class?" Lily blinked. "Oh. Am I dressed okay?"

Celia chuckled. "You'll do."

"No, seriously, should I change? I have other clothes."

"Wear whatever you like. We're going to Edinburgh on an Avanti West Coast, not the Orient Express. You look wonderful. Don't worry."

Celia noted Lily's cheeks brightening and turned to look at the crowds below them. She shouldn't be complimenting Lily on her looks, even if she did look absolutely adorable. They'd swept the whole issue of the kiss under the carpet but comments like that would only serve to bring it back up. Considering how Celia had twice recently found herself daydreaming about that kiss, she really didn't want to add that to the list of emotionally charged issues she had to contend with.

"I assume you work from home?" she said.

Lily leaned on the railing. "Most of the time, unless I'm invited into a studio to collaborate with someone. But usually at home. I used to work in admin and had to do all this." She gestured down to the people below. "Don't miss it."

Celia hummed her agreement and looked at the multiple departure screens. Their train was listed, but the platform was still blank.

"It's five hours, isn't it?" Lily asked.

"Five and a half."

"Excellent. I have two movies and two books. And a magazine. And obviously I'm going to talk to you until you get bored of me. It will fly by."

Celia appreciated Lily's attempt to lighten the mood but couldn't reply with much more than a hum. As the large station clock ticked closer to their departure time, the unsettled feeling in her stomach grew and grew.

❖

The train steward passed through the first-class cabin and smiled knowingly at Lily. Lily returned the smile. It was obvious she didn't want anything as she had already loaded up on treats and drinks that now filled the table.

She'd never been on a first-class train journey before and had no idea how much stuff they would happily give away. On the third time the steward passed through, Lily had run out of table space, much to Celia's amusement.

They sat opposite each other, a table with a fixed lamp between them, and the single seats meant there was no one to share the space with. Lily thought that was worth the price of the ticket alone.

Not that she knew the price of the ticket. Celia had refused any form of payment, insisting that Lily was doing more than enough by simply accompanying her. That had made Lily worry that Celia didn't have many friends, certainly not any she could rely on.

Then again, Lily felt the same. She had a lot of acquaintances, and while Cassie was the closest friend she had, there was still plenty she didn't tell her unless Cassie dragged it out of her. People often didn't understand what she was trying to say, and she found it too difficult or too emotionally exhausting to try to explain. So she often didn't bother.

It was only recently, with Asami and now Celia, that Lily had found people who seemed to understand her. Or, at least, accept her.

Asami was obviously a fraud, but Celia seemed to be the real deal. Someone Lily trusted and respected.

Celia had fallen asleep half an hour before, and Lily had quickly dived for her sketchpad and pencil. She felt a little naughty drawing Celia's portrait without permission, but surely it was illegal for someone to look so classy and graceful having fallen asleep on a train. She'd decided to accept her all-encompassing crush on Celia. It wasn't as if she was hurting anyone by harbouring feelings for the woman. Celia didn't have to know—no more sudden kisses would be shared. Lily could just privately luxuriate in the dreamworld where she and Celia could somehow be more.

Lily often sketched her friends. It was second nature to her. From a young age she had realised that she didn't necessarily have a natural talent for art, but she could persevere with it. Practice really did make— well, if not perfect, then at least better. As with most art forms.

She checked her watch and wished it was a little later so it would be lunchtime. The menu had looked delicious, and she was eager to try the pasta on offer. It would also mean that they were more than halfway through their journey.

They would arrive in Edinburgh in the mid-afternoon, and Celia had them booked into a hotel in the Old Town near the station. She'd neglected to mention which one, which made Lily assume it was a top name brand. She didn't know if Edinburgh had a Shangri-La or not, but Lily suspected they'd be staying in the equivalent.

Celia had blushed and stumbled her way through a quick statement to clarify that they wouldn't be sharing a room again. Lily had quickly nodded her understanding, hopefully not giving away any indication that she was either happy or sad about the fact.

She hadn't *expected* to share a room again but did feel a little sad at the acknowledgement that they wouldn't. Despite the horrible situation, she had fond memories of falling asleep in their separate beds, watching strange Japanese reality shows in the middle of the night. But those had been unique circumstances. Celia wasn't exactly hard up when it came to money, so she would have little realistic excuse to suggest sharing a room again.

Not to mention the optics of it, Lily suspected. An older, wealthy woman asks a younger woman to accompany her on a trip, suggesting she will pay for everything, only to book one room and propose they share the space.

Lily wouldn't mind as she knew Celia would never take advantage of her. A small jolt of excitement ran through her at the idea. Not being taken advantage of as such—there was *nothing* sexy about that—but the suggestion of Celia wanting more.

If Celia had pointedly looked at her over the edge of her takeaway coffee mug and proposed, with a suggestive tone, that maybe they could share a room, Lily would have nodded so quickly her head would have fallen off.

But that definitely wasn't on the cards. Neither was an innocent night under the same roof where they traded banter and slumbered on separate beds. So they would sleep in different rooms before meeting up the next morning with Andrew's friends in a local pub.

Celia was already clearly nervous about tomorrow, and Lily couldn't imagine what she would be like nearer the time. She sighed and looked at her travel companion again. At least she looked peaceful now.

Checking In

"The Hilton?" Lily looked at Celia with a glare.

"What? It's a hotel." Celia watched the taxi driver put their luggage into the back of the taxi. While it wasn't far to the hotel, it was up several long flights of stairs, and she had no intention of wrestling her travel case, even though it was rather light.

"I knew you were being cagey. You said it was a mid-priced hotel."

"It is mid-priced," Celia defended. "I usually stay at The Balmoral, which is four times the price."

Lily rolled her eyes. "I'm sure there's a perfectly nice Ibis around here."

"I think we have a difference of opinion in what *perfectly nice* means. Hilton doesn't equate to luxury, you know, it's all PR nonsense. Some of the Hiltons I've stayed in didn't even have a doorman."

Lily put her hand to her mouth in faux horror. "No. The monsters."

"Indeed. They cut corners. How else do you think that woman with the dog is dripping in diamonds?"

"Woman with the dog?" Lily questioned.

"The Hilton woman. Pippa?"

"Do you mean Paris Hilton?"

"That one. One less doorman for you and me means one more diamond necklace for her. Mid-price."

Lily shook her head but remained silent.

The taxi driver finished putting Lily's rucksack and Celia's travel case in the boot and slammed it closed.

"Ready, ladies?" he asked, clearly wondering if they were still going to the Hilton or if Lily would win the public battle they were engaged in.

"Yes, we're ready," Celia said, making the choice for all three of them. She got into the back of the taxi with Lily.

"I wish you'd let me give you some money for all this," Lily complained.

"It's really not necessary."

"I'm not poor, you know," Lily grumbled.

"I don't think you are," Celia said. "It's just, this is my mission to go on, and you're kindly joining me. It shouldn't put you out of pocket. But if it bothers you that much, buy me dinner."

"I will," Lily agreed.

Celia smothered a grin at Lily's fervour and turned to look out of the window. Lily was cute when she got riled up.

Celia didn't mean to demean her by paying. It was just in her nature. She earned a very good salary, had paid her mortgage off years before, and was happy to pay for the finer things in life—for herself, and those she cared about.

"Oh, I'm meeting my brother this evening, after dinner." Celia realised that she'd neglected to tell Lily her plan. "I'm going to enlist his help in killing Alan."

The taxi driver's eyes caught hers in the rear-view mirror.

"Alan's an inanimate object," she reassured him.

He didn't look convinced.

"You brought Alan?" Lily asked in surprise.

"Yes, he's in my case." She nodded to the driver, indicating, she hoped, that her case was far too small for an *actual* Alan.

Lily was clearly torn between being annoyed at Celia supposedly choosing an expensive hotel and being intrigued by the new Alan disposal plan.

"What's the plan?" Lily asked.

Celia didn't want to say too much in the taxi, as clearly they were being listened to. She couldn't blame the driver—she'd be listening intently to an apparent murder plot as well.

"I'll tell you over dinner. You can come and meet my brother if you like. You're more than welcome."

"I'm going to have to pass on that. I'm going to do some sketching for my portfolio if that's okay? It's not every day you get this kind of weather, and Edinburgh is gorgeous."

"Of course." Celia didn't know why she felt a slight burn of abandonment. They'd already discussed that Lily was free to spend the time aside from the memorial however she saw fit. But now that Lily had actually taken her up on that, Celia felt somehow rejected, even though she knew in her heart that Lily was probably just giving her time to herself with all the best intentions.

They sat in silence for the rest of the short journey. As the crow flew, the hotel was ridiculously close to the station, but Edinburgh was very hilly, and steep inclines and long flights of stairs were not the way Celia wanted to begin a trip she was already dreading.

At the hotel, the driver helped them with their cases and seemed to do his very best to get a good look at both their faces as he did. He'd probably be scouring the papers later for any mention of a man called Alan who had recently gone missing.

Celia paid him a tip and offered him a warm smile, but he didn't seem to care, getting back into the car and speeding away as soon as he was able.

"I blame you, you know," Celia said.

"What for?"

"The fact that people think I'm a murderer these days. You called it Alan."

"And you continue to call it Alan," Lily pointed out.

"Well, it suits him."

"It does," Lily agreed.

They entered the hotel lobby, and Celia approached the reception desk. As she arrived, she realised Lily wasn't beside her and turned to see her staring around the large lobby with wide eyes. Celia looked up at the chandelier and down at the marble floor and supposed it was rather nice.

"Good afternoon, welcome to the Hilton. Are you checking in?"

Celia turned her attention back towards the desk and the young woman in a smart suit who was smiling at her.

"Yes, two rooms, under the name Scott."

Lily approached. "This place is gorgeous."

"Scott?" the receptionist clarified, looking at Celia in what appeared to be shock.

"That's right," Celia replied, wondering what was wrong.

The receptionist shook herself out of her stupor.

"I'm sorry, I didn't realise you were staying here. I'm Kaye Lassiter, Andrew's housemate." Kaye reached her hand out, and Celia mentally kicked herself to reciprocate and shake the proffered hand.

"Ah," Celia replied.

She was at a loss for what else she could possibly say, not having prepared herself to meet any of Andrew's friends until at least the next day. Kaye did sound familiar to her, and her brain belatedly reminded her that Andrew had frequently mentioned the name. But right then she couldn't remember anything relevant or think of anything at all to say.

"I'm Lily. A friend of Celia's." Lily stuck her hand out and thankfully took some of Kaye's attention while Celia pulled herself together.

"Nice to meet you," Kaye greeted her.

"We're meeting at The Black Owl tomorrow, right?" Lily asked, obviously indicating that she'd also be attending the memorial.

Celia couldn't have felt more grateful in that moment to have someone with her while she was relatively dumbfounded.

"That's right. You can't miss it. It's up on this road—you'll see the rainbow flags hanging on either side of the door," Kaye replied.

"Is that because rainbow flags are pretty or because it's a gay-friendly pub?" Lily asked with a bright grin.

"It's owned by a gay couple," Kaye replied.

"Cool." Lily turned to Celia. "I'm going to like this place."

Celia smiled at her. "Yes, I rather think you might."

"There are a lot of LGBTQ places around if you'd like some recommendations," Kaye offered, her attention focused like a laser on Lily.

Celia looked between the two of them, realising she had suddenly become the third wheel in the conversation. It was something she didn't like at all.

"So, that's two rooms, under the name Scott," Celia said as casually as she could. This was one of Andrew's friends after all. She didn't want to start off on the wrong foot.

"Oh yes, sorry." Kaye managed to rip her eyes from Lily briefly enough to look at her computer and type. "Are you in town for long? I mean, after the memorial?"

Celia was about to reply when she realised that Kaye was asking Lily and not her.

Lily leaned on the counter. "Nope, flying visit. We're heading home the following morning."

"Well, if you have any spare time and want to see some sights or something, let me know. I'll be working throughout your stay, and I'd be happy to help."

"Cool, thanks."

Celia looked down at her body, wondering if she had somehow

become invisible. Lily and Kaye were fawning over each other as if she didn't exist. She bit her tongue while the check-in process continued at a slower-than-necessary pace as Kaye kept dropping flirtatious comments that Lily ate up.

Eventually, two key cards were placed on the counter. Kaye wished them a pleasant stay and had the audacity to say she was looking forward to seeing Celia the next day.

As if.

Celia and Lily walked towards the elevators, and Celia stabbed the button with more force than was necessary.

"Sorry if that was awkward," Lily whispered.

"It was." Celia stared up at the number indicator, wishing the car would hurry up so she could make her escape.

"At least she seemed nice," Lily added.

The doors slid open, and they both stepped in. Celia took a look at her key card, having already forgotten what floor they were on. She jabbed the correct button.

"Nice? Yes, she certainly was very nice to *you*," Celia commented as the doors slid closed.

Lily had the gall to look confused. "She was nice in general."

"She was mounting your leg. I was merely in the way."

Lily's jaw dropped. "Excuse me?"

"You heard me."

The elevator arrived at the designated floor, and Celia swept out and marched down the corridor, hoping she was going in the correct direction, or there would be an embarrassing U-turn in her future.

"She was being friendly," Lily argued when she caught up to her.

"To you, specifically." Celia stopped by a door and looked down at the key card. Seeing the numbers matched, she handed it to Lily.

"Are you jealous?" Lily asked.

Celia barked a laughed. "No. I am tired, though. I'm going to rest." She continued walking up the corridor in search of her own room.

"Are we having dinner together still?" Lily called after her.

"Only if you want to," Celia replied.

"I do," Lily said firmly. "And I'm paying."

"Very well."

Celia rounded the corner, thankful for some protection from Lily's gaze. She'd acted like a fool, a jealous fool. She didn't know why, other than that something had snapped in her when she'd finally made the decision to come to Edinburgh.

All common sense seemed to fall away, and she was left feeling like a shell of herself, a feeling she wasn't at all comfortable with. She hoped a nap would help, even though she'd already slept most of the day away.

She just wished she could somehow get her emotions under control and resemble a normal human being again. How long was grief supposed to last? She wouldn't be like this for the rest of her life, would she?

❖

Lily lay on the bed and stared at the ceiling. Part of her wanted to forgive Celia for her bad mood during an obviously stressful time, but a bigger part of her was annoyed by Celia's attitude.

Kaye had just been polite—surely Celia could see that? And if Kaye had been more than polite, which she hadn't, what would it matter to Celia anyway? It wasn't as if Celia owned her. Did she think she did? Did she think that Lily couldn't have other friends?

Lily looked at her watch. She didn't know when Celia intended to eat dinner or when they were supposed to meet. It had been a shitty power move to just walk off like that and leave her with all the questions and none of the answers.

Lily pushed herself up and off the bed. If Celia thought she was going to just sit around the hotel and wait for her to graciously say it was okay to leave, she had another thing coming.

She grabbed her rucksack, checked her reflection in the mirror, slid the key card into her back pocket, and left the room.

She'd been to Edinburgh a couple of times before. It was a great city to roam around, with beautiful architecture, intricate street designs, new and old rubbing shoulders seamlessly. It was an excellent place to sketch; literally anywhere you stopped would put you right in front of the perfect subject.

She left her room and walked to the elevator, briefly wondering if she should let Celia know she was going out.

"She's not my keeper," Lily muttered as she waited for the elevator to arrive. "She'll call if she wants me."

She got in the elevator and stabbed the button for the lobby. When the doors slid open again, she saw Kaye look up from the reception desk and smile warmly.

Lily knew it would be rude to ignore her, and she was due to see her the next day, so she went over to the desk.

"Hey, I'm just heading out for a while," Lily said, wondering why she felt the need to explain herself.

"It's a lovely day out there," Kaye agreed conversationally. "Going anywhere nice?"

"Sketching while the sun's still high in the sky," Lily replied.

"Oh, you draw?" Kaye's eyes lit up. "I love drawing. Well, painting, to be exact. I'm playing with oils at the moment, and it's a nightmare, but I'm going to crack it eventually." She held up her hand and pointed to some paint stains under her fingernails. "You'd think I bathe in it, but I do try to be careful."

Lily chuckled. "Yeah, oils do have a talent for getting everywhere."

"Is, um, Miss Scott going with you?" Kaye asked.

"No, I think she's resting," Lily replied. "She's finding all this a bit difficult to process."

It wasn't really Lily's place to say such things, but she wanted to give Celia some slack in Kaye's eyes. She remembered well when she had first met Celia and thought she was a bit of an unapproachable snob. At least Kaye hadn't been caught prodding any sandwiches.

Kaye nodded. "Yeah, it must be really hard to lose your son like that. I can't imagine it."

"No, neither can I," Lily admitted. "You were his housemate?"

"Yeah, there were three of us in the house. Diane had to move out after Andrew died—she couldn't take it any more. So we have two new people in there now, but it's still weird."

Lily bit her lip. She wanted to ask something that she never would have asked Celia, but she just didn't know if it was appropriate. Asking for details about someone's death could be considered macabre or insensitive. She knew he had taken his life, but nothing more.

"Did you know him very well?" Kaye asked.

"Oh, I didn't know him at all," Lily admitted. "I met Celia way after he died. I'm just here for moral support."

Kaye smiled. "That's really nice of you."

"She'd do the same thing for me," Lily said without a moment's hesitation. "Her bark is worse than her bite."

"Andrew said the same thing," Kaye admitted.

The phone on the desk rang, and Kaye looked apologetic. "I have to get this, sorry."

"It's fine, I'll see you tomorrow." Lily pushed away from the reception desk.

"Lily?"

She stopped and turned around.

"I'll be painting in Princes Street Gardens this evening, if you happen to be around. From six until the light gives out. You'll spot me—I'll be covered in oils and trying to get the castle just right but failing miserably." Kaye picked up the phone. "Good afternoon, Hilton Edinburgh, how may I help you?"

Lily smiled and turned, leaving Kaye to her work. She frowned as she wondered if Kaye *was* flirting with her after all. Had Celia picked up on it and Lily missed it entirely? It was possible, though it didn't explain Celia's angry reaction.

Unless Celia was jealous? Lily wondered. She shook her head. No, of course she wouldn't be jealous. Why would she be?

Apologies

Celia picked up her watch from the bedside table and fitted it to her wrist. She'd not slept, but she had managed to calm herself down and re-evaluate her behaviour.

And now she felt guilty and embarrassed.

It was time to think about going out to dinner, and she couldn't put off speaking with Lily any longer. She sucked in a deep breath and picked up the hotel phone and made the internal call.

It rang and rang and rang.

Eventually she hung up. Was Lily using the bathroom? She paced the room for a few moments, preparing her outfit for the next day and flipping through the news app on her phone.

When she thought a sufficient amount of time had passed, she called again.

After the tenth ring she started to worry. She hung up and made a call from her mobile to Lily's. All the while she wondered if she had finally pushed Lily away. She had been pretty awful to her, and she wouldn't be surprised if Lily had finally had enough. It wasn't as if she had to be there. Celia couldn't blame her if she'd turned around and checked out.

"Hey!" Lily greeted her when she answered the phone.

"Hi," Celia replied, uncertain.

"I'm in town," Lily said. "Sorry about all the noise."

"I'm sorry about what I said," Celia said before she lost the courage to do so. "It was wrong. I don't know wh—"

"It's fine," Lily reassured her. "We're okay."

Celia let out a breath of relief. She didn't know if they were really okay or if Lily just didn't want to have a conversation about it, but she'd take it for now.

"Thank you. I was calling about dinner."

"I'm on Grassmarket. Do you know anywhere good to eat around here? I can meet you," Lily suggested.

Celia brought up a mental map of the area. "Yes, there's a pub called The Red Lion."

"Isn't there always?" Lily chuckled. "Oh yes, I see it. When do you want to meet?"

"I can be there in twenty minutes."

"Great, I'll grab a table. See you soon."

Celia said goodbye and hung up the call. She stared at the handset for a couple of moments. Lily had seemed fine, but Celia couldn't be sure. Had she really forgiven her so easily?

She rubbed her forehead where a sizable headache was forming.

She set about quickly getting ready, and within a few minutes was out the door and on her way to the lobby. Sharp relief hit her when she exited the elevator to see Kaye was occupied with guests checking in. She really didn't have the energy for a second round with the chipper young woman.

The concierge smiled at her as she approached the desk and requested a taxi. She elected to wait outside, in case Kaye suddenly became available again and attempted to talk to her. Although she had to wonder if Kaye would bother; she had been pretty terrible to her too.

Celia presumed her behaviour had cemented whatever notion Kaye already had when it came to Andrew's awful mother. She shivered at the thought. She'd probably made the next day even more difficult than it needed to be.

Thankfully, a taxi pulled up and dragged her attention away from that particularly negative train of thought.

At the pub she quickly spotted Lily at an outside table. She weaved her way to where Lily was thoroughly focused on sketching. Celia smiled at the way Lily chewed on her inner cheek as she looked up at the surrounding buildings that she was attempting to capture.

"May I join you?" she asked in order to not scare Lily half to death when she did just that.

"Oh, hey! Has it been twenty minutes already?" Lily hurried to pack her things away.

"I'm a tad early," Celia admitted. "You don't have to stop—I don't mind."

Lily continued putting her pencils into a metal case. "No, no, it's rude. No drawing and no mobiles. My mum taught me well."

"I don't think it's rude," Celia said. "I like watching the artist at work."

Lily laughed. "Hardly."

Celia smiled. "Well, actually, completely. You are an artist. Had you forgotten?"

"I'm not. I illustrate children's books. It's like doodles in comparison to some people."

"Do you always compare yourself to others?" Celia asked.

"Absolutely. That's how we grow."

"Or constantly feel that we're never good enough," Celia added.

"Possibly." Lily nodded. "But I don't feel like I'm an artist. I'd like to be better, to do more with my art."

"Then I have no doubt that you will. But in the meantime, I'll consider you an artist," Celia said, picking up a menu from the holder.

"You make it sound like a threat," Lily said through a chuckle.

"It is." Celia glanced at the menu, glad to see it hadn't changed a lot since her last visit. "I am sorry about my overreaction earlier."

"It's fine. I know it's a bad time for you, and seeing Kaye without warning must have been a shock."

"It was. But still, no excuse, and I am sorry."

Lily picked up a menu. "Do you come to Edinburgh a lot? You seem to know it well."

"My brother has lived here for about thirty years," Celia explained. "I do love it here."

"What does he do?"

"He blows things up for a living."

Lily lowered the menu and looked at Celia with confusion.

"Seriously. He's a demolition expert. Also works with fireworks, that kind of thing. If you want something destroyed, Ben is your man."

Lily grinned. "Ah, so that's why Alan is here."

"Yes. I've spoken to him about it, and he has agreed that Alan has to leave this world. He has a secure area where he tests explosives and such, out in the middle of nowhere on his farm. You're welcome to come if you like."

"Are you inviting me to the middle of nowhere to blow stuff up?" Lily asked with a smile. "That sounds super dangerous."

"I'd protect you," Celia replied with a grin.

Lily laughed. "Well, as fun as that sounds, I have some more sketching planned. Unless you *want* me to come?"

Celia waved the thought away. "No, no, it's fine. You enjoy your evening."

A waiter came by, and they ordered drinks and requested a little more time for the meals. They focused on what to eat, discussing menu items of interest before deciding to go for the same thing, much to their shared amusement.

After the waiter had delivered the drinks and departed again, Celia took a sip of the homemade lemonade and steeled herself.

"You know, I was clumsy in how I said it, but Kaye *was* flirting with you," she said tentatively. "She seems very nice."

Celia had realised that her reaction to Kaye was some kind of misplaced jealousy. She didn't own Lily, and if she was a real friend, then she should help Lily find happiness. Even if that burned like an injustice within her. Was it that she wanted Lily to be alone and miserable just like she was? If so, that was not the kind of friend she wanted to be to Lily. Not the kind of friend Lily deserved.

Lily sipped her drink and looked away.

"Maybe you should follow up on it?" Celia suggested, realising that Lily wasn't going to reply.

"Maybe," Lily said. "What time are you meeting your brother?"

It was such an obvious deflection, but Celia wasn't about to give up that easily.

"Whenever we're done here, around six thirty or seven. What's wrong, aren't you interested in Kaye? Is she not your type?"

"Do you *want* me to date her?" Lily asked, staring at Celia.

"If you want to," Celia replied, not sure why Lily was getting defensive.

Lily huffed and shook her head. "Can we talk about something else?"

"Sure."

Lily, for some reason, wasn't interested in talking about Kaye's flirting. Celia wondered if it was too soon after the Asami situation, which had clearly left Lily heartbroken and wary.

"What else did you see this afternoon?" Celia asked, hoping to steer the conversation to safer ground. "It must be an artist's paradise in Edinburgh."

❖

After saying farewell to Celia and seeing her into a taxi to go and meet her brother, Lily had ended up strolling around the city without purpose. The good thing about Edinburgh was that there was always a new street, alleyway, graveyard, or park to discover.

Lily had made a deal with herself to forgive Celia for her outburst, but that deal had faltered when Celia again insisted on bringing up Kaye. Lily wasn't quite sure why it had angered her, but it had. Did Celia think she couldn't find a girlfriend for herself? Or did she think that any two lesbians would fit together regardless of personality? Or was it that she didn't want Celia to so willingly hand her over to Kaye?

It was strange to be annoyed by such a thing mere hours after feeling that Celia had treated her like her property.

Lily stopped walking as she entered a park. She pinched the bridge of her nose and tried to get rid of the headache that was developing. She needed to resolve whatever it was that was happening between her and Celia—or, more precisely, her own feelings for Celia.

She shook her head. Now wasn't the time. Now she was being the supportive friend. She'd promised herself that she'd keep her crush under wraps, but they were barely a few hours into the trip, and all the feelings were already breaking through her flimsy barriers.

She sucked in a big breath, enjoying the fresh air of the large park in the middle of the bustling city. She looked at the sign and realised she was in Princes Street Gardens, exactly where Kaye said she'd be.

It wasn't like Lily had anything else to do, and so she decided to seek Kaye out. Perhaps she could find out a little more about Andrew and be prepared for the memorial the following day.

She strolled around the park, only now realising how big it was and wondering where Kaye would have set herself up.

In the distance she saw Edinburgh Castle, high up on the hill of craggy rocks. It was less than a hundred metres away from her but perched so high that it felt impossible to get to. She imagined that was exactly what its creators had wanted.

Looking around, she considered the position of the sun in relation to the castle and headed in the direction where she would choose to set up if she was planning to draw the castle.

Her guess had been right, and a few minutes later she could make out Kaye in the distance, sitting on a bench with a large sketchpad on her lap.

Lily approached carefully, only now wondering if the invitation had really been meant or if it was only issued out of politeness.

She needn't have been worried. Kaye's face lit up when she saw her.

"Oh wow, you came!" Kaye covered her sketch. "Now I'm super embarrassed."

Lily chuckled. "No need to be. I won't judge, I promise."

Kaye gestured for Lily to take a seat beside her on the bench.

Lily glanced at the sketch of the castle. Kaye had a good outline, but she was definitely struggling with some of the perspective. Not that she'd say anything.

"It's a lovely park," Lily commented.

"It's great, gets a bit busy at times, but it's big and it's close to work. And you don't often get a view that nice." Kaye gestured up to the castle that towered over them.

"That's true. Edinburgh is certainly very pretty."

"It really is. I used to come to this park a lot with my housemates, when Andrew was alive. But we don't really come here that much any more. Too many memories, I suppose."

"Whose idea was it to have the memorial?" Lily asked.

"Anthony, Andrew's best mate. We didn't really get a chance to all get together at the time—it was exam season for a lot of us. It got delayed and delayed, and then we just stuck a date in the diary in the end."

"How many people are coming?"

Kaye blew out a breath and looked to the sky as she counted. "Forty? Maybe more."

Lily wondered if she could get forty people to come to a memorial for her. She doubted it. "Sounds like Andrew was popular."

Kaye nodded. "Yeah, he was. So charming and easy to speak to. Everyone loved him."

"Must have been hard to lose him," Lily commented, not sure what to say. She dearly wished she'd met the young man.

Kaye let out a sad sigh. "It was." She tried to perk up. "It's great that Miss Scott is here. Andrew idolised her, so it's good to meet her finally."

Lily blinked a little. Celia certainly hadn't given the impression that Andrew idolised her. If anything, she'd indicated that she was an absent mother with a son who had felt left behind. Why would anyone idolise that kind of behaviour?

"Really? Celia didn't mention."

Kaye smiled. "Oh yeah, they were thick as thieves. He was always on the train down to London, and she was always spoiling him rotten. He'd come home with new clothes and talking about all the cool things they'd done, what plays they'd been to see, that kind of thing."

Lily frowned. This really wasn't the picture Celia had painted at all.

"Presumably that changed, towards the end," Lily gently suggested.

Kaye shook her head. "No, I don't think so. What makes you say that?"

Lily hesitated a moment. She didn't want to put her foot in it, but she'd already started, so it would be hard to turn around now.

"Um, Celia mentioned that she was working a lot and worried that he felt ignored. I think."

Kaye laughed. "No, he never mentioned that. But I know she was working a lot—my God, we all knew about it."

"What do you mean?"

"He wouldn't stop going on and on about this big contract she was working on. It became a running joke in the house. We'd all ask him how it was going as a giggle because he'd talk about it so much. But then he *was* writing a paper on it, part of his business degree. I don't know what it was all about—it went over my head. But whatever she was working on went hand in glove with his paper."

Lily felt as if the bench was suddenly made of jelly. Had Celia misread the situation so badly? It did seem likely that it was something she would do. She could be opinionated, and jumped to the wrong conclusion on occasion.

Or was it Kaye, a relative stranger to Celia, who had no idea what was happening with Andrew and had herself misread his mental state?

If Kaye was right, then Andrew wasn't unhappy at Celia diving head first into work. In fact, he was pleased. Pleased enough to be boring his housemates with all the details of Celia's multimillion-pound contract. Pleased enough to make it the subject of his education.

"A paper?" Lily asked.

"Yeah, it was this huge deal, fifty percent of his final grade or something," Kaye explained. "Actually, it's on my drive at uni. When he died, the facilities department had to clear his part of the shared drive. But I knew he had pictures and stuff on there, so I begged and pleaded, and they agreed to give me access, and I just copied everything. Never deleted it all. It's sort of all I have left, you know? Just a folder marked *Andrew* on a shared drive I don't even own. Weird."

"I know this sounds really odd, but is there any way I could read that paper?" Lily asked, hoping she was keeping her desperation in check. "It's just, Celia is convinced that Andrew was upset because she was working so hard on this big case. If he wasn't, that would...that would really help her."

Kaye looked a little confused but seemed happy to help with the strange request. "Um. Yeah, sure. We can go to the library building now, if you like. It's still open for a while yet."

Lily quickly nodded. "That would be amazing, thank you so much. Sorry about this, it's just..." She trailed off, not knowing what it was. The paper might be nothing, but she felt filled with hope that it might be *something*. If she could heal even one percent of the hurt and blame that Celia felt, it would be worth it.

"It's hard when someone's gone," Kaye said.

"It is," Lily agreed.

Kaye quickly packed her things away and stood up. "And now I get to show you the university library. It's pretty cool. Beautiful building."

Lily smiled and stood as well. "Lead the way."

A TOAST

"D rink up."

Celia took the glass of whisky from her brother's hand and sighed. "I'd been trying to not drink as much," she admitted.

Ben took the folding chair beside her and balanced his glass on the armrest, looking at her suspiciously. "Any particular reason why?"

"I was drinking like a fish," she explained.

"You've always drunk a lot—you can handle it," he told her, sipping his drink.

"It's not a matter of if I can handle it or not. It's a matter of if I'm using it as a crutch." She looked at the glass of amber liquid. She didn't feel a pull to drink it, but she knew the taste of it would be exquisite, as her dear brother only drank the best.

"I'll get you some water if you like?" he offered, gesturing towards the open back door of the house.

They were sitting in the garden of his farm, or it would be a garden if anyone else lived there. But Ben lived there, so that meant it was enormous and grassy, with a fenced-off area in the distance.

They were miles from anywhere else, and all that could be seen was Scottish countryside—hills, wooded areas, a babbling creek in the distance. And the fenced-off area at the end of Ben's garden.

"No, thank you," she replied, taking a small sip of whisky. "It seems appropriate to toast his farewell."

Ben looked at her curiously. "You know it's weird that you refer to it as a him, right?"

"Yes, I'm aware."

"Why did you call him Alan?" Ben probed.

"Lily came up with it, and it stuck."

Ben didn't reply. She'd told him about the award, and Lily, and her inexpressible guilt, as best she could. He didn't really understand, she knew that, but he was her brother, and he was trying to be supportive in his own way.

Ben had never been one for examining emotions or maybe even having them. He'd come out of school and immediately joined the army. It had been a perfect fit, and he'd happily served his country for many years.

When he decided to retire, he used some of his experience with explosives to create a company. From fireworks displays to ground clearing to demolishing, Ben could help.

And that was why her award now sat in the fenced-off area at the bottom of the garden, strapped to what was effectively a bomb. It was far enough away that they were safe, but close enough that they would see and hear Alan's final passing.

"To Andy." Ben held up his glass.

"To Andrew," Celia corrected him as they tapped glasses.

A few moments of silence went by, and Celia could practically hear her brother's mind whirring.

"I'm really sorry about Andy, sis," he finally said.

"I know," she reassured him.

Ben was a closed book, but she knew he still felt things. He had been close to Andrew and had been devastated by his loss, in his own way, but that didn't mean tears and a depressive state. Ben just wasn't like that.

"I didn't really have much to say at the time, but that didn't mean I don't care," he continued, shifting uncomfortably in his chair.

"I know. It's fine, Ben, really."

"I didn't know you were suffering." He sighed at his clumsy wording and sat up a little in his chair. "No, I mean, I know you were grieving. Obviously. I just…I didn't…"

"You didn't know about how I'd neglected my son and felt guilty," she eventually said, helping him out of the hole he'd dug for himself.

"Yeah, exactly."

"We've never had that kind of relationship, Ben. You know that. It wasn't like I was going to call you in a wine haze and tell you how I was feeling. That's not something either of us could deal with." She chuckled at the very thought. "You're my big brother. You're for fixing my car when I was younger, taking my son fishing, and helping me to blow stuff up. And that's just perfect."

He smiled at her, a sad, soft smile that indicated that he wished he could be more but understood that it just wasn't in his wheelhouse.

She took another sip of whisky before adding, "I'm thinking of quitting work."

Ben stared at her as if she'd said she was investigating a new career as an astronaut.

"Come on, Celia. You love your job."

"I did," she corrected.

He continued to stare at her before shaking his head. "Your call."

"I'm not happy, Ben," she admitted.

"At work?"

"In life." She sipped the whisky. "Just...everything."

"You need a new man," Ben told her.

Celia laughed. "I said I wasn't happy, not that I needed a new challenge. Besides, who'd have me? Divorced, workaholic, son killed himself, middle-aged—but only if I haven't killed my liver, in which case, I'm rapidly approaching my expiry date."

Ben chuckled. "Wow. You're fun tonight."

"I was thinking of teaching. I've taught people at work throughout the years. It's quite enjoyable. You could consider it paying something back, or forward, or however you're supposed to pay it these days."

"Like teaching kids?" Ben asked.

"Well, I doubt five-year-olds care much about the reduction yield on an insecure portfolio. Maybe university age or older. I haven't figure out all the details yet. I'm just thinking about it."

"Sounds good. If it makes you happy."

"I kissed Lily," Celia blurted out. "At least, I think I did."

Ben raised an eyebrow, the only indication that he'd heard her.

"She might have kissed me, but I was certainly a participant in whatever happened." She looked at him. "What do you have to say about that? Your sister kissed a woman."

He shrugged. "Do I need to get you a card or something?"

"I don't think so."

He shrugged again. "Well, like I say, whatever makes you happy, sis."

Celia didn't know how to respond to that. She didn't even really know why she had brought it up other than the obvious fact that it was playing on her mind.

"I will mock you, though," Ben added. "Not for kissing a woman but for kissing someone half your age."

Celia considered it for a moment and nodded. "Well, yes, of course. Goes without saying."

They clinked glasses.

Library Research

Lily sat awkwardly on the chair as Kaye scrolled through folders on the computer. It had been a while since Lily had been in a university, and she felt completely out of place, as if everyone was staring at her and wondering who she was and why she was there.

Which was ridiculous because when she was a student, she would have never looked at anyone twice and wondered what their business in the library was. Her nerves were simply because of the very real risk that she was putting her nose where it wasn't wanted.

It was too late now. She'd all but begged Kaye to find the paper she'd spoken of, and now Kaye was busy hunting it down in a folder full of photos, documents, music, and more.

"He was always a mess," Kaye commented, leaning in a little closer as she slowly scrolled through the contents.

"It's the new messy bedroom, isn't it?" Lily asked.

Kaye nodded her agreement. "Yep. My photos on my phone are a disaster. Ah, here it is."

Lily tried not to lean in and look at the document, even though she was desperate to read it. Kaye clicked a few buttons, and a nearby printer sprang to life.

It was only a few moments, but it felt like a lifetime before a copy of the paper was placed in Lily's hands.

"It's not finished—he was meant to hand it in a week after he died. But there's a lot of it there, and he was working on it for months on and off," Kaye explained.

Lily put the papers down on the table and started to read. It was clearly an unfinished document with missing sections and the author's notes-to-self about what to put where. Comments interrupted the text to remind him to add or cut where necessary. Little of it made sense to Lily, since she had never been involved in corporate business, but what was overwhelmingly clear was that Andrew was proud of and excited by his mother's achievements.

He spoke about the contract in a way that a poet spoke of love. Admitting early on in the paper that his mother was the orchestrator of the deal and that he was probably biased, he went on to discuss and analyse the negotiation process in detail.

Lily tried to read between the lines, hunting for a sense of irony or sarcasm, but there was none to be found. It was a corporate love letter, from someone who understood the details of the deal that had been made and relished it.

Lily couldn't see how it was possible that the man who wrote the paper could possibly have been upset with Celia. It was obvious that he idolised her—and her work.

"I don't get it," Lily admitted.

"I can't help you with any of the business stuff," Kaye said. "It's way over my head."

"No, I mean, why did Andrew kill himself? Celia is convinced that he was upset with her for being busy, but that just doesn't ring true when you read this." Lily huffed and sat back in the uncomfortable plastic chair that university libraries were filled with.

Kaye was staring at her in shock, and Lily felt a deep sense of dread.

"What?" Lily asked.

"Miss Scott thinks Andrew killed himself?" Kaye asked, her voice barely more than a whisper. She jumped to her feet. "Oh my God, she would. She…she doesn't know."

"I'm confused," Lily confessed, hoping to shake Kaye out of whatever shock she was in and get some answers quickly.

"Andrew didn't mean to kill himself—it was an accident," Kaye explained.

"What happened?"

"Drugs," Kaye admitted with a sad shake of her head. "He knew this guy, well, Andrew knew everyone. But this guy was selling drugs for students to stay awake, you know? Stay sharp? That kind of thing." Kaye flopped back into her chair. "We didn't know he was taking them. He was working two part-time jobs and was falling behind with university work. We don't know when he started taking the pills.

Somehow, he overdosed. Or something was wrong with the pills. We don't know."

Lily felt all the breath leave her lungs.

"The thing is, there had been a spate of suicides on campus. Three students had taken their lives in the last six months. Some people who didn't know Andrew that well suggested that he had committed suicide, but we knew he hadn't. He was tired and he was stressed, but he wasn't suicidal." Kaye shook her head, the anger still obviously very raw. "All deaths in Scotland are investigated, but many of them get labelled sudden death or unexplained death when there's no clear idea of what happened. One of Andrew's lecturers, who barely knew him, told the authorities of the other student suicides and that they had taken the same pills. He was suggesting that it was suicide. But we all knew it wasn't."

"But there wasn't a note or anything like that?" Lily asked.

"No. Nothing. It wasn't clear what had happened. Some thought that he'd been depressed, some thought it was an accident. It was labelled as unexplained, but that doesn't mean suicide."

Lily stared at the paper. "But…" She swallowed hard. "You're sure?"

"Anyone who knew Andrew well knows that it wasn't suicide," Kaye said. "You'll meet them tomorrow. His real friends. I know that people who commit suicide often hide their real feelings from everyone, but I know that wasn't the case with Andrew. He just wanted to be able to work harder, and he started taking those stupid drugs. He wasn't depressed. I'd stake my life on it."

"Celia doesn't know," Lily whispered to herself.

"I had no idea that Miss Scott didn't know. I just kind of assumed that she would. But maybe the police told her what they thought, and she never spoke to any of us, so how would she know?" Kaye rubbed her face. "Ugh. I'm so stupid. I should have reached out to her. I didn't even think."

"No one told her?" Lily asked, dumbfounded.

"I don't think so. I mean, she only came up for the funeral. No one wanted to bother her. She was a grieving mother, and we all felt so bad for her. We offered our condolences but left her alone. I mean, none of us really knew her. We've never really spoken to her."

Kaye shook her head. "Gosh, even after the funeral we didn't talk to her. We boxed up Andrew's stuff, and his uncle arranged for it to be collected by a courier. Later we received a letter from Miss Scott thanking us for being wonderful friends and helping with the funeral arrangements. That was kind of the end of it."

Lily swallowed, forcing some liquid into her painfully dry throat.

"Celia thinks that Andrew killed himself. She also thinks that he primarily did that because she was too busy with work. She thinks she neglected him when he needed her most," Lily explained in a hushed tone.

Kaye's eyes widened. "No. No, no. That's not the case at all. He loved her. Like, *adored* her. And he wasn't suicidal." She tapped at the paper. "He was proud of her work. Like, he wouldn't shut up about it. Talking about fee rates and negotiations and bonds and whatever else. Every time he spoke to his mother, he came alive and started boring us all with more details of this multimillion-pound contract. Honestly, it was like she had discovered a cure for cancer. But that's what he was like, fascinated by business."

Lily struggled to process what she was hearing. Celia had been demonising herself for weeks and months because of this, but she was wrong to do so. There had been an immense miscommunication, and Celia had no idea of the truth.

Realisation struck her like a thunderbolt, and she jumped to her feet.

"I have to tell Celia." She pointed to the paper. "Can I take this?"

Kaye nodded. "Yes, sure. I'm sorry we didn't tell her before. We just kind of assumed she knew. We didn't put ourselves in her shoes. Feels stupid now."

Lily shook her head and grabbed the papers. "Not your fault. I can see it was a really hard situation all round. But I have to get to Celia before she, well...I have to go."

"I understand. See you tomorrow?" Kaye asked.

"Definitely. I—I'll catch you later."

Lily picked up the paper and dashed out of the library, through the corridors of the university, and into the street. She grabbed her phone and called Celia, hoping that she wasn't too late.

"Lily?" Celia answered the call, sounding a little confused.

"Have you blown Alan up yet?" Lily asked, breathlessly jogging through the narrow street. A passer-by looked at her with horror. "It's an object, not a person."

"No, we're about to. Did you want to come and watch?"

"Don't do it. I have something to show you, and I think it might give Alan a reprieve."

"What do you mean?"

"I need to show you."

There was a pause. "I'll text you the address."

NOTHING ACCIDENTALLY GOES BOOM

B en Scott handed Lily a glass of water.

"Thanks." Lily took a sip and then looked out the kitchen window. Celia walked around the garden, a tartan shawl around her shoulders to protect from the cool evening breeze. In her hands were the papers that Lily had delivered to her, along with a brief explanation of what she had heard from Kaye.

Celia had paled and asked for a repeat of almost everything Lily had said, desperately seeking clarification.

In the end she had taken the papers and announced she needed some time alone.

"Should one of us go out there?" Lily wondered out loud, hoping that Ben would take the hint that she meant him.

"She said she wanted to be alone," he replied.

Lily cast a glance at him. He was tall and well-built, with neatly cropped hair. The photos on the wall of his tours of duty and the medals proudly displayed from his military career were not a surprise. He seemed aloof, and she couldn't imagine for one moment him going outside and comforting his sister. So now they were both confined to the neat little farmhouse kitchen, clearly feeling uncomfortable.

"Sorry to intrude, I just felt she needed to know," Lily said, trying to begin a conversation to break the ice.

"She did," he agreed.

"So, you were going to blow Alan up?" Lily fished.

He sipped from a freshly refilled glass of whisky and nodded. "Yep."

"But, like, he's safe, right?"

Ben looked at her as if she was insane.

"I mean, he's not going to accidentally go boom, right?"

"Nothing accidentally goes boom," he told her.

"Okay, just checking. I think she's going to want Alan safe and sound."

Ben frowned. "Why?"

Lily sighed in exasperation. If Ben was the only emotional support Celia had, Lily understood why she had turned to wine.

"Because she wanted to destroy him because he represented a contract she won, one that she thought Andrew resented her for. When her emotions settle, she'll realise that Andrew was super proud of her. And would have been *really* proud of her getting the award."

Ben seemed to understand what she was saying and gave a small nod. "I'll go up to the enclosure and retrieve it."

He put his glass down on the counter and walked out the open back door, avoiding Celia by a long distance as he walked towards the end of his land.

"Coward," Lily muttered to his back.

It was obvious he was uncomfortable and using the first excuse available to do something productive that didn't involve offering emotional support. Not that she could blame him.

She swallowed as she remembered how Celia's face had dropped and contorted in pain as she recounted what she had found out from Kaye. Andrew was gone, but at least Celia now knew the truth. Whether she would find less anguish in accidental death remained a mystery to Lily. At the end of the day, Celia had still lost her son. She still had a mountain of emotions to process.

Lily pinched the bridge of her nose again. She wished she could take some of the pain away, that she could somehow shoulder some of the emotional turmoil that swirled around Celia at that moment.

She took a sip of water, put the glass down, and braced herself. It was time to go outside and see if she could be any help.

❖

A gentle hand took hold of her upper arm, and Celia looked up into Lily's concerned eyes.

"Hey, you okay?" Lily asked.

Celia realised belatedly that Lily had been talking to her for a while with no result. Celia was firmly in her own world, trying to recreate her history and reprogram what everything meant now that she had fresh information.

"I don't know," she said honestly. "I don't know much at the moment."

"I'm sorry," Lily said carefully.

"You have nothing to be sorry for. You're here, you came to Edinburgh, you put up with my moods, you found all this out." Celia waved the papers at her. "How long would I have had no idea about this without you? Possibly the rest of my life."

A hint of a blush touched Lily's cheeks. "It doesn't feel like enough. I hate seeing you suffer like this."

"It's life. Bad things happen, and you have to get on with it." Celia looked thoughtfully at the papers she gripped in her hand. "And sometimes not so bad things happen. He…he was proud of me, Lily."

"He was," Lily agreed. "Kaye said he idolised you."

"I idolised him. He was…Oh, Lily, I wish you could have known him. I think you would have gotten on very well." Celia shook her head. "Except for his naivety in trusting people. Drugs, I can't believe it. He always despised drugs."

She knew Andrew had been falling behind with some schoolwork. He had lamented the number of hours in the day more than once. She never thought he'd be as foolish as to take drugs to combat the situation, though he had been known to drink one too many energy drinks to stay up late on occasion. It wasn't beyond the realm of possibility that Andrew would be convinced by someone that medication was a solution to his time-poor situation.

No matter how many times she attempted to go back to the phone call informing her of Andrew's death, she was unable to pick out any details of the conversation. Those minutes were a blur. A mess of emotions combined with the desire to scream at the injustice along with the need to keep herself in one piece because she was at work.

She had no idea what was said, aside from the fact that Andrew was dead. Had she really just assumed suicide? Was her guilt at being absent so pronounced that she just naturally concluded that she had driven him over the edge with her thoughtless behaviour?

There was no other possibility. The call had faded into the background, and she had replaced any words spoken by the soft-voiced police officer with her own personally destructive narrative. She blamed herself when she wasn't at fault at all. Not that she could rejoice in that knowledge. Her darling Andrew was still gone.

She shivered at the chill in the air. Lily reached up and pulled the shawl further around her.

"Thank you," Celia whispered. "I'm sorry I'm not the best travel companion right now."

"It's okay. When you first met me you accused me of prodding sandwiches. It's gotten better from there."

Celia chuckled. "Why do you put up with me?"

The blush on Lily's cheeks became a little more intense, and she looked away. A penny dropped in Celia's mind, and she found it hard to breathe at the realisation. Lily liked her. Not that Celia had any idea what to do with that information then and there.

"Albert or whatever you want to call him is safe," Ben announced as he approached them.

They took a step apart.

"*Alan*," they said, correcting him in unison.

"Whatever." Ben handed the award to Lily.

Lily cleaned the award with her sleeve.

"This will come up as good as new," she said. "And Andrew would be proud of you."

Celia looked at the papers in her hand. Maybe Lily was right, but it would take a while before Celia felt it in her heart.

I'D CHOOSE YOU

L ily sat in the back of the Land Rover Defender and kept a close eye on Celia in the front passenger seat. Ben was driving them back to the hotel despite Celia's insistence that they could get a taxi.

Ben's farm was only twenty minutes outside the city, but he was determined to see Celia safely back to the hotel. Lily considered that was probably his way of showing that he cared. He seemed to be a very stoic man, more willing to give practical help than emotional.

"Will we see you tomorrow?" Lily asked Ben.

"No, I have a job up near Inverness that I have to go to, can't be moved," Ben replied.

Lily got the impression that Ben wasn't too sad about having an ironclad reason to not go and grieve with a group of people he didn't know.

"Ah, shame," she said.

"But you'll take care of my little sister, won't you?" His eyes met hers in the rear-view mirror, and for a second she saw real depth of concern in his expression.

"I will," she promised.

After a short, quiet journey, they arrived at the hotel. Ben wished them well before quickly departing again.

"He's not good with people," Celia explained to Lily. "He does care—he's just not very good at showing it."

Lily nodded, having already gathered as much.

The hotel lobby was busy with people either heading out for a night on the town or coming back from dinner.

"Should we take the stairs?" Celia suggested upon seeing the queue of people at the elevators.

"Sure." Lily tossed her rucksack onto her back and secured the straps. She'd tasked herself with carrying Andrew's paper and Alan, and the weight of the precious cargo felt good against her back.

She opened the heavy fire door and gestured for Celia to enter the stairwell. They climbed the few flights and arrived at their floor quickly enough. Lily didn't know what the plan was. All she knew was that Celia was exhausted and confused.

"Do you want company?" she asked as they walked down the long corridor towards their rooms.

"I think I need some time alone. I have a lot to think about," Celia confessed.

"Okay, but I'm only a phone call away. You know that, right?"

Celia stopped in the hallway in front of her room and looked at Lily fondly. "What did I ever do to deserve a friend like you?"

Lily swallowed. "It's a two-way street, Celia. You're a great friend to me."

Celia continued to look at her, a warm smile on her lips, and Lily realised how close they were. As close as they were the time they accidentally kissed. She realised she should say something but had no idea what.

"Could I have Andrew's paper? I'd like to read it again," Celia finally said.

"Oh yeah, sure." Lily quickly removed the rucksack and got the paper out, handing it over. "You want Alan?"

"Might as well, probably owe him an apology." Celia got her key card out of her bag and opened the door. She walked in, holding it open behind her. Lily took that to be an invitation to follow her.

She took Alan out of the bag, suddenly handling him with care and a reverence that she'd never bothered with before. She thought back to the Tokyo canal and chuckled.

"To think, we tried to kill him," Lily said, placing him on the desk.

"Less than an hour ago he was taped to some heavy-duty explosives," Celia replied, looking at the statue. "Poor Alan."

"He's held up really well, considering," Lily said.

"Maybe someone was watching over him?" Celia suggested.

"Maybe," Lily agreed.

"Lily?" Celia's voice was so soft that Lily nearly missed her name, despite standing next to her.

"Yeah?"

"It's none of my business, but…Kaye?"

Lily frowned. "What about her?"

"Did you arrange to meet her this evening?" Celia quickly shook her head and took a step away. "No, I'm sorry. Forget I asked that. It's none of my business."

"I didn't arrange to meet her," Lily explained. "She told me where she'd be, and I was walking and happened to end up in the same place."

Celia wrapped her arms around her middle, walked over to the window, and looked down at the street below. "I'm sorry. I shouldn't have asked."

Lily racked her brain to think of why Celia would ask, not daring to wish that Celia was jealous. Everything was complicated. Lily wanted to push and get to the bottom of what was happening, but the timing was wrong. Celia had been through enough, and Lily couldn't interrogate what Celia was thinking and feeling right then. She doubted Celia knew herself.

"I'm tired," Celia announced, her back still to Lily. "I should probably prepare for tomorrow. It's going to be a big day."

"It is. I better get going," Lily said. She approached the door to the room and paused in front of it for a second. "For the record, I'd choose you over Kaye every single time," she confessed before opening the door and making her escape.

THE WAKE

"This is a bad idea," Celia announced as she started to turn around. Lily stopped her and turned her back. "Come on, we're nearly there."

"Precisely why this is the best time to leave," Celia implored her.

Lily maintained a grip on Celia's arm and levelled a serious look at her.

"Do you really want to leave, or is this a spur-of-the-moment panic?" Lily asked.

Celia almost replied that it was obvious that she should leave but paused for a second and sucked in a deep breath.

It had been a long night, filled with strange dreams and an exhausted sleep so deep that she still felt disorientated hours after waking. She was mere steps away from the pub where Andrew's friends were meeting, and she still, despite recent information, felt as if she didn't really belong there.

"Come on. If you're uncomfortable while you're there, then we can leave," Lily reassured her.

"Lily!"

They turned to see Kaye walking towards them. Celia wished she didn't dislike the girl on sight, but there wasn't a lot she could do about the kneejerk reaction now. However, that didn't mean she'd spend more time in her presence than was absolutely necessary. Escape was essential.

"You're right," Celia announced. "I'll meet you in there."

Lily looked from Kaye to Celia and back again. "What? Wait, are you sure?"

"Very. I'll see you in there."

She walked away before Kaye got any closer and focused her

attention on trying to walk with as much confidence as she could towards the pub. It was a pub she knew well as she'd visited it with Andrew more than once. In fact, she'd probably introduced him to it.

As she entered the building, she glanced behind her to see Lily and Kaye hugging in the middle of the crowded street. She swallowed to push down the jealousy that quickly bubbled up her throat. Any notion that the jealousy was because Lily had found someone and Celia remained alone had been quashed in her mind. She wanted Lily for herself, even if that was never going to happen. And now was most certainly not the time to dwell on such matters.

Inside the pub was just as she remembered it—original flagstone tiles on the floor, low ceilings, and exposed wooden beams painted black. A proper original gem of Edinburgh's historical past.

"Miss Scott?"

She turned to see a smartly dressed young man approaching her with a questioning look.

"Please, call me Celia," she replied.

He held out his hand. "I'm Darren. We're so glad you could make it."

Celia shook his hand, remembering a Darren Andrew had spoken of.

"You worked with Andrew at Duke's, I believe?"

Darren beamed at Celia's recognition and nodded. "That's right. Can I get you a drink?" He gestured towards a roped-off area at the back of the pub. "We're sitting over there. We have a chair reserved for you."

"Because I'm old?" she joked.

Darren blushed. "No! No, because, well, we…we…"

She touched his arm to calm him down. "I'm only joking, don't worry."

He chuckled. "You're just like him."

"I came first—he's just like me," she said with a wink.

Lily and Kaye entered the pub, and Celia gestured to Lily. "This is a friend who was kind enough to travel with me. She never met Andrew, but I hope she'll feel like she knew him before long. Lily, this is Darren."

Darren and Lily shook hands, and Celia did her best to avoid eye contact with Kaye without seeming rude. She'd talk to her eventually, when she felt she could do so without being biting and bitter.

❖

Lily helped Matteo carry another two trays of drinks over to the table.

Not long after arriving, Celia had put her credit card behind the bar and announced that she wouldn't have students buying her drinks. Which Lily thought was a good call because she remembered being a student and being broke.

Lily had snagged a stool opposite her, a great position to keep an eye on Celia and allow everyone a chance to talk to her without Lily being in the way. She'd kept a close watch over Celia, looking for any sign of her being uncomfortable or wanting to leave.

Thankfully, after introductions were made and people started to settle in, Celia became more relaxed as she listened to their stories and shared her own.

Lily lowered her tray of drinks to one of the tables and started doling out the glasses, careful to quickly swipe Celia's lemonade so she could hand it to her personally.

"Oh, thank you," Celia said when the cool drink was put in her hand.

"You doing okay?" Lily whispered in her ear.

Celia took hold of Lily's hand and gripped it tightly. "I'm wonderful. Thank you for asking. And thank you for making me do this."

Celia's smile was warm and genuine, and Lily became lost in it for a few moments. Then Celia let go of her hand and looked away as her attention was sought by someone else.

Lily stood up and noticed Kaye watching her with a smile. Lily swallowed and looked away, returning to help Matteo distribute the latest round of drinks. Soon the drinks were in hand, and Lily had little more to do than take her seat, knowing what would come when she did.

Sure enough, Kaye approached.

"Hey, I'm sorry about earlier," Kaye whispered.

Lily could feel her cheeks heating up. "It's fine."

"It's not. I embarrassed you. I'm really sorry."

Lily saw Celia look up at her at that moment, an unrecognisable expression in her eye before she looked away again.

"Really, I'm fine," Lily reassured her in a way that clearly said she wasn't fine at all but wanted the subject dropped.

Kaye took the hint and stepped away and joined a group she had been chatting with earlier. Lily focused her attention back on Celia, listening as Darren finished up telling a story about a fishing trip he'd taken with Andrew the previous year.

Celia soaked up the story, and Lily couldn't help but smile and feel relieved that the event was going so well. She didn't have much to say, but that didn't matter. Everyone kept the conversation flowing perfectly. It was great to just sit and listen.

❖

As the hours passed, people apologetically started leaving the memorial as they had to go and work, study, or attend a class.

The group thinned and thinned, and eventually Celia announced that it was probably time that she also left. Contact details and hugs were exchanged, and soon Celia and Lily left the pub to walk back to the hotel.

Lily blinked in the sunlight.

They'd been in the dimly lit pub for hours, and she hadn't expected it to be so bright outside for some reason. It was late afternoon, and Edinburgh was teeming with people and noise.

"We don't have to dine together tonight, if you don't want to," Celia said, a slight edge to her tone.

Lily frowned. "What do you mean?"

"Nothing. Just…if you wanted to be alone. Or had other plans."

The change in Celia's mood was like a light being switched, from pleasant and charming to cold and standoffish. And Lily felt it was directed at her, for some reason.

"Um. No. No plans. Unless you want to be alone?" Lily asked.

"I'm quite indifferent," Celia announced.

Lily didn't know what to say to that, so they continued the rest of the walk to the hotel in silence. Her mind swam with theories on what had caused Celia's sudden turn. She couldn't fathom what it was or what she had done, but she was sure that she had done something.

When they arrived in the lobby and entered the waiting elevator, Lily couldn't take it any longer.

"Have I done something to offend you?" she asked.

Celia chuckled. "Offend me? No."

"Then why are you so obviously pissed off at me?"

"I'm not."

"You are."

"I'm not going to argue with you," Celia replied, turning her head to look at the elevator buttons rather than at Lily.

"What did I do?" Lily asked again. "Why can't we have dinner together?"

Celia sighed as if exhausted by the stupidity of Lily's question.

"I didn't say we *couldn't*. I said if you had other plans, I'd understand."

"And I told you I don't have plans," Lily repeated.

"Well, you tell me lots of things," Celia replied.

The doors open, and Celia stormed out, giving Lily a sense of déjà vu. Lily rushed after her.

"What's that supposed to mean?"

"Nothing."

"It's something," Lily insisted. "Tell me."

Celia suddenly stopped, and Lily nearly crashed into her.

"You said you had no interest in Kaye, and then you sought her out in the park. Then you said you'd choose me over her, and a few hours later you're hugging her in the street. And then in the pub she was making eyes at you. Go and spend time with her—I know you want to."

Celia spun around and stalked the hallway to make her escape.

"You're an idiot," Lily called after her.

Celia stopped and very slowly turned. The glare could melt plastic, but Lily held her own. If she was right, Celia had just shown her hand.

"Excuse me?" Celia asked, her tone deadly.

"You. You're an idiot." Lily gestured at her to make her point.

Celia placed a hand on her hip. "Care to tell me why?"

Lily hesitated for a moment but figured that she was already in Celia's bad books, and what she was about to say could only make a bad situation worse, which would mean never seeing Celia again. All things considered, that might be a good thing if what she was about to say was badly received.

"I didn't plan to see Kaye last night. It just happened. I don't have any interest in Kaye at all, not like that. But when I saw her last night at the library, I accidentally left my sketchbook on the table. She picked it up, and when I saw her today, she admitted that she'd looked at it."

Lily paused to swallow down her nerves.

"Is there a point to this?" Celia demanded.

"She saw what I'd been sketching, and she asked me about something I'd been trying to hide."

Celia continued to stare at her, waiting for the point.

"You."

Celia frowned. "Me what?"

"I'd been sketching you," Lily explained. "Kaye saw it and she knew."

"Knew what?" Celia asked, frustration clear.

One of the doors in the hallway opened, and a middle-aged woman stepped out, buttoning up a cardigan.

"She's been sketching you because she likes you. Keep up, dear." The woman looked at Celia and then at Lily and smiled. "She's a bit old for you."

Lily bit her lip to cover up the smile and looked away for a moment. Having a loud conversation in a hotel hallway clearly wasn't the best idea. She looked up at Celia and asked, "Should we talk somewhere else?"

Celia nodded, and they both apologised to the woman before rushing away. Celia paused by Lily's door, and Lily realised they were going to have this discussion in her room. Her heart was thudding against her ribcage as she unlocked the door and Celia breezed in.

Celia stopped in the middle of the room and turned to face Lily, her arms folded over her chest.

"Was that nosy woman right?"

Lily entered the room and softly closed the door behind her.

"Yes," she whispered, still facing the door and unable to look Celia in the eye just yet.

The silence dragged on until Celia finally spoke. "I…I'm not right for you, Lily."

Hearing the rejection stung, but Lily immediately kicked into gear to recover the situation. She spun around and tried to smile.

"I know. I'm just, you know, mentioning it to you. I know you're straight. And I respect that, really I do."

Celia laughed. "I'm old and rude. You could do far better than someone like me." She approached the tea-making facilities. "Drink?"

Lily nodded, her mind swimming with what Celia had just said. It seemed a strange response. An evasive one.

"*Are* you straight?" Lily asked as Celia walked past with the world's smallest kettle, to fill it from the bathroom tap.

Celia chuckled. "What a question."

Lily waited, but there was nothing further forthcoming. "Is there any answer?"

Celia exited the bathroom, stepping around Lily and seemingly refusing to make eye contact. Lily bit the inside of her cheek as she gathered every scrap of information she had learnt about Celia and came up with a plan for how best to go forward.

Celia busied herself making tea for the two of them, and Lily was struck by how familiar it all was. They'd both made drinks for one another in their short time together. Lily had friends who still didn't know how she took her tea.

"I care for you," Lily admitted, "and I think it's become more than that. No, actually, I know that it's become more than that."

Celia chuckled.

"Please don't laugh at me. These are my feelings." Lily sighed, sitting on the edge of the bed.

Celia spun around. "I'm sorry, I didn't mean to belittle your feelings. That was rude. I just, it seems so ludicrous that you'd be wasting your time on someone like me. That's all."

Lily furrowed her brow and looked at Celia as if she was the most complicated puzzle she'd ever seen. "Someone like you? You mean kind, considerate, funny—well, sometimes funny," Lily teased.

"I'm hilarious," Celia informed her with a deadpan expression.

"You were jealous of Kaye," Lily said, slipping in her ace while Celia was unaware.

Celia slumped a little and remained quiet for a few seconds, which ended up seeming like a lifetime. "I was. But that was immature and foolish of me. Kaye looks like a good fit for you, Lily."

"I'm not interested in Kaye," Lily said for what felt like the millionth time. How could Celia not see that Kaye wasn't right for her?

"Well, if not Kaye, then there will be someone else, I'm sure," Celia said. She turned and regarded the half-made tea. "You know, I'm not thirsty. In fact, I may have a little lie-down before dinner. It's been an exhausting day."

Lily was up off the bed and blocking Celia's escape route, before Celia had a chance to get to the door. She needed to have this discussion now, before Celia's emotional walls went back and it was too late.

"Celia," Lily begged, "please talk to me."

"There's nothing to talk about." Celia's gaze focused on the carpet.

"You were jealous of Kaye and me, you won't tell me if you're straight or not, you didn't say you *weren't* interested in me, just some line about you being old and rude." Lily threw all her top-ranking cards out, one after the other, and hoped that they would pierce Celia's shell.

Celia looked up at her. "You're a wonderful young woman, Lily."

Lily waited for more, but it never came. They ended up staring at one another as the seconds rolled by.

"What does that mean?" Lily asked.

Celia sighed in frustration and looked away before taking a step back and sitting on the small sofa.

"Lily, I'm wrong for you," Celia whispered, looking up at her beseechingly.

Lily's mind swam with the possibility of what might have just been said. She knelt in front of Celia.

"You don't get to make that decision for me. They're my feelings," Lily said. "Do you have feelings for me?"

Celia looked so small and fragile sitting on the smallest sofa in Edinburgh, and Lily held her breath while she waited for an answer.

"Yes, but—"

Lily jumped back, a wide smile on her face, holding up her hand to stop Celia from saying anything else.

"Lily," Celia implored, "let me finish."

"You think you're too old. Or I'm too young. Or a mix of the two. What would my friends and family say? What would yours? Am I rebounding from Asami? You're not even sure you have feelings. What would the future look like? What if someone else came along? You don't want to be hurt again. Am I right?"

Celia blinked a couple of times. "Well, most of that, yes."

Lily felt her heart soar across the room, out the window, and across the sky. She hadn't felt so happy in a long time. Feelings she'd long since forgotten took over, hope and anticipation.

Now wasn't the time to cement anything—recent events were still too raw. No decision made now would be fair to either of them. But it was an open door with possibilities just beyond.

"Can we just hang out?" Lily asked. "No expectation, but open minds?"

Celia shook her head. "I can't promise you anything, Lily."

"I'm not asking you to. I'm asking you to spend time with me and see how you feel. I won't expect anything. I won't push. I…we've already been dating, when you think about it."

Celia opened her mouth, obviously to refute the claim, but then stopped. Her brow furrowed, and she considered the point.

"And we've kissed," Lily added. She was now surer than ever that Celia had initiated the kiss. Lily had never done such a thing before, and now that she knew Celia must feel *something* for her, it seemed to fit.

The blush on Celia's cheeks was adorable. "Lily," she said admonishingly.

"Let me take you out for dinner tonight," Lily said.

"No."

Celia shook her head, and Lily's heart sank. She'd done everything she could. There was nothing left to say. Celia wasn't going to go for the idea.

"No," Celia repeated. "Let me take you out for dinner. You took me out last night."

Lily knew she probably looked like a grinning fool, but she couldn't help it. Becoming friends with Celia would be better than nothing. But Lily didn't think that was all that lingered between them. She was sure there would be more than a friendship as long as Celia was open-minded to the idea.

"No promises," Celia said firmly. "Just...see where it goes. Yes?"

Lily nodded sharply. It wasn't a no, and right now that meant the world to her.

SORRY, ALAN

Celia looked at her reflection and guided the earring into position. She was making more effort than she usually would for a simple dinner with a friend, and she knew exactly why.

She smiled to herself and stepped away from the mirror to get a better look at her overall appearance. She decided she looked good. Old, but good.

Knowing that Lily had developed feelings for her had certainly been an ego boost, but Celia knew that was no reason alone to get involved with Lily. They both deserved better.

Celia had been through an emotional roller coaster lately, and although she'd recently overcome several huge hurdles, she was still in a place of upheaval. And Lily was hardly any better, still processing her whole Tokyo debacle.

Which was one of the many reasons Celia had been so keen to keep Lily at arm's length after that first kiss. To give Lily the space and time she so obviously needed in order to heal. But Celia's jealousy and underlying emotions had bubbled to the surface on more than one occasion, giving Lily the way in she needed.

Celia couldn't be too unhappy about that. Maybe exploring the obvious connection between them would be a good thing.

Maybe it wouldn't.

She felt so very confused.

In some ways, things wouldn't change much. They'd dine together, take walks, and spend time talking and learning more about one another, which was what they had been doing during their time together already. And which sounded an awful lot like dating, anyway.

They'd shared a kiss, the memory of which still caused Celia go warm all over and made pleasant goosebumps appear on her arms. She wasn't blind to Lily's attractiveness. In fact it was becoming harder and harder to ignore.

She left the bathroom and walked into the bedroom area to tidy up a couple of things before she left to meet Lily for dinner. Her eyes rested on Alan, lying on his side on the desk.

"Sorry, Alan," she mumbled as she stood him upright.

She looked down at the award, the culmination of a tremendous amount of work. What was once a statement of what a terrible mother she had been was now something else. Would Andrew have been proud of her? She wondered. She crouched and looked at the award, the beautifully crafted, bevelled edges, the exquisite engraving. Alan had been through a lot, but somehow he hadn't been damaged at all.

She'd taken such poor care of the award, hoping it would shatter in the way her heart had when she'd first received news of Andrew's death. But Alan hadn't shattered. He hadn't dented, chipped, or even scuffed. He was as immaculate as the night she picked him up.

"Maybe we can start over?" she asked him. "We met when I was in a bad place. But I think I'm starting to feel better now."

A STARFISH CALLED BASIL

One month later, Celia sipped the non-alcoholic cocktail and looked around. Lily was late, but as she was learning, Lily was often late. Just a few minutes here and there, and often because Lily seemed to end up coming out of the wrong station exit or getting lost in shopping centres.

It had become quite the running joke.

For Celia, that was. Lily was desperately trying to prove that she could be on time. Which meant miserable failure each time. Much to Celia's delight.

Lily arrived via an escalator. Her red cheeks were the first thing Celia saw.

"Not a word," Lily said as she approached.

"Would I dare?" Celia asked.

"Yes, the second I sit down." Lily kissed her cheek in greeting. It was a thing they did frequently now. Celia relished it.

Lily sat down and looked at Celia expectantly.

"Okay," Celia began, "I just have to ask why you were downstairs. How did you even get down there?"

"Why do you insist on meeting in this maze of a place?" Lily gestured around the Canary Wharf Estate. "It's all islands, bridges, underground labyrinths, and a thousand different Tube exits."

Celia snorted a laugh. "Because I work here, and I really don't think it's as difficult as all that. Everyone else seems to manage it."

"You enjoy this. You like it that I can't find my way around here," Lily teased.

"I like the rosy glow of your cheeks when you've clearly been running, but you pretend you haven't been," Celia confessed. She gestured to the bartender, and he nodded to acknowledge he'd be there soon.

"I haven't been running," Lily denied. "It was just…hot. On the Tube."

Celia knew it was a lie and offered her a smile that said just that.

"How was work today? Did you get the colouring finished on that sequel?" Celia asked, picking up a menu despite already knowing she was having the chicken salad.

"Yes. And I heard some exciting news about *Olly the Jellyfish*."

Celia smirked. She'd become very familiar with the impressive back catalogue of books Lily had worked on. "Oh yes? What news does Mr. Jellyfish have?"

"He's going to be an audiobook. Which probably means another book. So another sequel."

The bartender arrived, and Lily ordered a pineapple juice.

"That's good news. I know you love a sequel," Celia said.

"Yep. So much easier when you have everything already decided. It's just money in the bank." Lily picked up a menu.

"You heartless capitalist, you," Celia joked.

"Yeah. Just churning out them kids' books to make the change," Lily replied with a smile.

Celia knew the truth was that Lily was attempting to make a move to other artistic pursuits, and to do so she needed to spend a little bit less time on her day job without reducing her income. Sequels were a great way to do that—easier to draw and the same level of pay.

"I heard from the cybercrime department," Lily said, her voice softening. "They found the guy pretending to be Asami and have arrested him. The Japanese authorities are going to prosecute him."

Celia wanted to jump for joy but knew that the whole experience was still raw to Lily. She didn't want to be insensitive to her feelings. She placed her hand on Lily's atop the bar and squeezed.

"Excellent. I know it was hard to file the report, but it was absolutely the right thing to do. And now you're saving anyone else from going through the same."

Lily slowly nodded her agreement but kept her attention focused on her menu, still too embarrassed about the episode, Celia knew, to look up at her. She took the opportunity to lean over and press a kiss onto Lily's soft cheek. "I'm proud of you," she whispered in her ear.

Lily's cheeks lit up like red beacons immediately, and Celia bit her lip at the adorable response.

"I'm having the pizza," Lily announced. "And you're obviously having the chicken salad because you've gone on about the glaze for weeks."

Celia sat back and took a sip of her drink. Lily wanted to move on from the Asami chat, and Celia was happy to oblige.

"Yes, and you'll try a bit—because you always do—and then you'll be horribly jealous," Celia told her.

The bartender came with Lily's drink and took their food orders, punching the details into their tablet before disappearing to serve other customers.

"How was your day?" Lily asked.

"All good, I'm looking forward to the end of the week."

Celia had made the decision to cut down on her hours and spend some of her time working at a local business school. She was looking for a new professional challenge and had the opportunity to try to inspire the next generation, so she took it. Howard had taken the news remarkably well, presumably because he knew the good PR spin the company could get out of it.

This week was her final week of full-time work. Then she had a week off to prepare before starting to train for giving lectures. It wouldn't be a complete change of direction, as she'd often taught within the company, and so a lecture hall wouldn't be too much of a stretch.

"Can I call you *Professor*?" Lily asked cheekily.

"Only if you want to stay after class in detention," Celia played along.

"Sounds fun." Lily waggled her eyebrows.

The flirting had been intensifying, from both of them, over the last few weeks since they returned from Edinburgh. And Celia found that she loved it. As promised, Lily had kept to her word that things would progress slowly and at a natural pace. With the pressure off, Celia had found herself quickly falling for Lily in a much harder way than she'd expected.

They met up frequently and exchanged phone calls and texts when they weren't able to see each other in person. Celia found herself daydreaming in the office and wondering how Lily's day was going. When they met up, Celia often wore clothes that were a little tighter and a little more revealing than normal. The glint in Lily's eyes and the harsh swallow that followed were reward enough.

For now.

"Seriously, though, I'd love to come and watch you teach. Is that possible?" Lily asked.

"I'm sure I can sneak you in," Celia said, "but I'm also sure you'll find it pretty tedious."

"Depends on the teacher. I think I could watch you talk about anything."

Celia chuckled. "Excellent, I'll make sure you sit in on a talk about compound interest."

"Sexy."

"It is rather interesting, actually. I was doing some research on the origins of the method of—" Celia stopped as Lily raised her hand.

"Don't spoil it now," Lily joked. "I want to be surprised."

Celia smirked. "If you insist. There will be a test after."

Lily pouted.

"By the way, I'm heading up to Edinburgh next week," Celia explained. "Last-minute thing that Ben needs help with. So I'll have to cancel our lunch, but I can do later in the week?"

Lily shook her head sadly. "I can't. It's my nephew's birthday, and I have to go to Denmark to see the family, remember? On the bright side, we're going to Tivoli. On the other hand—Mormor."

Celia did remember. Lily was equally looking forward to it and dreading it, and Celia couldn't blame her. She hated the idea of Lily dealing with Anette alone, and an idea popped into her brain and out of her mouth before she had time to stop it. "How would you like some company?"

Lily's eyebrows raised. "In Denmark?"

"Yes. Is it too soon?" Celia asked, suddenly concerned that she'd broken their agreement to take things slowly. They'd never decided what slowly was. Celia was ready for more, and she thought Lily was too, but she didn't know for certain.

Lily quickly shook her head. "Not for me."

"Nor me," Celia confirmed, her gaze fixing on Lily to emphasise her meaning. "I'd like to meet your family. And give you some protection from Anette."

"You don't have to do that," Lily said gently.

"I want to. And you're going to Tivoli, a place I enjoy. I'll pay for the hotel. We can watch your grandmother's jaw drop when she knows we're together."

Lily swallowed visibly. "You'd tell her that we're together?"

"Of course."

"She might be mad," Lily warned.

"She'll have to get used to it. Besides, she liked me. I'm delightful."

Lily smiled. "Take some time to think about it, but if you really want to come, then I'd love for you to be there."

"I've thought about it," Celia insisted.

"Thank you," Lily whispered gratefully.

Celia took the opportunity and leaned forward, this time not for the friendly kiss on the cheek that they had been sharing. This time she did so with every intention of claiming a real kiss on those soft, plump lips that kept her awake at night.

Lily leaned in and met her halfway. Celia closed her eyes and luxuriated in the feeling. Although it wasn't their first kiss, it did feel like it. That first kiss had been tired emotions and a potential mistake. This was deliberate and yet undemanding. If any doubt lingered in Celia's mind, it was banished by the sweet, sensual kiss.

Aware that they were in a public restaurant that was open to a large shopping centre, Celia regretfully pulled back after just a few seconds. Lily moaned gently and Celia chuckled.

They smiled at each other and sighed happily before turning back to their drinks.

"So, Olly the Octopus," Celia began.

"Jellyfish."

"Why on earth is he called Olly if he's a jellyfish?"

"I don't know. I didn't write him. I'm just the illustrator."

"But surely he should be James or Jeremy? Alliteration is a very important thing in literature," Celia explained.

"Well, I'll be sure to tell that to the author," Lily replied.

"Do. I suppose there's a submarine called Julia?" Celia laughed.

"No, but there is a starfish called Basil."

Celia shook her head. "Utter madness."

"You're not the target demographic," Lily reminded her. "It's for three-year-olds."

"And this is getting a sequel?" Celia asked. "Madness."

"Kiss me again?" Lily requested.

Celia swallowed nervously but soon agreed to the invitation and leaned in. Lily quickly took control of the intense though woefully short-lived kiss. Celia felt a passion she'd never experienced before, but it was over almost as soon as it had begun.

Lily returned to her drink as if nothing had happened, but Celia was left a little breathless. She was happy they had taken things slowly, but now she was equally happy that they had come to an unspoken agreement about a new direction.

Now she was looking forward to a romantic stroll in Tivoli Gardens more than ever. And to putting Anette in her place, politely but firmly.

REWRITING THE PAST

Six Months Later

Lily woke up and stretched out luxuriously in the king-sized bed.

"Sorry if I woke you," Celia whispered.

Lily opened her eyes and sat up. "'S okay," she mumbled. She looked around to try to remind herself where she was and what was happening. The familiar-looking hotel room snapped into place in her memory, and she smiled.

"What time is it?" she asked.

Celia was unpacking clothes from her suitcase into the wardrobe, obviously unable to sleep. "Here or back home?"

"Here."

"Nearly five in the morning. I'm sorry if I woke you, really."

"You could apologise by coming back to bed," Lily suggested.

Celia returned to the bed and gracefully got in her side and pulled the sheets back up over her naked form.

"It's okay. I don't think you did wake me. I think I just woke up naturally." Lily let out a yawn and stretched again. "Trouble sleeping?"

She turned onto her side to face Celia. She looked tired, but her eyes were bright and wide awake, a clear sign of jetlag having hit her hard.

"Yes, I'm just awake. Even though I feel so tired," Celia admitted.

"Then let's get up," Lily suggested.

Celia chuckled. "And do what?"

"We'll get ready and then eat breakfast. By the time we've done that, it will be, what, six? We can walk around, look at the imperial gardens. I'm sure we can find something to do in Tokyo at six in the morning. Then we can come back and have a nap at lunchtime."

"Shouldn't we be trying to reset our body clocks?" Celia asked.

Lily shrugged. "Sometimes you just have to listen to your body."

"You wouldn't mind getting up now?"

"Sure. I'm awake now. It will be fun to explore."

Celia smiled that smile that Lily loved so much. It lit up her face all the way to her eyes and shone with an intensity that blew Lily away every time.

The return to Tokyo had been Lily's suggestion, a throwaway comment one lazy Sunday morning in bed. It was a casual statement that she had been looking forward to seeing Tokyo, and Asami—or Riku, to give him his real name—had ruined that for her. In fact, Lily was even struggling to go to her favourite sushi bar in London because she'd become disenchanted by the entire country. All because of the actions of one man.

A few days later, Celia had a plan in place. A birthday present, she claimed. A ludicrously expensive birthday present, Lily had argued, but Celia's mind was made up. They'd redo the trip, but this time as a couple and without any of the drama.

No Asami. No muggings. No layover in Denmark. No terrifying awards ceremonies. Just the two of them playing tourist and enjoying the delights that Tokyo had to offer, rewriting history and fixing the bad memories that they both had lurking in their minds.

Lily edged forward and pressed her mouth to Celia's in a soft kiss.

"I'm glad we did this. Thank you," Lily said.

"We haven't done anything yet," Celia reminded her.

They'd arrived the day before and had immediately eaten a big meal and then gone to bed. The taxi from the airport to the hotel was the only part of Tokyo they had seen so far.

"But even this," Lily admitted, "it's healing, in a way. To come back and, I don't know, replace those shitty memories. They weren't all shit, of course."

"I know what you mean," Celia said. "I think it was both the best time in my life and the worst all at the same time. I'm looking forward to papering over the bad bits and remembering the good."

Celia gave Lily a peck on the cheek before rolling out of bed and starting to get dressed.

"In fact," she said, "I should thank Asami—Riku, whatever. Otherwise I would never have met you. Maybe I should send a gift basket. Do you know which prison he's in?"

Lily laughed. "You're *so* mean!"

"I know. You love it."

"I do," Lily said. "I really do."

A pile of underwear was thrown on the bed, and Celia pointed from it to Lily.

"Come on, let's get moving. There's a whole beautiful city out there to explore," Celia commanded.

Lily leapt out of bed and wrapped her arms around Celia's neck, pulling her in for a kiss. Celia's arms wrapped comfortably around her. Lily couldn't believe she was lucky enough to get to do this whenever she wished.

"I love you," Lily whispered when they parted.

"I love you too," Celia replied, staring intently at her. "So very much."

Lily smiled and took a deep breath, feeling as if every old memory of this place and the time that had gone before was slowly being replaced with something new and something pure. It had been under a year, but it felt like a lifetime. She was struck by how quickly everything could change.

"Are you sure you don't want to sleep some more?" Celia asked, looking at her with mild concern. "I don't want you struggling on because of me."

"I'm sure," Lily promised. "I know you'll look after me if I start to get tired."

"I will," Celia said with such conviction that Lily couldn't help but fill with joy. "Always."

Lily kissed her nose. "Let's go and explore."

About the Author

Amanda Radley had no desire to be a writer but accidentally turned into an award-winning, best-selling author. Residing in the UK with her wife and pets, she loves to travel. She gave up her marketing career in order to make stuff up for a living instead. She claims the similarities are startling.

Books Available From Bold Strokes Books

A Far Better Thing by JD Wilburn. When needs of her family and wants of her heart clash, Cass Halliburton is faced with the ultimate sacrifice. (978-1-63555-834-0)

Body Language by Renee Roman. When Mika offers to provide Jen erotic tutoring, will sex drive them into a deeper relationship or tear them apart? (978-1-63555-800-5)

Carrie and Hope by Joy Argento. For Carrie and Hope, loss brings them together but secrets and fear may tear them apart. (978-1-63555-827-2)

Detour to Love by Amanda Radley. Celia Scott and Lily Andersen are seatmates on a flight to Tokyo and by turns annoy and fascinate each other. But they're about to realize there's more than one path to love. (978-1-63555-958-3)

Ice Queen by Gun Brooke. School counselor Aislin Kennedy wants to help standoffish CEO Susanna Durr and her troubled teenage daughter become closer—even if it means risking her own heart in the process. (978-1-63555-721-3)

Masquerade by Anne Shade. In 1925 Harlem, New York, a notorious gangster sets her sights on seducing Celine, and new lovers Dinah and Celine are forced to risk their hearts, and lives, for love. (978-1-63555-831-9)

Royal Family by Jenny Frame. Loss has defined both Clay's and Katya's lives, but guarding their hearts may prove to be the biggest heartbreak of all. (978-1-63555-745-9)

Share the Moon by Toni Logan. Three best friends, an inherited vineyard, and a resident ghost come together for fun, romance, and a touch of magic. (978-1-63555-844-9)

Spirit of the Law by Carsen Taite. Attorney Owen Lassiter will do almost anything to put a murderer behind bars, but can she get past her reluctance to rely on unconventional help from the alluring Summer Byrne and keep from falling in love in the process? (978-1-63555-766-4)

The Devil Incarnate by Ali Vali. Cain Casey has so much to live for, but enemies who lurk in the shadows threaten to unravel it all. (978-1-63555-534-9)

Secret Agent by Michelle Larkin. CIA Agent Peyton North embarks on a global chase to apprehend rogue agent Zoey Blackwood, but her commitment to the mission is tested as the sparks between them ignite and their sizzling attraction approaches a point of no return. (978-1-63555-753-4)

Journey to Cash by Ashley Bartlett. Cash Braddock thought everything was great, but it looks like her history is about to become her right now. Which is a real bummer. (978-1-63555-464-9)

Liberty Bay by Karis Walsh. Wren Lindley's life is mired in tradition and untouched by trends until social media star Gina Strickland introduces an irresistible electricity into her off-the-grid world. (978-1-63555-816-6)

Scent by Kris Bryant. Nico Marshall has been burned by women in the past wanting her for her money. This time, she's determined to win Sophia Sweet over with her charm. (978-1-63555-780-0)

Shadows of Steel by Suzie Clarke. As their worlds collide and their choices come back to haunt them, Rachel and Claire must figure out how to stay together and, most of all, stay alive. (978-1-63555-810-4)

The Clinch by Nicole Disney. Eden Bauer overcame a difficult past to become a world champion mixed martial artist, but now rising star and dreamy bad girl Brooklyn Shaw is a threat both to Eden's title and her heart. (978-1-63555-820-3)

The Last First Kiss by Julie Cannon. Kelly Newsome is so ready for a tropical island vacation, but she never expects to meet the woman who could give her her last first kiss. (978-1-63555-768-8)

The Mandolin Lunch by Missouri Vaun. Despite their immediate attraction, everything about Garet Allen says short-term, and Tess Hill refuses to consider anything less than forever. (978-1-63555-566-0)

Thor: Daughter of Asgard by Genevieve McCluer. When Hannah Olsen finds out she's the reincarnation of Thor, she's thrown into a world of magic and intrigue, unexpected attraction, and a mystery she's got to unravel. (978-1-63555-814-2)

Veterinary Technician by Nancy Wheelton. When a stable of horses is threatened, Val and Ronnie must work together against the odds to save them and maybe even themselves along the way. (978-1-63555-839-5)

16 Steps to Forever by Georgia Beers. Can Brooke Sullivan and Macy Carr find themselves by finding each other? (978-1-63555-762-6)

All I Want for Christmas by Georgia Beers, Maggie Cummings & Fiona Riley. The Christmas season sparks passion and love in these stories by award-winning authors Georgia Beers, Maggie Cummings, and Fiona Riley. (978-1-63555-764-0)

From the Woods by Charlotte Greene. When Fiona goes backpacking in a protected wilderness, the last thing she expects is to be fighting for her life. (978-1-63555-793-0)

Heart of the Storm by Nicole Stiling. For Juliet Mitchell and Sienna Bennett a forbidden attraction definitely isn't worth upending the life they've worked so hard for. Is it? (978-1-63555-789-3)

If You Dare by Sandy Lowe. For Lauren West and Emma Prescott, following their passions is easy. Following their hearts, though? That's almost impossible. (978-1-63555-654-4)

Love Changes Everything by Jaime Maddox. For Samantha Brooks and Kirby Fielding, no matter how careful their plans, love will change everything. (978-1-63555-835-7)

Not This Time by MA Binfield. Flung back into each other's lives, can former bandmates Sophia and Madison have a second chance at romance? (978-1-63555-798-5)

The Found Jar by Jaycie Morrison. Fear keeps Emily Harris trapped in her emotionally vacant life; can she find the courage to let Beck Reynolds guide her toward love? (978-1-63555-825-8)

Aurora by Emma L McGeown. After a traumatic accident, Elena Ricci is stricken with amnesia, leaving her with no recollection of the last eight years, including her wife and son. (978-1-63555-824-1)